# DANCING WITH CLARA

*Further Titles by Mary Balogh from Severn House*

A CHRISTMAS PROMISE
THE IDEAL WIFE

# DANCING
# WITH CLARA

## Mary Balogh

This title first published in Great Britain 1993 by
SEVERN HOUSE PUBLISHERS LTD of
9–15 High Street, Sutton, Surrey SM1 1DF.
First published in the U.S.A. 1993 by
SEVERN HOUSE PUBLISHERS INC., of
475 Fifth Avenue, New York, NY 10017.
by arrangement with New American Library,
a division of Penguin Books USA Inc.

British Library Cataloguing in Publication Data
Balogh, Mary
  Dancing With Clara
  I. Title
  813.914(F)

  ISBN 0-7278-4543-8

Typeset by Hewer Text Composition Services, Edinburgh.
Printed and bound in Great Britain by
Redwood Books, Trowbridge, Wiltshire.

# 1

Bath in the summertime. It was a beautiful city, perhaps the most beautiful in all England. The Honorable Mr. Frederick Sullivan conceded that point. Nevertheless, he had frequently felt during the week he had spent there that he would rather be anywhere else on earth. That was a rash exaggeration, of course. He consoled himself with the realization that he could probably think without any great effort at all of a dozen places on earth he would like a great deal less. Suffice it to say that he was not enjoying being in Bath.

He had taken up residence at the York Hotel, though perhaps it had been somewhat extravagant to do so, had paid his courtesy call on the Master of Ceremonies, had paid the subscription that gave him access to all the gardens and libraries and social events of the city, and had had the satisfaction of seeing the announcement of his arrival in the Bath Chronicle. He had visited the Pump Room and both Assembly Rooms, had strolled in Sydney Gardens and in the Royal Cresent, had read the newspapers at one of the circulating libraries, and had in short done everything that one was expected to do when in Bath.

He was bored.

He could, of course, be at Primrose Park in Gloucester-shire for the wedding of his cousin, the Earl of Beacons-wood, to Julia Maynard. Surprisingly he had been invited. Or perhaps not so surprisingly when one considered the fact that the family had always been close and neither Dan nor Jule would want to cause any upset within family

1

ranks by pointedly omitting him from the guest list. But he had not accepted. He had penned an excuse and left it for them when he departed from Primrose Park. He was quite sure that the two of them would be breathing as great a sigh of relief as he was. That was one wedding he had certainly not wanted to attend.

Or he could, of course, be in London, though it was summertime and not at all the fashionable time to be there. He could be at Brighton, then. That was the fashionable place to go and the place where he would choose to be if he were free to go wherever he pleased. There would be the company of friends and acquaintances there and plenty of activities with which to amuse himself. But he could not go there.

His creditors had found him at Primrose Park before he had left there more than a week ago. How much more easily they would find him and pester him if he went to Brighton. And yet if he did not go there, how was he to bring himself about and acquire the money with which to pay off all his debts? Or the most pressing of them anyway – no one would expect a gentleman to be totally without debt. He would be considered queer in the head.

There was really only one way to bring his fortunes about in Bath. He had tried gambling and seemed even to have run into a streak of good luck. But his winnings were more frustrating than exhilarating. Playing deep was strictly forbidden in Bath. Gaming was intended to be merely a pleasant social exercise there. And so his winnings in total would make scarcely a dent in the smallest of his debts. No, one did not come to Bath in order to recoup one's fortune at the tables. One came to Bath to look for a rich wife.

The best place to do that, of course, was London during the Season. The great marriage mart. It seemed the obvious place at which Frederick should shop. But for two particular reasons he could not do so. First, he could not afford to wait until the following spring to find himself a wife. It was likely he would be in debtors' prison

2

long before then unless his father paid his debts for him – he shuddered at the thought. Second, no father or guardian, looking out for the interests of his daughter, would give even the smallest consideration to the suit of the Honorable Frederick Sullivan.

Frederick could only hope that his reputation had not followed him to Bath. But whom was he to find there anyway? The story that Bath had become home to staid octogenarians and folk of shabby gentility seemed hardly exaggerated. The only youngish women of any beauty he had encountered since his arrival were all very obviously without fortune. In the course of the week he had narrowed down his matrimonial possibilities to three, none of which was particularly appealing. But then, he reminded himself, he was not considering marriage from motives of romance or love or personal gratification.

He thought of Julia Maynard and how he had tried to coerce her into marriage at Primrose Park and grew cold at the thought. He preferred not to think about it.

There were three possibilities in Bath. There was Hortense Pugh, the youngest of the trio, seventeen years old, plump and pretty and singularly unappealing. She was the daughter of a hat manufacturer who had made himself very wealthy and thought to establish himself socially by marrying his only daughter to a member of the *beau monde*. Father and daughter were courting him with singleminded devotion. He should rush into the marriage with mindless gratitude. It was exactly what he needed. But he could not keep himself from thinking that even debtors' prison might be preferable to the girl's vulgar and emptyheaded prattle for the rest of his life. The superior state of her wardrobe and her jewelry box were her chief topics of conversation.

Lady Waggoner would be more to his taste. A buxom, handsome widow, who was perhaps seven or eight years his senior, she was also in possession of a sizable fortune. And she fancied him. He had had enough experience with women to know that he could climb into her bed any night he set his mind to doing so. The prospect was distinctly appealing. But would she marry him? That was the key question. The woman was as expert at dalliance as he was, he guessed. He suspected that she might be just as adroit at avoiding marriage. He might waste the summer on an affair that would be satisfactory physically but in no other way. He could not afford to take the chance.

That left Miss Clara Danford – perhaps the most distasteful prospect of the three. And perhaps too the wealthiest of the three. Her father, a gentleman, had made what was reputed to have been a fabulous fortune with the East India Company in India, and had left everything to his daughter on his death. She was in her mid-twenties, Frederick guessed, perhaps no older than his own twenty-six years. She had been courteous when he had arranged an introduction to her at the Upper Assembly Rooms one afternoon, and had appeared quite ready to converse with him for a few minutes during each morning after that at the Pump Room. It might be altogether possible to persuade her into marriage. From their first meeting he had taken great care to use all his practiced charm on her.

And yet the thought of marrying Miss Danford could make him break out in a cold sweat. He stood in the Pump Room early one morning – fashionably early – conversing with a few newly-made acquaintances and amusing himself with observing the distaste with which those who drank the waters raised their glasses to their lips. And watching Clara Danford at the other end of the room, talking with her faithful companion, the young and pretty and lamentably unwealthy Miss Harriet Pope, and with Colonel and Mrs. Ruttledge.

He must go and talk with her, he thought. There was no time for a leisurely courtship. He must close his mind to his reluctance for the match and press onward. She was as unlovely a woman as his eyes had ever dwelled on. She was thin, probably from the inactivity caused by her condition. She was crippled and was always seated in a wheeled chair whenever he saw her. Her arms were thin

4

and her legs, outlined against the light wool of her morning dress, looked as if they were too. Her face was thin and unnaturally pale. From what he had heard, she had lived for several years in India with her father and there had contracted the illness that had left her an invalid.

She had too much hair. On any other woman perhaps it would have been seen as her crowning glory, being thick and shining and very dark. But it was too heavy for Miss Danford's head. And her eyes were too dark for such a pale face. He had thought at first that they were black, but they were in reality a dark gray. They would be fine eyes in a different face. Or perhaps they were fine anyway. Perhaps he was adversely affected by the fact that they looked so directly and so deeply into his own whenever he spoke with her, that it seemed they were stripping away the carefully imposed mask of charm that he wore for her and seeing the truth.

She was no prize for any man – except for the enormous fortune that was now hers. Frederick excused himself from the group with which he stood and strolled gradually closer to her across the Pump Room, nodding and smiling at acquaintances as he went. There were three matrimonial possibilities in Bath. And yet he could narrow them down to one without any great thought. And felt his breath constricting with near-panic. Miss Clara Danford.

He fixed his eyes on her as he drew close in the way he knew could melt nine female hearts out of ten, or perhaps ninety-nine out of one hundred, and smiled the half smile that he knew could make those melted hearts beat at double time.

She looked back at him from those eyes that could seem to see beyond the artifice, and smiled.

"Here he comes," Harriet Pope said as Colonel and Mrs. Ruttledge moved away to begin a promenade about the Pump Room and Mr. Frederick Sullivan left his group at the other side of the room almost at the same moment and began strolling slowly their way.

5

"Yes," Clara Danford said, "as you predicted he would, Harriet. And I did not disagree with you, did I? Come, you must confess that he is by far the most handsome man in the room. In all of Bath, in fact."

"I have never denied the fact," Harriet said.

"No." Clara smiled slightly and looked up at her friend. "Your objection to him is only that he is also probably the most unprincipled man in Bath. I have not disagreed with that, either."

"And yet you will persist in encouraging him," Harriet said.

"He is very handsome," Clara said.

Harriet tutted, "And knows how to use his looks," she said.

"Granted." Clara smiled at her again.

They had talked about him before. Particularly the evening before after he had sat with them for tea at the Upper Rooms, having sat with Miss Hortense Pugh for a while first.

"He is a fortune hunter," Harriet had said with some scorn. "He is in search of a wealthy wife, Clara. Miss Pugh or you."

Clara had agreed. Even apart from her crippled state, she knew that she had no looks with which to attract a gentleman of Mr, Sullivan's almost godlike appearance. If he was going to be smitten by love, then surely his eyes would turn to Harriet, who was undeniably lovely with her very fair hair and delicate rose-petal complexion. Yet he had scarcely glanced at Harriet since his introduction to them almost a week before. Of course he was a fortune hunter. She had met a few in her time, mostly before the death of her father. She had only recently emerged from her year of mourning for his death.

"I suppose," she had said, "that it is permitted to marry for wealth, Harriet. A man who does so – or a woman – is not necessarily a blackguard."

"Mr. Sullivan is," Harriet had said. "Those eyes, Clara, and that smile. All the charm."

6

Yes, the eyes were dark and looked on the world from beneath heavy eyelids. And the smile revealed very white strong teeth. The charm was just that, but devastatingly attractive even so. His person was even more so. Tall, athletically built, with long legs, slim hips and waist, and powerful chest and shoulders and arms – it would be difficult to find a single fault with his looks. Dark hair, from which a truant lock frequently fell across his forehead, strong, handsome features, and those eyes and that mouth – it seemed almost unbelievable that one man could possess such total beauty. And health and strength.

"He is beautiful," she had said.

"Beautiful!" Harriet had looked at her with some surprise and laughed. "That is a word for a woman."

It suited Mr. Sullivan. Though there was nothing even remotely feminine about him.

"You must discourage him," Harriet had said. "You must let him know in no uncertain terms, Clara, that you recognize him for what he is. You must send him on his way. Let Miss Pugh have him. They deserve each other."

"Sometimes," Clara had said with a smile, "you can be quite nasty, Harriet. Poor Miss Pugh is merely trying to move up in the world. And Mr. Sullivan is trying to secure a fortune for himself. Why not mine? I have little enough use for it. And I would have all that beauty in exchange."

She had laughed at Harriet's horrified expression and made a joke of the matter. And yet, thinking about it afterward, she was not quite sure that it had been a joke. She spent most of her life on a chaise longue at home or in a wheeled chair when out. She had Harriet for company and several other friends, mostly couples, mostly older than her own twenty-six years. Her prospects of marrying were slim. Her prospects of marrying for love or even affection were non-existent. The only man who would consider marriage with her was the man who had an eye to her fortune.

7

She was lonely. Dreadfully lonely. And she had needs that were no less insistent than they could be in other women despite the fact that she had no beauty and was unable to walk. She had needs. Cravings. Sometimes she was so lonely despite Harriet's friendship and despite the existence of other good friends that she touched the frightening depths of despair.

She could have Mr. Frederick Sullivan. She had realized that on their first meeting. If he had thought to court her with some tact and patience, he was wasting his time. She had known from the first why he had effected the introduction to her and why he visited the Pump Room each morning, after her daily immersion in the waters of the Queen's Bath. He wanted to marry her. He wanted control of her fortune.

She had always turned from fortune hunters without even a second thought. In other words, she had always turned from every suitor she might have had. Mr. Sullivan was the first to whom she had given any consideration at all. He did not love her or feel any affection for her. Probably he did not even like her or hold her in any esteem at all. Perhaps he even cringed from her. That was the reality of the situation and must be faced if she were to be mad enough to consider marrying him. Perhaps he never would feel any affection for her.

It would not be a good marriage. It would never be the sort of marriage she dreamed of just like any other woman. But would it be better than no marriage at all? That was the question that had plagued her all night. She was not in love with him, she thought as he drew closer across the Pump Room and almost visibly turned on the charm with which he always dealt with her. She could never be in love with a man who played a part and one who came to her only because of her money. But he was beautiful and strong and healthy and she was wondering if the combination would prove irresistible. She rather thought it might.

"He is so very beautiful," she said to Harriet now before

smiling at his approach. He was too close for Harriet to have a chance to reply.

"Miss Danford." He took her thin cool hand in his, decided not to raise it to his lips, but held it with both his own for a few moments longer than was necessary. "I trust you did not take a chill in going to the Upper Rooms yesterday?"

"When the day was so warm?" she said. "No, sir, I thank you."

He relinquished her hand to straighten up and make his bow to Miss Pope. If only the two figures could be switched, he thought regretfully. If only it were Miss Pope who was in the chair and in possession of the fortune. But Miss Pope, he had discovered from discreet inquiries, was the daughter of an impoverished widow, whom Miss Danford had met and befriended several years before while in Bath with her father.

"For my own part," he said, returning his attention to Miss Danford, "I think the custom of taking tea at the Rooms quite delightful. Bath is surely one of the loveliest places on earth and should be enjoyed as much as possible."

"I agree with you entirely, sir," she said. "Tea is always more enjoyable when taken in congenial company."

She turned her attention to a gentleman who had approached to greet the ladies and exchange civilities before inviting Miss Pope to take a turn about the room with him.

"By all means," Miss Danford said when her companion looked inquiringly at her. "That will be pleasant for you, Harriet."

Miss Pope looked doubtfully at Frederick.

"I shall keep Miss Danford company until your return," he said, "if I may be permitted to do so."

Miss Danford smiled at him. "I would be grateful, sir," she said.

"Grateful." He gave her his full attention. "It is I who should be feeling the gratitude, ma'am. I admire

9

your courage. You remain cheerful and serene despite an obvious and unfortunate affliction." He resisted the urge to stoop down on his haunches beside her.

It seemed as if she had read his mind. "One disadavantage of always having to be seated," she said, "is that I must often crane my neck in order to look up at someone standing beside me. Would you care to push my chair closer to that bench, sir, and seat yourself?"

It was encouraging. She obviously wanted to converse with him. He did as she asked, and they were able to talk without the inconvenience she had spoken of and without the usual presence of a third person. Her eyes *were* fine, he thought, except that he found himself wanting to draw back his head in order to be a few inches farther away from their very direct gaze.

"Are you finding the waters beneficial?" he asked.

"I find them relaxing," she said. "I bathe in them but I do not drink them. Fortunately I have no illness that might be cured in such a way. I believe I would have to be very ill indeed to drink a daily draft. Have you tried the water?"

He smiled deep into her eyes. "Once," he said. "Once was enough. I am glad the baths are helping you. Are you happy in Bath?"

"As you remarked," she said, "it is a beautiful place, and I have some agreeable acquaintances here. I came here several times with my father before his death."

"I am sorry about that," he said. "It must have been distressing for you."

"Yes," she said. "Are you enjoying being here, Mr. Sullivan?"

"A great deal more than I expected to," he said. "I was intending to spend no more than a few days here. I thought I would look in on the city since I was in this part of the country. But now I find myself reluctant to leave."

"Oh?" She was looking very directly at him. He had piqued her interest, he could see. "It is more beautiful than you expected?"

10

"Yes, I believe it is," he said. "But it is people who make a place, I am sure you would agree. There are people here from whom I am reluctant to part." He let his eyes stray to her mouth before raising them again to hers. "I might even say – one person."

"Oh." Her lips formed the words though she made no sound.

"I have been touched by your quiet patience and by your cheerfulness and good sense," he said. "I have been accustomed for several years to mingle with the young ladies of *ton* who flock to London for the Season. I have become almost immune to their charms. I have never met anyone like you, ma'am. Am I being impertinent? Am I speaking out of turn?"

He fixed his eyes on hers, very aware that Miss Pope and her escort were approaching. He willed them to take a second turn about the room. They obeyed his will, though he fancied that Miss Pope looked at him very intently as they passed.

"No," Miss Danford said, her voice a mere whisper of sound.

He touched his fingers lightly to hers as they rested on the arm of her chair. "I have thought myself jaded and immune to the charms of women," he said. "I have been unprepared for the intensity of my reaction to making your acquaintance, ma'am."

"It was less than a week ago, sir," she said. She was all dark eyes in a pale face.

"It could be an eternity," he said. "I did not know that so much could happen within the span of one week. So much to the state of one's heart, that is."

"I am unable to walk," she said. "I am unable to be out in the air as much as I could wish." Her eyes gazed deeply into his. "I have no claim to beauty."

It was a point he must deal with carefully. "Is that what you have been told?" he asked. "Is that what your glass tells you? Sometimes when we look in a glass, we do so impersonally, seeing only what is on the

11

surface. Sometimes beauty has little to do with surface appearances. I have known women who are acclaimed beauties but are quite unappealing because there is no character behind the beauty. You are not beautiful in that way, Miss Danford. Your beauty is all inner. It shines through your eyes."

"Oh." He watched her lips part. He watched her eyes dart to his own lips before looking into his again.

"Am I embarrassing you?" he asked. "Am I outraging you? I would not do so for the world. Perhaps you do not believe what I am saying either about your beauty or about my feelings for you. I would not have believed the latter myself a week ago. I thought myself beyond falling in love."

"Falling in love?" she asked him.

"I believe that is the appropriate term," he said. He smiled slowly and deliberately. "The term over which I have always sneered."

"Falling in love," she said. "It is for very young people, sir. I am twenty-six years old."

"My age," he said. "Do you feel yourself beyond youth, then, ma'am? I have felt like a boy in the past week – eager, uncertain, gauche, and, yes, in love."

She opened her mouth to speak and closed it again. "I find this hard to believe," she said at last very quietly.

She must live a lonely life, he thought suddenly. She must have had her share of fortune hunters but very few genuine suitors, if any. Did she dream of loving? Of being loved? That was the trouble with him – he thought too much. It was what had happened with Julia, though in that case he could not say he was sorry that he had stopped to think. He felt quilty enough as it was.

Should he feel guilty now? Was he catering to a dream that he could not after all fulfill? But why could he not? If he married her, he would treat her well. He would give her affection. He would give her some of his time and attention. He was not trying to lure her into a dreadful marriage of total neglect.

12

"Believe it," he said, leaning a little toward her and looking into her eyes with more genuine sympathy than he had expected to feel. "We are in a public place. It is neither the time nor the place for a formal declaration. But with your permission I would like to find that time and that place. Soon."

Was he being too hasty? He had not come to the Pump Room that morning with the intention of going so far. But the opportunity had presented itself in the form of the gentleman who was strolling with Miss Pope. And Miss Danford seemed receptive.

"You have my permission, sir."

She spoke so quietly that he was not sure at first that she had said the words. When he was sure, he felt elation and – panic. He felt rather as if he had taken an irrevocable step. Her words suggested that she understood him fully and was prepared to listen to a formal offer. Probably to accept it. Why would she be willing to listen if she had no intention of accepting?

He leaned back away from her again. Miss Pope and her escort were approaching. They would probably not take a third turn about the room.

"Tomorrow?" he asked. He shied away from the thought of today. He needed time in which to sort out his thoughts, though there was nothing really to sort out. He needed to marry wealth soon and now he had a better chance than he could have hoped for. "May I call on you tomorrow afternoon, ma'am?"

She hesitated for a moment. "The next day, if you will, sir," she said. "I am expecting a visitor from London tomorrow."

"The day after tomorrow, then," he said, getting to his feet and turning her chair to face the room so that she could watch the approach of her friend. "I shall live in fearful anxiety until then."

He spoke nothing more than the truth. She was going to accept him, he thought. It could not be this easy, surely. And yet there was panic and terror. He looked down at her thin figure in the wheeled chair, at the pale face and the too-thick masses of her dark hair beneath the pretty bonnet. It seemed altogether possible that she was to be his wife. He was going to tie himself to her for life merely because of an accumulation of debts that might be wiped out in one evening at the tables if luck was with him. A lifetime as set against one evening.

She looked up at him and smiled just before her companion joined them. "I shall look forward to it, Mr. Sullivan," she said.

# 2

Clara really did have a visitor the following day. He strode into the drawing room of the house she had rented on the Circus during the afternoon, following hard on the heels of the housekeeper.

"Clara, my dear," he said, stretching out his hands to take hers as he crossed the room toward her. "I came as soon as I heard from your messenger." He bent to kiss her cheek.

"Mr. Whitehead," she said, smiling warmly up at him and returning the pressure of his hands. "I knew you would. I hope it was not a dreadful inconvenience."

But they could say no more until the Misses Grover, twin sisters of indeterminate years, and Colonel and Mrs, Ruttledge took their leave after paying an afternoon call. Clara introduced the new arrival as Mr. Thomas Whitehead from London, a dear friend of her late papa's.

Harriet saw the visitors to the front door. She looked back before leaving the room. "I shall be in my room if you need me, Clara," she said. "I hope Mr. Whitchcad will be able to talk some sense into you."

"Ominous," Mr. Whitehead said whcn thc door had closed. He moved to a chair beside Clara's and smiled at her. "What is this all about, my dear? Some trouble?"

"I hated to drag you all the way from London on such short notice," she said. "You did not bring Mrs, Whitehead?"

He chuckled. "Miriam would need a week to get ready even for an emergency visit," he said. "Actually she is preparing to close the house for the rest of the summer.

We are removing to Brighton. A week later and your messenger would not have found me at home. What is the problem?"

"Oh, dear," she said, "I am not sure it is a problem. Perhaps it is. I am considering marriage."

He raised his eyebrows and took one of her thin hands in his. "But this is splendid news," he said. "Miriam will be sorry indeed that she did not come. Who is the fortunate man?"

"He has not made an offer yet," she said, "though I believe he is about to. The problem is that he is a fortune hunter. I think he is probably impecunious."

Mr. Whitehead's rather bushy eyebrows shot together. "Clara?" he said. "What is this? Are you in love with the fellow?"

"No," she said. "But I think I am going to marry him if he does indeed ask. Harriet is very vexed with me, as I am sure you could tell."

Mr. Whitehead released her hand and sat back in his chair. "I think you had better tell me everything," he said. "I assume that is why you summoned me here."

She smiled. "I summoned you because since Papa's passing I have thought of you almost as a second father," she said. "As you have insisted. Actually I need financial advice more than anything. When I marry, all my property and fortune will be my husband's?"

"In the normal course of events, yes," he said. "But it is possible for a marriage settlement to state otherwise."

"Ah," she said. "That is what I needed to know. You must explain it to me if you will. You helped me organize my affairs after Papa's death. I do not know how I would have managed without you. You gave the practical assistance and Mrs, Whitehead and Harriet gave the emotional support I needed. You have helped me make wise investments. I trust you absolutely, you see."

"I should think so too, Clara," he said. "Your papa was my colleague in India and my closest friend, after all. Now, who is this man? Anyone I know?"

16

"Mr. Frederick Sullivan," she said. "Elder son of Lord Bellamy. Do you know him?"

"Sullivan?" He frowned. "There is no point in saying that I hope you are not serious, is there, Clara? You would not have summoned me from London if you were not. What do you know of him?"

"That he is handsome beyond belief," she said, half smiling, "and charming. Oh, yes, and that he has conceived a violent passion for me."

"Has he?" Mr. Whitehead got to his feet and stood staring broodingly down at her. "The rogue."

Her smile became rueful. "Is it so impossible to believe?" she asked. But she held up a staying hand. "You are not expected to answer that question. Of course it is impossible. I have not been deceived for a moment."

"And yet," he said, "you are seriously considering marrying the scoundrel, Clara? This is most unlike you. What am I missing?"

"A great deal," she said. "Is he a scoundrel, then, Mr. Whitehead? What do you know of him?"

"Bellamy is wealthy enough, by all accounts," he said, "and generous enough. But Sullivan is wild, Clara. Totally irresponsible. He is a gambler and – yes, it must be said. He is a womanizer too. I believe he is still received in good company, but I have heard it said that men with eligible daughters keep them well beyond his reach. Now I can see the wisdom of their actions."

"It is as I thought, then," she said. "You have not told me anything I had not guessed for myself. So I will need a carefully drawn up marriage settlement, you see."

"Clara." He stood looking down at her for several silent moments before seating himself again. "Knowing the truth, you cannot seriously consider continuing with your plans, surely. You have realized for yourself the insincerity of his protestations of affection, and you have admitted that you do not love him. Or was that not the truth? *Are* your feelings engaged?"

17

"Not at all," she said. "I am not blinded to anything that might lead me on into false expectations. I will not be disappointed because I do not expect a great deal. But I have not changed my mind."

He stared at her, speechless.

"It is the human factor you have missed, you see," she said. "I am still young enough and I am certainly wealthy enough to attract a husband. I cannot expect to win any man's affections. There are too many factors against it. No, don't try contradicting me. You would be kind to me, but I know the truth. Only my money can buy me a husband. It seems sordid and horribly unwise to you that I would allow such a thing to happen to me. But there is the human factor. I need a husband. I need marriage."

"But not where there is no fondness," he said, pleading with her, reaching for one of her hands again. "Not where there is no reasonable expectation of its developing, Clara. Don't do something you will forever regret. And you will regret this, my dear."

"Perhaps," he said. "But perhaps not. Or not as much as you fear. I believe that continuing as I am would eventually become insupportable to me."

"Clara." He patted her hand with his free one. "Come to live with Miriam and me. You would be a daughter to us and company for Miriam. You said no after your father's passing. Say yes now. You do not need to live alone. You do not need to be lonely."

"I am neither," she said. "At least, not in the way you mean. Harriet is a dear friend and I have others. Although I like to go out whenever possible, I do not need to do so in order to have company, you know. This afternoon's visits were by no means unusual. But if the offer is made tomorrow – he is to make a formal call during the afternoon – I shall accept."

"But why Sullivan, Clara?" he asked. "We can find you a better husband than he. Someone who would be attracted by your fortune, perhaps, but prepared to treat you kindly. Sullivan is a wastrel."

18

"A handsome wastrel," she said. "Perhaps I am willing to buy beauty, Mr. Whitehead. There is so little of it in my life."

He released her hand once more. "I wish Miriam were here," he said. "I have never had any skill at giving personal advice, Clara, only financial advice. But you do not sound like yourself at all. You have always been so sensible."

She smiled. "Don't worry about me," she said. "It is your expertise I need. You must advise me if you will on how I am to prevent my beautiful wastrel from making a beggar of me."

And so the conversation turned finally to the marriage settlement that would be offered to Mr. Frederick Sullivan if indeed he did make the expected proposal the next day. Clara had always trusted the financial astuteness of her father's dear friend and more lately hers, and she trusted him on this occasion. But on one point she was stubborn.

Her dowry must be large enough to pay Mr. Sullivan's debts. That, after all, was doubtless why he was going to marry her. They did not know, of course, how large those debts were. Clara adamantly refused either to allow Mr. Sullivan to be asked or to allow inquiries to be made.

"I will not marry a man whom I have just humiliated," she said, "or one on whom I have just spied."

"But we have no other way of knowing, Clara," he said.

"Are his debts likely to be higher than ten thousand pounds?" she asked.

He grimaced. "One would certainly hope not," he said. "It is unlikely that even with such a man they are as high, Clara."

"Then my dowry is to be twenty thousand pounds," she said. She refused to be budged from her decision despite Mr. Whitehead's repeated assertion that she was being foolishly over-generous.

Mr. Whitehead was willing to act as Clara's man of

19

business and discuss the marriage settlement with Mr. Sullivan. He could hardly pretend to be her guardian, he explained, since Clara had been of age for several years. But he could pretend that he was trustee of her father's estate and fortune and that she was not entirely free to dispose of them as she wished. A generous dowry was to be given at her marriage. The rest of her fortune was to be kept in her name.

Clara pondered the lie. She did not want to enter a marriage of deceit, though of course there would be plenty on his side. And yet neither did she want to enter a marriage in which her husband would feel the humiliation of knowing that she was responsible for the fact that he was not to be entrusted with her total care, as other husbands were. She did not want him to know the truth.

Her heir, on Mr. Whitehead's advice, was to remain a distant cousin, at least for the time being.

Mr. Whitehead rose to take his leave eventually. He leaned over Clara to kiss her cheek once more. "I will meet with the scoundrel once the offer has been made and accepted," he said. "Consider very carefully, my dear, and listen to the advice of Miss Pope, who is a sensible young lady. Don't do something you will regret for the rest of your life."

"I don't intend to," she said, smiling up at him. "Thank you for coming so far at a moment's notice. I will never be able to tell you how grateful I am and how much better prepared I feel to face tomorrow."

He shook his head ruefully and left the room after promising to return later to take dinner with the ladies.

Clara sat watching the closed door after he had gone. It was all going to be very anticlimactic if Mr. Sullivan failed to put in an appearance tomorrow after all, or if his call turned into merely a social visit. She had not seen him today. Although she had bathed early in the Queen's Bath, as usual, she had not gone to the Pump Room afterward. She had had her servant carry her out to her carriage and had come straight home.

It was hard now to believe that he really would come. It was hard to believe that she would ever see him again. And would it be a great escape for her if he did not? Harriet would say so, and so would Mr. Whitehead. And her good sense. But she would be disappointed, she knew. Bitterly disappointed. For she had made up her mind, and with the decision had come the full knowledge of just how empty and lonely her life had been for years, especially since the death of her father. It had all come flooding out of her, just as if a dam had been released.

She wanted him. Mr. Frederick Sullivan, that was. She wanted all that health and strength and beauty to belong to her. Almost as if she could make them her own, she thought wryly. Almost as if she could transform herself by marrying him. Common sense told her how foolish she was being, but her heart yearned. And the heart was very difficult to silence when one was twenty-six years old and crippled and unlovely. When one's life was dull. Totally without excitement.

She hoped he would come. She did not quite believe that he would, but she hoped.

Frederick dressed with nervous care, discarding neckcloth after neckcloth when it would not fall into folds to suit his taste and finally having to call on his valet to do it for him. He was not a dandy and never had been. He despised dandies. Only dandies fussed over their neckcloths on the conviction that a simple knot just would not do.

He wished that he felt a little more alert and peered at himself more closely in the looking glass. Were his eyes bloodshot or did they just feel as if they were? He had sat up late at cards the evening before, though late nights were frowned upon in Bath, and had won again – a mere paltry sum again. And then he had escorted Lady Waggoner home, sensing both that she would allow him to and that she would allow him more than that. It was easy to sense such things when one was experienced at the same sort of game as that played by the lady.

There had seemed no further point in not being reckless and no harm in trying for a last minute reprieve from an almost certain fate. He had accepted the tacit invitation and spent an energetic and virtually sleepless night in the lady's bed. Indeed it would have been a thoroughly satisfactory night if he had not been obliged to make a marriage proposal to another lady the following day. The timing of the start of the affair had been wretched. And of course affair was all it was or ever would be. When he had broached the subject of marriage as though jokingly, Lady Waggoner had settled her ample body against his with a sigh of sleepy satisfaction and put all his slim hopes to flight.

"Marriage is not for the likes of you and me, Freddie," she had said. "It would drive us both insane within a fortnight. I believe a fortnight is as long as I was faithful to my late husband. He was not at all pleased with me."

"You are right, of course," he had agreed, kissing her lazily as they settled themselves for one of the brief interludes of sleep they had allowed themselves. "Far better a torrid and short-lived passion for people like us."

"Mmm," she had said. "You are a man after my own heart, Freddie."

And so he had left her far too late in the morning to make his appearance at the Pump Room, though that perhaps was just as well. And now he was drowsy and eager with anticipation of the coming night all at the same time. Not at all as composed as he would like to feel when on his way to make the first marriage offer of his life.

The thing to do was to treat it as a piece of business. The thing was not to stop and think of it. It was, after all, a business proposition he was about to make, though he would not use those words to Miss Danford. Her money in exchange for his name and protection. She would be a married lady. Such a status was important to women.

He would have a baroness's title to offer her one day, though heaven knew he wished no ill health on his father. He was fond of him. Too damned fond. Sometimes he wished there were no such thing as family.

He took one last look at his image in the glass – at the blue coat, Weston's finest, and white linen, the buff-colored pantaloons and shiny Hessian boots with their white tassels. His eyes were not bloodshot. He put on his hat, drew on his gloves, and took up his cane. It was time to go. She would be expecting him.

He was twenty-six years old, for God's sake, he thought as his steps took him toward the Circus. He had not expected to have to think of marriage for another five or six years at the least. Whenever his thoughts had touched on his future bride, he had pictured a young girl, exquisitely lovely, an ornament for his life and his home. Not love. He did not believe in love, only in lust and in friendship. But he would have liked a friendly relationship with his bride. He and Julia had always been friends – but he resolutely put from his mind thoughts of the new Countess of Beaconswood.

He thought with distaste of Miss Clara Danford as he lifted the brass knocker on her door. She was crippled. Did that mean, he wondered, that she would not be able to . . .? He fully expected that it meant just that or that anyway she was of such delicate health that she would not be able to endure the exertions of the marriage bed. He hoped that was the case, though he bore her no ill will. He intended to treat her with kindness when they were married. But not that. He had never found himself forced to bed a woman he found unappealing. An unconsummated marriage would suit him very well.

But it was not a thought to be pursued at the moment. The door opened and he stepped inside.

Harriet talked determinedly about the weather and about the people she had met during a morning shopping trip on Milsom Street until Clara looked steadily at her and

23

Frederick, more direct, asked if he might have a private word with Miss Danford.

Harriet left them together with obvious reluctance. She glared tight-lipped at Frederick as he opened the door for her.

"I believe I have offended your companion," he said quietly as he closed the door and turned back into the room.

"Harriet believes I need a chaperon," Clara said.

He stood looking down at her for a few moments before resuming his seat opposite her. "She has a care for your happiness," he said. "I can only honor her for that. Would she feel better, I wonder, if she knew that I share her concern?"

Clara said nothing.

"You are looking lovely this afternoon, ma'am," he said.

Without her bonnet, her very dark hair looked even thicker and heavier. It had been dressed very carefully into a topknot with ringlets adorning the back of her head and wisps of waves framing her face. The pale blue of her dress had been chosen with care to take away any impression that her pale complexion was sallow.

"Thank you," she said, but she did not smile. Such words were blatant flattery and not at all welcome. She might have returned the compliment with perfect sincerity, but one did not pay such compliments to a gentleman.

"I missed you this morning," he said. "I am sorry that business kept me from the Pump Room."

"I was not there either," she said. "I was tired after taking the waters and came home."

"I trust you are not unwell?" he asked.

"No." She shook her head.

It was an impossibility, she thought. The difference between them was so extreme that it was laughable. She must find kind words with which to send him on his way. He looked even more handsome and virile

24

sitting in her drawing room than he did in the Pump Room.

"You must know why I asked permission to pay this call," he said, getting to his feet with sudden agitation. Was it genuine or feigned? she wondered. "You must know that admiration and affection have grown in me during the past week until I can only put the word *love* to my feelings for you, ma'am. I love you. Do you find my declaration offensive?" He looked at her intently from those dark eyes, which must have been felling female hearts for years. They looked anxious.

She shook her head. "No, sir," she said.

He closed the distance between them, leaned over her, and possessed himself of one of her hands. His hand seemed very large and very brown in comparison with her own, yet well-formed. And warm. She looked down at it and at her own thin, pale wrist.

"Dare I hope," he asked her, "that you have any tender feelings for me, ma'am? I know myself quite unworthy."

She wished she could just look him in the eye, tell him that she understood, and explain that they could marry each other in all honesty for their own very separate reasons. But she could not do so. There were conventions to be observed.

"I am not indifferent, sir," she said. "Though my feelings are not as violent as those you describe."

"I would not expect them to be," he said, setting one knee on the floor. A man kneeling to make a proposal of marriage did not look nearly as ridiculous as she had always imagined, she found. In fact, he looked enormously attractive. "You are a lady, ma'am. You cannot know how you have delighted me by the admission that you are not indifferent to me."

She watched him raise her hand to his lips and hold it there for a long moment. A man's lips, she found, were warm, warmer than his hand. His breath fanned the back of her hand. She found herself swallowing involuntarily.

25

"Miss Danford," he said, "will you make me the happiest of men? Will you marry me?"

"Yes," she said. It was a strange unreal moment. She felt almost as if she were standing a distance behind herself, observing the scene. She felt almost as if someone else had spoken the single word. It had happened, then. He had made the offer and she had accepted.

He was gazing up into her face. "Yes?" he said. "You said yes? I have hardly dared hope. Even now I hardly dare believe the evidence of my own ears. Say it again."

"Yes," she said. "I will marry you, sir, I thank you."

He smiled then, slowly, a smile that spread from his eyes to his mouth and finally to his whole face. She could well imagine that a woman with more reason to believe in his sincerity might have her stomach performing somersaults at the expression. She felt a wave of sadness that she could not suddenly be beautiful and youthful and agile. But she would not dwell on it. She had reconciled herself to reality long before.

"You have done it," he said, and he laughed and tightened his hold of her hand. "You have made me the happiest of men. How – how happy I am!"

She found herself returning his smile. Yes, she thought, he probably was happy. So was she. God help her, so was she. "And so am I, sir," she said.

"Sir." He laughed at her again. "My name is Frederick, ma'am. Freddie to my family and friends. You are going to be both."

"Freddie," she said. She was going to be his family and his friend. Yes, definitely the first and perhaps the second. There was no reason, surely, why they could not become friends. "I would like to be both. I am Clara." She smiled again. "To my family and friends."

"And now," he said, "the first and highest hurdle safely over, I am all impatience. When will you be my wife, ma'am – Clara? Soon? I cannot bear the thought of waiting even for the banns. I shall go to London for a special license. Shall I? Tomorrow? Don't say no."

26

"A special license, yes," she said. "But not tomorrow, Freddie. My man of business is in Bath – he arrived yesterday by design, though neither of us realized when it was arranged just how opportune a time it would be for his visit. He is also the trustee of my father's estate. He will want to talk with you about a marriage settlement."

She might have imagined the flicker at the back of his eyes since she was looking for it. If it was there, it was well controlled. He laughed. "Marriage settlement," he said. "How coldly mercenary that sounds. Is it necessary? I suppose it is, but all I can think of is you, Clara, and making you my bride. Are you going to be the voice of good sense in our marriage? Very well, then, I shall delay for one day in order to speak with this ogre who will demand to know how I am to support you. My father will be generous, I do assure you. We will not be paupers, my love."

*My love.* She did not realize how much her heart had yearned to hear the words directed at her until Freddie spoke them – and did not mean them. She would have liked so dearly to be some man's love. But she must not wish for the moon now that she had the stars. She had never expected the stars either. She was going to be married – to the most beautiful man she had ever seen. She would be content with that.

"No, of course we will not," she said. "My fortune is vast, Freddie, and Mr. Whitehead is not ungenerous. But I warn you that he is very protective of my interests. He will probably treat you as if you are a fortune hunter whose only motive is to part me from all my possessions."

He took her other hand in his free one and squeezed both. "I like him already," he said. "I am glad you have had someone to protect you since the death of your father, Clara, and to continue to do so even after our betrothal and marriage. Soon enough he will know that the only treasure I want from our marriage is the one I am gazing at at this very moment."

"Thank you, Freddie," she said, drawing her hands

27

from his before she could forget that it was all charade, before she could forget that he would spend an anxious night wondering if he had trapped himself into a pointless marriage, wondering if there were any honorable way out. "I shall try to be a treasure to you."

He got to his feet and smiled down at her. "I have been so nervous," he said. "I slept scarcely a wink last night."

"If you pull the bell rope behind you," she said, "Harriet will return. I think we should share our news with her, Freddie."

"Of course," he said, turning quickly. "I must not keep you too long alone, my love." He turned back to her after pulling on the rope. "She does not like me, does she? She suspects my motives. She too will learn the truth soon enough. I love you, Clara."

She smiled at him.

# 3

Frederick had not looked a great way beyond the proposal. If he had, it was with a vague notion that he would rush to London in person for a special license and marry in haste and near secrecy in Bath, only the requisite two witnesses present apart from the clergyman and the two of them. Things did not turn out quite that way.

First there was that infernal Whitehead, who turned out to be quite as humorless as Frederick had expected and quite as adamantly protective of Clara Danford's interests as she had warned. The two men spent all of three hours together on the morning following the proposal, supposedly sitting over breakfast at the White Hart, to which hotel Frederick had been summoned, apparently conversing affably and agreeing on all major items of business. But in fact fencing with each other, sizing each other up, trying to decide if they liked each other and trusted each other. Trying to decide how much the other liked and respected Clara and had her interests at heart.

On one point at least Frederick was relieved. Enormously relieved. Although he was to receive only a dowry with his bride, it was far more generous than he had feared all through a pleasurable but distracted second night with Lady Waggoner. Twenty thousand pounds! It would pay all his debts with some to spare. It was tempting at first to consider which debts were pressing enough that they must be paid immediately and which ones could be conveniently forgotten about until in time they fell into the first category. But he would not give in to temptation. He would pay them all off, every last one of them. It would be a novel feeling to be debt free.

It was going to be a novel feeling to be married, he thought when he was finally climbing the hill back to his own hotel. He still felt something like panic at the prospect. But he needed to think of it coolly and rationally. There was no getting out of it now. He was going to have to reform his ways. No more gambling, he decided, or not for high stakes, anyway. He had learned his lesson. And no more womanizing, or not to the extent he had carried on during the last several years anyway. He would find himself a mistress, something he was not in the habit of doing, and keep only one at a time. It would be infinitely more healthy than whoring. He had made no further assignations with Lady Waggoner after the night before. It was the wrong time for a long-term affair, pleasurable as it would undoubtedly have continued to be.

Lord, he thought as he entered the York Hotel and nodded affably to those employees who were on duty in the lobby, he was not even married yet and already he was planning a complete transformation of his life. Would it be possible? Did it snow in July? He let himself into his private sitting room.

And found his mother seated there and his father standing at the window. Who the devil had told them? he wondered foolishly during the first moment of surprise. And then his mother was on her feet and he was hugging her and kissing her cheek and reaching out a hand to his father.

"What is this?" he asked, laughing.

"We were on our way home from Primrose Park," Lady Bellamy said, "and decided to come out of our way here to call on you, Freddie."

"Well," he said, "I am delighted you did. Where is Les?"

"Your brother went to London," Lord Bellamy said, "with some bee in his bonnet about traveling. He wants to go to Italy for the winter, it seems. Julia put the idea

30

into his head apparently that he had always wanted to be a traveler."

Jule. There was no getting away from his guilt, was there?

"We wondered why you did not stay for the wedding, Freddie," his mother said, "but rushed away almost without a word to anyone."

He grinned at her. "You know me, Mama," he said. "Always restless. Always eager to be on to the next adventure."

His father cleared his throat. "We thought it might have had something to do with Julia," he said.

Oh, good Lord, had they heard?

"We thought perhaps you had offered for her yourself and been disappointed at her refusal," his mother said. "We know you have always been fond of her, Freddie."

They had not heard. He grinned again, with relief this time. "It was wicked of Uncle to state in his will that Primrose Park would go to whichever nephew Jule agreed to marry," he said. "Of course I was interested for a while, Mama. It is an attractive property and I am fond of Jule. I even offered for her. But my feelings were not engaged. I wish her happiness with Dan. Did the wedding go well? Did the rest of the family stay for it?"

"Everyone except you," his father said.

Frederick shrugged. "I was afraid they would be embarrassed with me there," he said. "Since I had proposed to her and all that – and Dan knew it. I would have been embarrassed. I have some important news." The understatement of the decade, he thought.

They both gave him their full attention.

"I got myself betrothed yesterday," he said. "I am going to be married within the week."

His mother sat down abruptly again. His father frowned. Frederick laughed.

"Are you not going to congratulate me?" he asked. "Are you not going to ask who she is?"

"Who is she?" his mother asked.

31

"You dark horse, Freddie," his father said. "Someone you fancied before, is she? And you heard she was in Bath? That is why you rushed away and did not stay for the wedding?"

"Who is she?" his mother asked again, her voice more impatient.

"Miss Clara Danford," he said. "Of Ebury Court in Kent. Her father was the late Sir Douglas Danford."

"But why did you not tell us about her before, Freddie?" his mother asked. "How long have you known her?"

"A week, Mama," he said. "I met her here and fell headlong in love with her. It sounds out of character, I admit. It took me by surprise too."

His mother's eyes lit up and she clasped her hands to her bosom.

"Danford?" Lord Bellamy said with a frown. "The East India Company Danford, Freddie? He was as rich as a sultan, wasn't he?"

"I think maybe he was," Frederick said with a shrug, "according to something Clara said yesterday when I was making my offer to her and according to what her man of business has just been telling me."

"She inherited everything?" his father asked.

"Apparently, yes," Frederick said. "A nuisance actually. She is wealthier than I am. A man likes to feel that his wife will depend upon him for everything. But we will not let it spoil things for us."

His father looked at him fixedly and shrewdly. "We must have a man-to-man talk later, Freddie," he said. "Right now it is time for luncheon."

"When may we meet your betrothed, Freddie?" his mother asked. "Oh, does not that sound strange and wonderful, Raymond? Clara is her name? A sensible name. Is she beautiful? But of course she must be. What a foolish question. No one has more of an eye to beauty in women than you. I just hope that she really is sensible too. Oh, this is turning into a marvelously exciting day. I am only just beginning to comprehend what you have told us,

32

Freddie." She laughed. "There is to be another wedding. Our own son this time. We are to have a daughter-in-law. Perhaps even a grandchild by next summer."

"Luncheon, Eunice," Lord Bellamy said firmly, setting a hand beneath his wife's elbow.

Frederick's cravat was feeling too tight suddenly.

"But when may we meet her, Freddie?" his mother asked again.

Clara was agitated when a note was brought from the York Hotel early in the afternoon asking if Mr. Sullivan might call later and bring with him his parents, Lord and Lady Bellamy, to present to his betrothed.

"Harriet," she said, her face looking even paler than usual, "I did not think to have to meet his family so soon. They will know, will they not? As soon as they set eyes on me? That I have grabbed an opportunity to be married at the expense of their son?"

Harriet's voice was angry. "Perhaps they will know too," she said, "that he has grabbed an opportunity to enrich himself at your expense."

"I wonder how much he has told them about me," Clara said. "Do you think he has told them everything, Harriet? I cannot refuse to meet them, can I? Can I pretend to have had a sudden attack of smallpox? Or typhoid?" She laughed. "What shall I wear? My blue again? And what can I do with my hair? It is so unruly."

It really was something she had not expected. She had imagined a quiet wedding in her own drawing room, no one present except her and Freddie and the clergyman, with Harriet and perhaps Mr. Whitehead as witnesses. She supposed she must have realized that at some time in the future she would have to meet his family, but she had put the prospect comfortably to the back of her mind. She did not even know how large a family he had.

And Mrs, Whitehead would be coming for the wedding. She would not miss it for worlds, Mr. Whitehead had said during a brief visit before luncheon, during which he had been able to assure her that everything had been agreed most amicably between him and Freddie.

Suddenly the truth of what she had allowed to happen during the past few days was being borne in upon Clara. Harriet was not pleased.

"Oh, Clara," she had said as soon as Frederick had left the previous afternoon, "what have you done? Have you really considered? What does he mean by calling you his love and looking at you with such melting glances?"

"He means to convey the impression that he is in love with me," Clara had said.

"Oh, Clara." Harriet had looked sorrowful. "Send him away. Tell him to go on the stage where he belongs."

They had come near to quarreling for the first time.

"You must not say such things any longer, Harriet," Clara had said quietly. "He is my betrothed. He is soon to be my husband. I will not hear anyone maligning him."

Tears had stood in Harriet's eyes and she had bitten her upper lip. "I am sorry," she had said. "I am so sorry, Clara. Do you care for him after all, then?"

"Whether I do or not," Clara had said, "he is to be my husband, Harriet. You must not expect me to discuss our relationship with you from this moment on."

"I shall look about me for another position," Harriet had said. "They are not difficult to come by in Bath. And Mama is here for me to live with while I wait. I am grateful that for more than two years my employer has also been my friend."

Harriet should be the one marrying, Clara had thought suddenly. She was the beautiful one. It was just a lamentable fact that she was without fortune. She was the one who should be marrying Freddie. They would suit each other in splendor. He could probably even come to love someone like Harriet.

"Don't leave, Harriet," she had said. "Please. Not

34

unless you will find the situation intolerable. I will need you as much as ever after I am married. My husband will have his own life, as all gentlemen do, but I will not be able to join him in as many activities as other wives enjoy. I will be able to share only a corner of his life. I will need your companionship and your friendship. Stay with me."

And so they had both cried a little and assured each other that their friendship was too deep a one to be broken so easily. Of course she would stay, Harriet had said. She would have stayed for friendship's sake even if she did not value the employment. And yet Clara had felt her pity – pity for a woman who was to be married within the week but who could hope for only a corner of her husband's life.

She did not pity herself. It was more than she had hoped for until a week before. It would be enough to push back the loneliness. It was not as if she loved Freddie, after all. She merely wanted to have a part in the type of life most people took for granted.

But she was nervous at the thought of meeting his parents. Lord and Lady Bellamy. They were only a baron and baroness. Her father had been a baronet. They were not so far above her in station. And yet she was awed by their titles. They would have expected more for their son. She wondered how much Freddie had told them about her.

Obviously it had not been a great deal. There was a horribly embarrassing moment when they were all admitted to her drawing room and Harriet rose out of respect – and the baroness's face lit up as she began to stretch out her hand. And there was the strange look cast upon her by both the baron and the baroness when they finally realized that she was the one and she did not rise to greet them. It was a blank look. An identical blank look that spoke volumes to Clara's anxious heart. They were deeply shocked. She wished absurdly that she had worn the blue again after all instead of the rose pink. As if a dress could have made an iota of difference.

"Clara is unable to walk," Frederick was explaining. He had come up beside her chair and smiled warmly into her eyes and took her hand to raise to his lips. "How are you, my love?"

But she was too aware of his parents to do more than smile stiffly up at him.

"Please do excuse me for having to receive you like this," she said, withdrawing her hand from Frederick's and extending it to his mother.

"My dear," Lady Bellamy said, taking her hand and bending over her, concern in her face, "was it an accident or an illness? No, don't try to move. I shall seat myself here beside you and we shall have a cozy chat."

"It was an illness, ma'am," Clara said. "A lengthy childhood sickness when I was in India. One of those mysterious tropical illnesses. The physicians never did seem to know quite what it was."

The baroness was kind, she thought in some relief. She must also be in some shock. The baron merely made his bow to her and seated himself in a chair indicated by Harriet and looked levelly at her. Frederick was sitting beside her, on the other side from his mother, and holding her hand again.

"Seeing Clara's cheerful patience," he said, smiling down at her and then looking at his mother, "can you wonder that I have tumbled into love with her, Mama?"

But of course, Clara thought, he must be quite as anxious as she at this meeting. It was obvious that he had not told them the full truth, that he was trying to deceive them as well as her. But they knew him better. They would know even better than she was expected to do just how incredible his story was. How could they look at her and believe that he had fallen in love with her?

"Harriet," she said, "would you be so good as to ring for tea?"

36

It was as well, she thought, setting herself to entertain her visitors and very aware of the warm strength of her betrothed's hand about her own, to get this over with. Perhaps after all it would have been more of an ordeal to meet the baron and baroness after a secret wedding.

The wedding did not take place for another four days. Though there was no particular hurry, Frederick realized. If any of his creditors had traced him to Bath, they would not have pressed their claims too hastily knowing that he was about to be married and to whom he was about to be married. He was safe.

He did not after all go to London the day following his meeting with Mr. Whitehead, as he had planned. His father had arranged a meeting at breakfast with him while his mother was still in her room. And an uncomfortable meeting it was, too. The baron demanded to know the truth.

"And don't give me that cock-and-bull story about having fallen in love with Miss Danford, Freddie," he said. "Have more respect for my intelligence. No offense to the lady, but she is very far from being a beauty. How big are your debts?"

Frederick was forced to admit to debts about half as large as they actually were. He submitted himself to a paternal lecture and promised faithfully that he would reform his ways. It was a speech and a promise that had repeated themselves with painful regularity over the past seven or eight years.

"But this time, Freddie," his father said, "you have more than yourself to consider. You are going to have a wife. My guess is that the lady has endured more than her share of suffering during her life. I'll not have my son causing her more."

Frederick promised with even more vehemence. And meant every word. But then he had always done so. He had always resolved to turn over a new leaf every time his father had bought him out of some deep hole of his own digging. He wondered again if it ever snowed in July. If only someone with a long memory could prove to him that it did, that once in history it had, then perhaps there would be hope for him.

"But I do love her, Papa," he said in conclusion, feeling compelled to justify himself in his father's eyes. Somehow his father, endlessly patient and unwaveringly loving, could make him feel like a schoolboy again with one sorrowful look. "I love her more than life. I would marry her if she were a beggar."

His father gave him that look – the one Frederick always dreaded more than any other. He even preferred anger to that level, knowing, and disappointed stare. "Don't over-do it, Freddie," he said. "Words mean little. Show her that you love her more than life. Make me proud of you, boy."

Lord, it was enough to make his eyes sting. It would be the final humiliation to cry in front of his father. More than anything else at that moment, he wanted to make his father proud of him. It was a ridiculous admission for a twenty-six-year-old man to make, even to himself.

The afternoon had to be given over to another meeting with Mr. Whitehead, that gentleman and the baron finalizing the marriage settlement with Frederick as an almost silent third member of the party. His yearly income was to be increased after his marriage – it was to be called an income now, no longer an allowance. And there was to be a town house. Bachelor rooms would no longer be suitable for a married man, it seemed, even though it was unlikely that Clara would ever want to visit London with him. Ebury Court was to be their country home.

It was strange, Frederick thought, how one seemed to lose ownership of one's own wedding once the proposal had been made. His mother spent the better part of the day at the house on the Circus with Clara, discussing things like flowers and wedding breakfasts. He saw Clara only briefly when he went to fetch his mother back to their hotel for dinner.

It was the next day before he finally set off for London and the special license. And once there he had to find out his brother to give him the news, and nothing would do but Lesley had to come to Bath too for the wedding. Italy could wait another day or two, he insisted, beaming his pleasure at his elder brother's approaching happiness. Weddings and happiness were synonymous in Lesley's vocabulary.

And so another day was lost while Lesley, uncertain what he should wear at the wedding – would it be quite the thing to wear the same outfit as he had worn at Dan and Jule's wedding so recently? – packed two large trunks with almost all his possessions and had to be persuaded to reduce his luggage by at least half. And then he remembered that he had a new coat awaiting him at Weston's, no less. Frederick found himself tossing glances at the ceiling and doing a deal of chuckling, something that always seemed to happen when he was with Les.

But finally they were back in Bath and back in the atmosphere of unreality. Everything had been arranged in his absence. Out of deference to Clara's condition, the wedding would take place in her drawing room instead of in a church. The baroness explained all the details. In addition to the minister and the bride and groom, the groom's parents and brother were to be in attendance, and the bride's companion, Miss Pope, and her dear friends, Mr. and Mrs. Whitehead, Colonel and Mrs. Ruttledge, and the Misses Grover.

Frederick wondered how they would all crowd into the drawing room, but he supposed it was not so very many people really. Just a deal more than he had originally expected.

The Misses Grover were to take Miss Pope home with them after the wedding breakfast, her own mother being from home at the time, and she was to remain with them for a week, after which time the baron and baroness would bring her to Ebury Court. The newly married couple, it seemed, were to proceed there the day after the wedding.

And so they were to have a honeymoon alone, Frederick discovered. He had not thought of honeymoons. He still did not know if there was any possibility of its being a normal marriage in any way.

There was a horribly confused mingling of reality and unreality in Frederick's mind as he retired to bed on the night following his return from London. His mother had seemed to be describing some alien event, something that had nothing whatsoever to do with him. And yet – good Lord! – he was going to be a married man by this time tomorrow.

He found himself wishing that he had not eaten such a hearty dinner.

Clara meanwhile was just closing her eyes after lying staring at the canopy over her bed for a long time. She could still see the pleats of the drapery outlined against her closed eyelids.

It had all become frighteningly real. Somehow as long as their impending marriage had concerned only her and Freddie, it had seemed quite reasonable. They were each marrying for a very definite reason. They each had something to gain from the marriage. It might turn out tolerably well.

But now other people were involved and she had the panicked feeling that she had started something that had developed a life of its own and was galloping along beyond her control. Several of her acquaintances had learned of her betrothal and had come with their smiles and kisses and handshakes and congratulations, and with their observations on the good looks and charm of Mr. Sullivan. Some of her closest acquaintances had called while Lady Bellamy was with her and had promptly been invited to the wedding.

Lady Bellamy had been very kind and very eager to ensure that the wedding would be an event to remember. Clara guessed that she was disappointed that it was not to be a large society wedding. But she had made the best of the situation. Clara discovered that there must be flowers everywhere, including the bride's hair, and that a special wedding breakfast must be prepared. She discovered that a seamstress must be summoned in all haste since she must have a new dress for the wedding and a new carriage dress to wear when she and Freddie left for Ebury Court the morning after their wedding. It was only a pity that there was insufficient time to have a whole wardrobeful of bride clothes made.

Lady Bellamy had arranged for Harriet to leave the house on the wedding day and to stay away for the first week of the marriage. Clara found the whole unexpected idea frightening and rather embarrassing. She wondered how Freddie would react to the idea of a week-long honeymoon.

It was that thought that made Clara close her eyes. A honeymoon. One week. She would have that, at least. He would surely stay with her at Ebury Court until his parents came at the end of the week, bringing Harriet home with them. At the age of twenty-six she would finally discover tomorrow night what it was like to be fully a woman. She would discover it in company with all that strong and splendid masculinity.

It was an exciting thought. A terrifying thought. And one not at all conducive to sleep. Yet she must sleep. If she did not, she would be even paler than she usually was in the morning. And there would be shadows beneath her eyes. She was plain enough without those added defects.

She willed herself to sleep. And felt rather nauseated and dizzy. And breathlessly excited.

# 4

The damned neckcloth was being stubborn again. Having to summon his valet to tie it for him – again – did nothing to soothe the irritation of Frederick's mood. His mother, fortunately, had been easy to banish. She had preparations of her own to make. Lesley was another matter. He hovered, grinning and nodding like the imbecile he was and mouthing the sort of foolishness one expected of Les. Things like liking Clara, though he had met her only once and briefly the afternoon before, and liking the idea of having a sister-in-law. Damn Les.

Though nothing was Les's fault, Frederick was forced to admit. And it was unfair to call his brother an imbecile, though he had not done so aloud. Les was slow, but he usually got where he was going eventually provided he was given time. And he was unfailingly goodnatured.

No, everything was his own fault. He was the imbecile – letting himself in for a life sentence merely because of a few paltry debts. Silk knee breeches in the morning, for the love of God! He looked down at them in distaste and at his white silk stockings and leather dancing shoes. He growled when a knock sounded on the door.

Good Lord, Clara's drawing room was going to be full to overflowing, he thought on first sight of his visitor. Was everyone and his dog coming to his wedding? And then he grinned at his friend's expression.

"Archie!" he said. "I never thought to see you in Bath."

Lord Archibald Vinney looked from Frederick to Lesley and back again. "Strange place, Bath," he said, fingering the ribbon of his quizzing glass but not lifting it to his eye. "I was appointed family envoy to bring greetings to my aunt – her eightieth birthday on the horizon, you know. Or is it her ninetieth? Something like that. The old girl dragged me off to the Pump Room at some unholy hour this morning and I heard quite by chance that the Honorable Mr. Frederick Sullivan was in residence. More than in residence. Actually you are the talk of the town, Freddie. I thought there must be some mistake. You know how gossip can twist things. But knee breeches at this time of day? And Les too?"

Frederick grimaced. "It's my wedding day," he said.

"What the devil?" his friend said, strolling into the room and raising his quizzing glass at last. "I was preparing to have a good laugh with you at the gossip, but it was all true. Who is she, Freddie my boy? The name that was mentioned meant nothing to me. I cannot even recall it now. Any beauty I know?"

"No," Frederick said shortly. "I met her here a week ago. Look, Archie, you had better come to the wedding. I need all the moral support I can get."

Lord Archibald whistled. "A whirlwind courtship," he said. "It does not sound in your line, Freddie. Or marriage at all, for that matter. Badly dipped, are you? Very wealthy, is she? And you turned on that famous charm and convinced both the chit and her papa that you have conceived a violent passion for her."

"Her father is dead," Frederick said irritably. "And she is no chit. She is twenty-six years old, Archie. I needed only her consent."

His friend whistled once more. "Twenty-six years old," he said. "The devil, Freddie. An antidote, is she? My commiserations, old chap."

Frederick's hands curled into fists. "She is to be my wife, Archie," he said.

Lord Archibald held up his hands defensively, palm out.

"I like her," Lesley said, smiling and nodding and saving a tense moment from exploding.

43

There was no chance to converse further. There was another knock on the door. The baron and baroness were ready, apparently, and the baroness was reputedly pacing her room in dire anxiety lest they be late. Or so Lord Bellamy reported, chuckling and then turning his attention to the new arrival.

Frederick tossed a look at the ceiling. "Mothers!" he said. "There is almost an hour before the wedding service is due to begin, and we have a ten-minute journey, if that."

"Nevertheless," his father said, "we had better be on our way, Freddie. Mothers suffer enough to bring sons into the world. It is a matter of simple courtesy for the sons and husbands to do all in their power to make that suffering seem worthwhile."

But Frederick did not hear the words. He heard only the echo of his own. The wedding service was due to begin in less than an hour. *Less than an hour.* He was thankful – very thankful – that he had been unable to eat any breakfast earlier. It had been hard enough on his stomach to watch Les devour a hearty meal.

She was sitting in her wheeled chair. With so many people expected and with the necessity of moving from place to place, it seemed easier. She would hate to have to be carried from one chair to another in sight of so many people. She was wearing the new white muslin gown Lady Bellamy had insisted was necessary, and she had to admit that it was beautiful and that she felt good in it. The short sleeves and hem were trimmed with a deep border of embroidered blue flowers. The silk sash beneath her bosom and her slippers were of a matching blue. Her hair, dressed higher than usual, was threaded liberally with live flowers.

"Do I look foolish?" she asked Harriet when guests had begun to arrive and she sat in solitary state in the dining room waiting to make a grand entrance just like any ordinary bride. "Flowers in the hair are for girls, aren't they?"

44

Her friend's eyes looked suspiciously moist when she bent to kiss Clara's cheek. "You look beautiful," she said. "You *are* beautiful."

Clara laughed. "Thank you, Harriet," she said. "I like his family, don't you? They must all be dreadfully disappointed, but they have been very kind. Is not Mr. Lesley Sullivan a dear?"

"Yes," Harriet said. "I like him. And Lady Bellamy is a true lady. You will be fortunate in your in-laws at least, Clara."

Clara smiled. But not in her husband. Harriet did not need to say the words aloud. And she would not do so. Clara had been adamant enough on the point that she would hear no more criticism of Freddie.

The housekeeper came into the dining room eventually to announce that Mr. Sullivan had just arrived and that all the expected guests were now waiting in the drawing room. So was the clergyman. There were ten minutes to go before the planned start of the service.

"Then we might as well begin," Clara said, drawing a slow and deep breath. "Will you send Mr. Whitehead in, please?" Mr. Whitehead had agreed to stand in her father's place.

And so this was it, she thought as Harriet bent again to kiss her, one tear trickling down her cheek, and then left to take her place in the drawing room. This was it. Mr. Whitehead came into the dining room, took both her hands in a firm clasp and bent to kiss her too. And then he was pushing the wheeled chair into the drawing room and she felt herself smiling.

It seemed bewilderingly full of people. And of flowers. And the scent of flowers. It seemed like a totally strange room. But she did not really see it or the people in it. If it had been full of strangers instead of her friends and his family, she would perhaps not have known it. For Freddie was standing before the fireplace with the clergyman, and he looked so unbelievably handsome dressed as though about to attend a formal ball that the breath caught in her throat. He was looking at her with intent, smoldering eyes and it was easy to believe in the unreality of the moment that the look meant what it said.

Mr. Whitehead pushed her chair to her bridegroom's side and the service began. A short service, without any frills. Without any music. So short that it was over before she could calm her mind sufficiently to concentrate. Freddie had her hand in his. He had put a gold ring on her finger that looked strange there and shining and very new. And he was bending his head to kiss her firmly on the lips.

"My love," he murmured, smiling into her eyes.

She should not have done it, she thought. Mr Whitehead had been right. She could have found another husband, someone more like her. Freddie was dazzlingly beautiful, like someone who inhabited a different planet from her own. Harriet had been right. They could never know happiness together, she and her husband.

*Her husband!*

"Freddie," she whispered back to him. She thought she was still smiling.

It seemed as if it was to be the last moment they were to have together for a long time. There was a murmuring about them and then a definite babble of voices. And a smattering of applause. And laughter. And then she was being hugged and kissed and cried over – by Harriet, by Lady Bellamy, by Mrs. Whitehead.

"My daughter, Clara, dear," Lady Bellamy said. "I have dreamed for many years of being able to say those words."

"Welcome to our family, my dear," Lord Bellamy said, squeezing her hand almost painfully. "We are proud to have you as a member."

"Clara." Harriet hugged her tightly for a long while. "I wish you happy. Oh, I do wish you happy."

"My sister." Lesley Sullivan was beaming down at her and taking both her hands in his. "I've always wanted a sister. I like you, Clara."

46

She felt tears spring to her eyes. "Thank you, Lesley," she said. "I like you too. And I have always dreamed of having a brother."

"Now you have one," he said. "A fortunate man is Freddie."

It was Lesley she should be married to, Clara thought foolishly. He was sweet and kind and open in manner – and as unlike Freddie in looks as it was possible to be. He was fair and goodlooking rather than handsome and not very tall.

"Here is Archie come to meet you," Lesley was saying, and she looked up to see a tall, brown-haired, aristocratic looking stranger at his side. "Lord Archibald Vinney, Clara."

"Mrs. Sullivan," the stranger said, taking one of her hands and raising it to his lips. "May I offer my congratulations, ma'am? I am your husband's friend, newly and opportunely arrived in Bath. I hope you do not mind that he invited me to your wedding without being able to consult your wishes first."

"You are very welcome here, my lord," she said. *Mrs. Sullivan.* Yes, she was. Clara Sullivan. How strange it sounded. But there was no time to dwell on the novelty of her new name and status. The Misses Grover were pressing about her and bending to kiss her. It was her wedding day, she told herself in some wonder. It was her wedding day.

"Les, my dear chap," Lord Archibald was saying as they drew back from the bride and he glanced in some amusement at his poor friend, who was going to be busy enduring hugs and kisses and handshakes for some time to come, "present me to the delectable little blond in green, if you will be so good."

The guests began to leave in the middle of the afternoon. The Misses Grover took with them a rather tearful and anxious Harriet. Mr. and Mrs. Whitehead stayed longer, and the baron and baroness and their younger son were still at the house on the Circus when it was very close to dinnertime. So close, in fact, that Frederick began to entertain strong hopes that they intended to stay. But when Clara invited them, they rose to their feet to take their leave.

Suddenly the house seemed very empty and very quiet.

Lord, Frederick thought as he returned to the drawing room after seeing his family on their way, his face felt almost sore from the smile he had kept pasted on it all day long. And he could not let go of it even now. There was a charade to be kept up.

"Well, my love," he said, reentering the room and smiling at his bride. She was sitting on a chaise longue, where Mr. Whitehead had placed her after the wedding breakfast, her legs resting along it. "We can relax at last."

Which were about the falsest words he had uttered all week, he thought. He had scarcely exchanged a word with Clara since the wedding service hours ago. He had been able to lose himself in conversation with their guests. She had appeared to be doing the same thing. He had been able almost to relax. Now he felt as taut as a bow.

"Yes," she said. "It was kind of so many people to come, Freddie. I had pictured a wedding with only two witnesses. This was very pleasant."

"Was it?" he asked, crossing the room to stand with his back to the fireplace. "It was not too much for your strength, Clara?"

It was hard to believe, he thought even as he spoke, that this woman was his wife. This pale, thin stranger with her pretty wedding dress, and flowers still twined in her too-thick hair. His wife. For the rest of their days.

"No," she said. "I am not ill, Freddie."

He stared at her. The subject had to be discussed before night came. Now was the opportune time since it had been broached already. Lord, they were married. This was their wedding day. Their wedding night was galloping up on them.

48

"What did happen to you?" he asked. "And in what degree of health has it left you?" He walked across the room to her and took a chair beside her.

"I was very ill for many months," she said. "So was my mother. She died after four months. I was left weak and bedridden and had recurrences of the fever all the time my father and I remained in India. I recovered my health after our return to England."

"But not your strength," he said.

"No," she said. "Papa was so afraid of losing me. I was all he had left. I believe he was exceedingly fond of my mother though I remember her only dimly. He made sure that I never went anywhere where I might take some infection."

It was peculiar watching a stranger become more of a person before his eyes. She had had a sad and sickly childhood. Someone had loved her to distraction. She had been everything in the world to her father, this plain, thin woman whom he had married without any regard to her personhood.

"Are you paralyzed?" he asked her. Her cheekbones were high and finely sculpted, he noticed as his eyes roamed over her face. She might have been almost lovely if she had had more flesh and more color.

She shook her head. "Only totally without strength," she said. "Papa would never let me exert myself in any way or go outdoors a great deal. He was afraid the illness would come back. But I think perhaps it was just the climate of India that did not agree with me."

God! he thought. "There is no pain?" he asked.

"No," she said. "Only aches and pains if I sit or lie in one position for too long. You do not have a sickly wife, Freddie. Only one whose body does not work for her as other people's do." She smiled.

Lord. He had had his answer. He reached for her hand, held it with both of his, and raised it to hold against his cheek. "I am so glad, my love," he said, gazing intently into her eyes. "I would suffer too if you had to suffer.

49

You look very lovely today. I have not had a chance to tell you that, have I?"

"And you look very splendid, Freddie," she said.

They were interrupted at that moment by the arrival of the housekeeper, who had come to announce that dinner was ready. A burly manservant stepped past her.

"Robin always carries me to the dining room," Clara explained.

Frederick got to his feet. "Thank you, Robin. That will be all," he said. "I will take Mrs. Sullivan in this evening." He turned to smile down at her after the servants had withdrawn. "How many husbands have this chance to get so close to their wives outside their private apartments after all."

He lifted her up into his arms while she twined an arm about his neck. She weighed nothing at all. God, she felt as fragile as a piece of fine porcelain. It was no wonder that a man who had loved her had feared constantly for her health and her very life. He carried her through to the dining room and set her down gently on her chair. She had indicated a chair at the side of the table, adjacent to its head, he noticed. And then she indicated that he was to sit at the head of the table – where he had sat at the wedding breakfast, while she had sat at the foot.

"Has this always been your place?" he asked her.

"It was my father's before his death," she said. "Now it is yours."

He set himself to charm her while they ate. He told her about London, with which she was not at all familiar, and recounted lively and humorous stories from his experience – ones that were suitable for the ear of a gently nurtured woman. They both laughed a great deal.

He wondered if she was in love with him. She had claimed to have some regard for him, nothing more, on the day when he had made his offer. It seemed like half a century ago. He hoped she did not love him. He would not hurt her for worlds. He wanted to show her kindness as far as he could. After all, she had already done him a

50

great service. Once he had got past all this strange tension of a wedding day, he was going to feel enormous relief at the knowledge that soon he would be debt-free. It was going to feel as if a heavy load had been removed from his back. He owed that feeling to her.

He was going to be kind to her. Because he wanted to be. Because he owed it to her. Because perhaps it would soothe his conscience somewhat. His conscience had been badly battered recently, what with that business with Julia and this deception with Clara.

And he needed to be kind to her. His mother and father would expect it of him. And he needed to prove to that tight-lipped little ice maiden of a companion that he was no ogre. And there was Archie. He had said nothing, of course, but there had been a look in his eyes after the wedding – part amusement, part sympathy – that had told Frederick that he understood perfectly. Sympathy! No, he did not need anyone's sympathy. Sympathy for him meant insult to Clara.

He would let no one insult Clara. She was his wife. He would prove to everyone that he knew how to care for a wife, even a plain and crippled one.

"Shall I have Robin summoned to take me back to the drawing room?" she asked when they had finished eating. "I used to leave Papa to enjoy his port alone."

"Not tonight," he said, setting a hand over hers and curling his fingers beneath it. "This is our wedding day."

And so he carried her back to the drawing room and sat beside her on a sofa, her hand in his, telling her more stories at her request until the gaps between them became longer and he could feel her growing agitation and his own. It was still early. But there was no point in torturing themselves for another hour or two. This was something he wanted to get over with. A wedding night should be something eagerly anticipated, he knew, especially if it was to be with a woman he had not had before. But not this particular wedding night.

"Would you like me to carry you up to your room, my

love?" he asked gently when she had failed to respond to one of his funnier stories.

She turned her head sharply and looked up at him.

"I shall summon your maid when we get there and leave you to her services," he said. "Is that how it is usually done?"

"Yes," she said.

"Clara." He raised her hand to his lips. "I must know. Do you wish this to be a normal marriage, my dear, or one in name only? It must be as you wish. I do not want to distress you."

For once there was color in her cheeks. A whole arsenal of roses. "I am your wife, Freddie," she said.

He searched her eyes and nodded. Ah, so she wanted it, then. She had not married him for the mere respectability of marriage. He just hoped . . . Oh, God, he hoped she was not in love with him. He would feel a worse blackguard than he already felt, if that were possible.

"You will become my wife fully this night, Clara, my love," he said, intensifying his look before getting to his feet in order to take her up into his arms again. He could not quite imagine himself making love to this thin and apparently frail body. "It has come at last. I have thought in the past few days that time had transformed itself into a snail just in order to torture me."

She set her head on the arm she had wound about his neck and laughed.

She lay on her bed after her maid had left, staring upward, trying to breathe steadily and slowly, wondering how long it would be before he returned. Half an hour, he had said after setting her down on the chair in her dressing room and summoning her maid. Half an hour. That must have almost passed already.

She should have had her hair braided, she thought. There was far too much of it to lie loose over her shoulders and down her back. Her father had never allowed her to cut it. Perhaps he had thought that as with Samson in the

Bible the little strength she had lay in her hair. She smiled at the thought. She should have braided her hair, except that braids seemed very juvenile and virginal.

Virginal. Her cheeks grew hot at the thought.

It would be strange to have a man in this room. In this bed. This had been her room ever since Papa had started bringing her to Bath after their return from India.

It had been a wonderful day. She had not expected the day itself to be wonderful, only the fact of her marriage. But it had been lovely. Everyone had been warm and kind. Everyone had seemed genuinely happy for her. Lord Bellamy had welcomed her into his family. He had said they were proud to have her as a member. She had believed him. Lesley – dear Lesley – had told her that he liked her. He had called her his sister. And Freddie had been charming – even after they were married and after all their guests had left and it might have been expected that he would lower his mask and put an end to the charade.

She had very much enjoyed dinner, despite the feeling of near-panic she had felt when his parents had refused her invitation to dinner and had left. Freddie had been charming and amusing and interesting. She liked his laugh. It was an amused chuckle.

She wondered how long he would continue to be charming. Until the morning perhaps? Until after the marriage had been safely consummated? Her stomach performed something of a somersault.

He had given her the chance to avoid this. Perhaps he had thought her health would make a normal marriage impossible. Perhaps he had welcomed the thought. Perhaps he had no wish to make a proper marriage out of it. But she would not be able to bear that. This was why she had married him. It was perhaps a shameful admission to make even in the privacy of her own heart. No lady surely would admit as much. But she had not married him just for the sake of being able to say she was a married woman. She had married him because she wanted him. Because she wanted a man. A strong and virile man.

53

She had paid dearly for Freddie. Twenty thousand pounds and perhaps more in the future. Perhaps he would drain away large portions of her fortune if she found herself unable to refuse him. And she knew what it was she had paid for. It was this. This that was about to happen to her. As a man might pay dearly for an extraordinarily beautiful courtesan. She did not expect that he would continue to charm her or to keep up the facade of calling her his love. She did not really expect his friendship or much of his company. Just this occasionally.

Yes, it was a shameful admission. But it was the truth and she had been alone with herself long enough to know that only the truth to herself was comfortable to live with. She had bought Freddie's beauty and strength and virility.

There was a tap on the door. It opened before she could gather herself together sufficiently to call to him to come in.

# 5

It felt like a new experience. But then it *was* a new experience. He felt almost as if he were the virgin, not knowing how to approach her, what to say to her, what to do to her. He did not know quite what she wanted apart from the consummation. He had never been with a woman under circumstances even comparable to these.

He smiled as he approached the bed. "It struck me after I had been shown to my room," he said, "that I did not know which one was yours. I had to guess that this was the one."

"Oh." She laughed.

She looked younger when she laughed. And with her hair brushed out loose. It was thick, shining, healthy-looking hair. He sat down on the edge of the bed and twined a lock of it about his fingers.

"I should have had it braided," she said.

"No," he said. "It is lovely as it is." It was rather lovely too. It looked better loose than piled on her head. She was looking at him with wary, questioning eyes and he realized that there was nothing in his experience to carry him through this moment. It was all new to him, this consummation of a marriage with a woman he found in no way appealing. And yet he owed her kindness, loyalty. What did she want? He wished he knew.

He lowered his head and kissed her. She was warm and apparently relaxed. Her closed lips trembled slightly beneath his closed lips and then pushed back against them. Ah, she was beginning to answer his unspoken questions. He smoothed back the hair from one side of her face and ran one knuckle of the other hand along her jawline, over her lips, along her nose.

"My love," he said, setting his lips to hers again, "you must tell me immediately if I cause you pain or discomfort. Will you?"

But she was pressing her lips to his again, and her hands were first on his shoulders and then about his neck. He felt the fingers of one of her hands twine in his hair. She wanted it, then. She was not merely going to endure for the sake of duty or in order to make the marriage valid. She wanted it. There was a restrained and inexperienced eagerness in her embrace.

So be it, then. He would give her what she wanted. He owed her that.

He got to his feet to remove his brocaded dressing gown and watched her eyes move over his form, clad only in a nightshirt. God, there was heat in her eyes. Desire. With some relief he felt the stirrings of arousal. There was something slightly erotic about being wanted when he did not want. He drew back the bedclothes, snuffed the single candle that stood on the table beside the bed, and lay down beside her.

"My love," he murmured to her, sliding one arm beneath her and leaning over her to find her lips with his again. He parted his own, wondering how she would react. But she followed his lead almost immediately, her mouth opening beneath the teasing of his own. She was warm and moist. She tasted good. And smelled good. There was a clean soap smell about her hair and her skin. He could feel her hands lightly exploring the muscles of his back and shoulders.

"Freddie," she said when he moved his mouth to kiss her eyes and her temples and her throat. Her voice was low and husky.

It was going to be easy to make love to her after all, he thought. She was inexperienced, but she was not shy. He just hoped that his weight would not cause her harm when it came time to cover her. He ran one hand lightly

56

down her side. She was so very slender. He spread the hand behind her and brought her over onto her side against him. Slender and warm and surprisingly supple. And more shapely than he had noticed. Strange really that he had not done so. Perhaps it was because he had never really looked at her as a woman, as any sort of sex object.

His hand verified the impression his chest had given him. Her breasts were not large, but they were firm and well-shaped. He caressed them through the filmy cotton of her nightgown and set a thumb against one hardening tip.

"Mmm," he said, finding her mouth with his own again, both open this time. He licked at her lips with his tongue, teased it up behind the tender flesh of her upper lip. "Beautiful." He was fully aroused at last. It was not going to be an impossibility after all. Or even difficult. He was infinitely thankful. Her mouth and her hands and her body told him that she wanted pleasure. He was glad he was going to be able to give it her.

He stretched down with one arm, grasped the hem of her nightgown, and raised it. He intended to raise it only to her hips, but there was no resistance in her, no shrinking. He drew it up to her waist, to her breasts, and then she raised her arms and he pulled it off altogether and tossed it over the side of the bed. And then he felt surprise – not totally unpleasurable – to feel her hands dragging at his nightshirt. He helped her and threw it to join her nightgown somewhere on the floor.

Her legs were thin as were her body and her arms. He could feel her ribs with the hand that explored, her skin was warm and silky. Her breasts were taut with desire. Her kiss demanded, and he gave, moving his mouth over hers, deepening the pressure, darting his tongue inside. One of her hands was spread over his chest. The other was moving over his back, her palm pressing against the muscles there and moving down even to his buttocks.

It was time, he thought. She was ready and somehow

57

he had persuaded himself into desiring her. Perhaps it was that he felt pity for her and gratitude for what she had unknowingly done for him. But whatever it was he was ready for her. Ready to give her pleasure. And afraid of giving her pain. She seemed so fragile, so thin as he turned her onto her back again and came over on top of her.

"My love," he murmured against her mouth, "I don't want to hurt you. But I fear I must in a moment. It will not last. It will be for a moment only. Am I too heavy for you?" He could have taken her on top of him, but she would have been unable to kneel over him.

"No," she whispered. "No, Freddie." And then she moaned a little as he positioned himself at the entrance to her and began to push slowly inward.

Small. Warm. Virginal. An untraveled path. And soon the barrier. He did not want to hurt her. He nudged forward when instinct would have had him plunging. And then the barrier gave way at the same moment as she gave an almost inaudible whimper, and he mounted all the way into heat and wetness. Into woman. She was as much woman as the most voluptuous courtesan of his experience, he thought in some surprise.

He was afraid that his weight was squashing her. He was afraid that her legs would be paining her from being spread wide by his own. He raised himself on his elbows and looked down at her. Her eyes were closed, her lips parted. God, he thought, she was enjoying this. She looked to be in near ecstasy. He felt a totally unexpected rush of tenderness for her. She opened her eyes. They looked huge and dreamy in the dimness of the room.

"Am I hurting you, my love?" he asked.

She shook her head and reached up her arms to his shoulders, drawing him down to her again.

And so he began to move in her, withdrawing and thrusting slowly until he was sure that she felt no pain, and then pleasuring her with a firm, steady rhythm. He was doing something he had never done before, he realized. For several years, ever since he had developed

58

some expertise, he had prided himself on giving pleasure to his women as well as to himself. But he had never concentrated more on his woman's pleasure than on his own. Not until now. This was not for his pleasure. It would have pleased him better to have accomplished the consummation with one swift inward thrust and a speedy spilling of his seed.

He worked to give pleasure to his new wife, stroking her until she relaxed and rocked to his rhythm, slowly building speed and depth with a skill of long practice to bring her toward climax, moving his hands to her buttocks, holding her steady while he finally held deep and hard and still in her once, twice, three times before all the tension shuddered out of her with one long, satisfied sigh. He held still in her until she was totally relaxed again and then finished swiftly before disengaging from her and moving to her side.

She turned her head and nestled her cheek against his shoulder. Her eyes were closed, he could see. There was a half-smile on her lips. The smile of a woman who had just enjoyed good sex. He was used to seeing it on the faces of the courtesans and whores he took frequently to his bed. There was something strangely moving about seeing it on the face of this woman. His wife. She was as much woman as they, he thought again. It was not her fault that she looked less alluring. And yet, strangely, beneath the bedsheets she had felt not a great deal less desirable than they. And she had been flatteringly eager.

"Well," he said, his voice low against her ear. He kissed her cheek and her mouth softly. "Now you are irrevocably Mrs. Frederick Sullivan, Clara. For life. Any regrets?"

Her eyes fluttered open. "No, Freddie," she said. "None. And you?"

He kissed her again. "I love you, my darling," he said. He wished he meant it. He tried to mean it as much as he could. He wanted her to be happy. He would make it one of the goals of his life to make her happy.

She closed her eyes again, made a sound that was almost

like a purr in her throat, and was asleep. She had not responded to his words, he noticed.

He had not gone back to his own room. That was the first thought she had when she woke up. She had been afraid that he would. She had expected that he would. As far as she knew, most husbands and wives slept in separate rooms. But he was still there beside her. He was not holding her, but her cheek was pressed snugly to his shoulder and all down the length of her body she was touching him. All that splendid warm maleness was against her.

Naked maleness. She remembered suddenly their unclothing each other, the shock and wonder of his firm, bare flesh beneath her hands and against her own equally naked flesh. Strangely there had been no terror, no embarrassment. Only an exultation in his muscled strength and an almost swooning desire to be possessed by him.

She could almost have believed during those minutes that she loved him, that the desire she felt, the desire that surged at his touch, was for Freddie himself, not just for his body. She even whispered his name more than once. And indeed, she thought now in her own defense, it had not been all purely carnal, what she had felt. She had been aware at every moment while the strange, delirious new delights were happening to her body that it was Freddie with whom she was doing those things. Not just any man, but Freddie. Freddie's splendid body.

Not Freddie himself, but only his body? Clara turned her head so that her lips were against his shoulder, and her nose. He smelled good, partly of soap, partly of sweat. But there was nothing unpleasant about the latter smell. It was masculine and virile. It reminded her of how that sweat had been generated.

There was something shameful, surely, about loving a man's body but not the man inside it. It was what men must feel for whores. Was there nothing more in her feelings for her husband? She despised him – his marrying her for her

60

money and pretending to different motives. She wished he would not keep calling her his love or his darling. She wished he would not keep telling her that he loved her.

And yet she did not really despise him, she thought. She had felt gratitude toward him earlier. And a certain tenderness. Inexperienced as she was, she knew that it could have been different. She knew that he had deliberately taken the time to give her pleasure. She knew that he had used patient skill on her. He need not have done so. She had not really expected that he would. She had expected to have to snatch pleasure in any way she could.

He had given it to her. As a sort of wedding gift perhaps. And a wonderful gift it had been too. She had expected pleasure to come from the mere touch of his body. To have that beauty and that strength against herself, inside herself – it had seemed the pinnacle of all that was wonderful. She had not expected pleasure to act on her own body, making her ache and pulse and tense and yearn. She had not expected the wonderful flow of peace and sheer joy that had come at the end. Or almost at the end. There had been a little more for him. She had felt the warm gush of his seed after she was relaxed and almost swooning with happiness.

He had asked her if she had any regrets. She had none. God help her, she could live for this. She felt like a woman, warm and desirable and beautiful. A foolish notion. And of course it would not last. His expertise had been obvious even to an innocent like her. It was inconceivable that he would be satisfied with her for the rest of his life. She resolutely shut her mind to the possibility that he might even have found their coupling distasteful. Certainly she was going to have to share him with other women. Many other women. She must not let the thought hurt her. After all, she did not love him.

No, she had no regrets. If there could be occasional nights like this one to look forward to, then she would be content with her life more or less as it had always been. It was too late now to dream of love. It had always been too late. She was not the sort of woman to attract the love of any man, and the circumstances of her life were such that she could not hope to find even a satisfactory relationship.

This was satisfactory. It was all she needed.

"You cannot sleep, my love?" She was startled by the sound of his voice. She had not realized he was awake. "Would you be more comfortable if I returned to my own room? I fell asleep here, I'm afraid."

"I have just woken up," she said, "and I am very comfortable, thank you, Freddie."

He turned onto his side, set an arm beneath her head, and kissed her mouth. She had not realized that kisses between a man and woman could be openmouthed. She liked the feeling. It was – intimate.

"Are you sore?" he asked her.

She understood suddenly what he was asking. Yes, she was rather. She was sore. Very pleasantly so and throbbing too now that he had spoken.

"No," she said.

And then his hand was there, causing her to tense with shock for a moment. But he set his mouth to hers again, and explored her gently with his hand, his fingers stroking lightly, circling over particularly sensitive areas, parting, probing. He pushed one finger up inside her and then two. She could hear wetness – and the pounding of blood through her temples.

"Does it feel good, sweetheart?" he whispered against the mouth.

"Yes." She had that feeling again of being about to swoon.

"No soreness?"

There was an aching soreness there where his fingers were. The ache was in her breasts too and in her throat. And in her lips.

"No." She ran her hand up his arm, from the wrist to the shoulder. It was covered with fine hairs and rock-hard with muscle. "Freddie."

62

She had not expected that he would do it to her again. She had not dreamed of it. It had seemed too momentous an act to be performed more than once in a night. But he came over her again and into her again. She was indeed sore. Very sore. He was hurting her enough to make her bite her lip. But the ache was more insistent than the soreness, and the throbbing pulsed through her body, all but deafening her. Release came almost instantly – it had almost come with just his hand. As before, he waited for her to finish shaking and to relax and then continued what he had been doing before – pushing himself deep, partially withdrawing, and plunging inward again. She lay still and enjoyed it despite the raw soreness. She had left him far behind this time. There were a couple of minutes to be simply enjoyed.

He was Freddie, she told herself as he worked and as she enjoyed. She had her arms about him, holding him warmly. He was the handsome, charming rogue she had spotted for what he was right from that first time at the Assembly Rooms when he had been presented to her. It was he making love to her in exchange for a twenty thousand pound dowry. She wondered if he regretted his decision, if he found the prospect of being married to her for life insupportable.

And yet, she thought, he had not been compelled to stay in her bed after the consummation. He had not been compelled to do this again.

She set her cheek against his shoulder as he sighed and stilled in her. Perhaps, she thought, they might come to like each other if they both wished for it. Enough anyway so that he would not feel utterly trapped by what debts had forced him into. And enough that she would not feel so wanton and guilty for lusting after his beauty and his health and strength.

He was lifting himself off her and moving to her side again but keeping one arm about her this time. He kissed her, settled her comfortably against him, and drew the blankets up about her naked shoulders. He did not say anything this time but was asleep almost instantly.

She was glad he had not said again that he loved her.

She was glad that he had still not returned to his own room.

She sighed with sleepy satisfaction.

Lord and Lady Bellamy arrived early the next morning, before breakfast, to see their son and new daughter-in-law on their way to Kent. They sat down to breakfast so that the newly married couple had no chance for private converse. His wife had good taste in clothes, Frederick thought. At least he could say that in her favor. Her pale blue carriage dress looked elegant and becoming.

His mother was looking curiously at both him and Clara all through breakfast. Trying to decide if the deed had been done, Frederick guessed. He looked at Clara himself. Was it in any way obvious? Was there a tinge of color in her cheeks or was it merely the reflection of the flowers that adorned the table, left over from the day before? Was there a glow in her eyes, or did he merely imagine it? She was talking about Ebury Court, the estate her father had bought on his return from India, and about the house he had built there to replace the moldering Tudor mansion the previous owners had allowed to fall into ruin.

And was there anything in his face for his mother to see? Frederick wondered. It seemed hardly likely since he had been bedding women with some regularity for the past seven or eight years. And yet his mother contrived to take him apart after breakfast before they left while his father was still asking Clara questions about India.

"Freddie," the baroness said, linking her arm through her son's and squeezing it, "all is going to be well, as I have been telling Papa since you first broke the news to us. I do not care what the truth is about those foolish debts – and I do hope you have learned your lesson this time, dear. Nor do I care that dear Clara is not quite the beauty I would have expected you to choose and that she

64

cannot walk. I have seen this morning that you are fond of each other, and that is all that matters when all is said and done. You *are* fond of her, aren't you, Freddie?"

He patted her hand. "I love her, Mama," he said.

She sighed. "I am glad after all that you did not marry Julia," she said. "I know the two of you have always been fond of each other, but I always thought you were more like sister and brother than anything else. You were not disappointed when she chose Daniel instead of you, dear?"

"If I was, Mama," he said, "it was quickly forgotten. If I had married Jule, I would never have met and fallen in love with Clara, would I?"

"That is very true," she said. "And Julia seems excessively happy with Daniel. And he with her, though one would not have expected it. He never seemed particularly to like her until she surprised us all by announcing their betrothal. Though really it was he who announced it, for dear Julia mumbled so that no one heard what she said."

He was perhaps the only one who had not been taken by surprise with that announcement, Frederick thought. He had seen it coming and that was why he had done what he did. But he did not want to think of it.

His father was not so easily taken in as his mother. "Well, Freddie," he said, extending a hand to his son while the baroness was taking a prolonged farewell of Clara, "it remains to be seen what you make of this marriage. Your wife's handicap will make life difficult for you and your reason for marrying her will make it more so. But she is a woman of sense and breeding, son, and deserves better perhaps than what she is getting. Unless you surprise me. I hope you surprise me."

Frederick put his hand in his father's and looked him in the eye. "I love her, Papa," he said. And he almost believed his own words. She had wanted him the night before – both times – and he had felt a certain tenderness for her as he had given to her. She was his wife. He would look after her. Even the suggestion that he might not annoyed him. "I will see to it that I do deserve her eventually. You will see."

His father shook his hand warmly. "It is time you were on your way," he said. "Your mother will cry over your wife until noon if you allow it." Father and son exchanged a rare conspiratorial grin.

Frederick carried his wife out to the waiting carriage, and they were on their way, Clara with tears in her eyes waving to the baroness, who had tears running down her cheeks.

"They are so kind," Clara said, turning finally to smile at her husband. "I feel almost as if I have parents again, Freddie."

"You do," he said, taking her hand in his. "They both seem to be agreed that I have done very well for myself. Better than I deserve. Do you miss your own parents, my love?"

She nodded. "Especially yesterday," she said. "And perhaps this morning. I wanted Papa to be there."

"Tell me about him," he said.

They did not lack for conversation all through the long journey to Kent. It was one thing that surprised Frederick. He had never conversed a great deal with women since he had always had only one important use for them and that had had nothing to do with talk. Certainly he would not have expected to find himself able to converse with the very quiet, respectable, and surely dull Miss Clara Danford. Mrs. Clara Sullivan, he corrected himself mentally. But in fact she liked to talk about her father and about her life in India and in England afterward. And she enjoyed listening to the stories he told about his family – about the aunts and uncles and cousins who had always gathered during the summers at Primrose Park, home of his uncle, the Earl of Beaconswood. The late earl. Dan had inherited the title a few months before, of course.

Frederick would not have expected his wife to enjoy his humor. But she had done so the evening before and she did so now during their journey. She chuckled a great deal and laughed outright with him at some of his stories of boyhood mischief – usually involving him and Dan.

"I did not know you were of such a large family," she said. "I thought it was just you and your mother and father and Lesley. It must be wonderful to be part of a large, close family." Her tone was wistful.

"They are yours too now, my love," he told her, raising her hand to his lips. "You will be a part of the next gathering."

He wondered if Dan and Julia would perpetuate the custom of inviting everyone for the summers. Primrose Park actually belonged to Julia. Dan had given it to her for a wedding present, Frederick's mother had told him. But even if they did, and even if everyone decided to continue going, he would not be able to join them there. If he never had to look either of those two in the eye again, it would be rather too soon. A pity really. He had cut himself off from his own past and from two of his dearest friends through an act of desperate stupidity.

"What is it?" Clara asked. She was gazing up into his eyes.

"Nothing," he said. "I was just remembering that my uncle died only a few months ago. He was something of an eccentric, you know. He ordered in his will that we were all to put off our mourning immediately."

"It is oppressive to wear black for a whole year," she said. "I would have preferred to remember Papa in my own thoughts than to be forced to remember him in such a morbid way. I hate black. You were fortunate, Freddie."

He surprised both himself and her, he guessed, by leaning across the seat and kissing her mouth. He really was fortunate. He could be riding now with a cold and sour stranger.

"I love you," he said.

She smiled slightly and turned to look out of the window.

It was a pleasant journey, the tedium eased by the

67

conversation that filled most of the time. Frederick lifted his wife in and out of the carriage on the few occasions when they stopped, scorning the assistance of her servant. She was as light as a feather.

"Besides," he murmured against her ear on the first occasion when he had turned the servant away, "it gives me an excuse to get close to you in public, Clara. Most men would not dare touch more than the fingertips or the elbow of a lady in such a place, even if she were his wife."

She looked at him, her arm twined about his neck, and laughed. "How absurdly you talk sometimes, Freddie," she said. "Are you never serious?"

"Sometimes," he said, looking into her eyes with that intense gaze that he knew usually had a melting effect on women. "Especially when I am busy doing things that don't require words."

Comprehension dawned in her eyes and she actually blushed. "Set me down," she said. "You have been standing before this chair for all of two minutes, Freddie. Put me down."

He chuckled and held her for a few moments longer before setting her down on the chair and turning to the innkeeper to order their tea.

# 6

She enjoyed watching his face as they approached Ebury Court. There were three miles of rolling tree-dotted lawns stretching either side of the winding driveway. She had always thought it must be happiness itself and freedom itself to ride a horse across those three miles, to feel strength and speed beneath her, to feel the wind against her face. She had never ridden.

And she enjoyed watching his reaction to the classical symmetry of the house with its pillared portico and marble steps. She was glad that her father had been a man of taste, that he had not used his great wealth for vulgar ostentation. It was a beautiful and stately house, though new.

"Somehow," Frederick said, "I had a mental picture of a manor of modest size set in a few acres of grounds. This is magnificent, Clara."

"I love it more than words can say," she said. "To me it was everything that is England after all those years in India. I used to sit at my window and marvel at the green grass and trees. I always felt selfishly glad that Papa had had no sons and that it would all come to me. Though at a price, I must confess. I would have liked to grow up with brothers and sisters."

He carried her up the marble steps and into the great hall, and there was a great rush to fetch her a wheeled chair – and some laughter too – since she wanted to be with him when he met her servants. And she wanted to be the one to show him the grand salon with its gilded frieze and coved ceiling painted with a scene from mythology.

She wanted to show him the huge formal dining room and the reception rooms. She saw them so rarely herself. She spent most of her life on the floor above in the living rooms or in her own rooms above that again. She wished she could walk at his side, her arm linked through his.

They were tired after their journey. They did not spend a long time downstairs, but she was warmed by the appreciation he showed for his new home. It meant so very much to her.

"We will go outside tomorrow if the weather holds," he said when they were sitting in the drawing room drinking tea. "You can show me the park in more detail, my love."

She laughed softly, but her voice was wistful when she spoke. "I can show you only what can be seen from the terrace, Freddie," she said. "I cannot walk, if you will remember."

"Then we will take an open carriage," he said, "and see whatever can be seen from the paths."

"There is no open carriage here," she said. "Papa was always afraid that I would take a chill."

He stared at her. "Even in the summer?" he said.

"It always seemed so cool here after India," she said. "He was terrified that I would become ill again. Sometimes I would persuade him to allow Harriet to wheel my chair along the terrace, but only if it was warm and there was no suggestion of a breeze. And only if I wore a blanket over my knees and a shawl about my shoulders."

He continued to stare for a few silent moments. "Life must have been unbearably tedious for you," he said. "Did you never rebel?"

Only in hot tears shed privately. "I loved my father," she said, "and respected his judgment. There are horses in the stables, Freddie. You can ride out tomorrow and see everything for yourself. And then you can come back and tell me if you will. I am an avid listener."

"There are sidesaddles in the stables?" he asked.

70

"Yes," she said. "Harriet rides occasionally and sometimes there are lady visitors."

"Then you will ride tomorrow too," he said. "There must be a horse or two strong enough to bear the two of us. You weigh nothing at all. I shall lift you into a sidesaddle and ride up behind you. You are going to see this land that you love so dearly."

"Freddie." She stared at him and laughed. And yet there was a great welling of unexpected longing at this mad make-believe scheme. "I could not ride on a horse. I would fall. It is a mad idea."

"You should talk to my cousins," he said. "I have never been at a loss for mad ideas, most of which I have put into practice." He grinned at her. "Are you chicken-hearted, Clara? Are you afraid to try it? I would not let you fall, you know. You have my word on it."

She was afraid. Terrified. Her heart pounded with fear – and with excitement. It could not be possible, surely. It was beyond the bounds of imagining. Her father had never allowed her to ride even in an open carriage. But Freddie's eyes were smiling at her, daring her.

"It will probably rain," she said.

He laughed. "But if it does not you will ride?" he said.

She had no riding habit. "I have nothing to wear," she said.

"A carriage dress will be just the thing," he said. "You can throw excuses at me for the rest of the evening, my love. I shall have an answer for each. I have a resourceful mind."

Why was he being so insistent? Why had he even thought of it in the first place? Would he not welcome the thought of a few hours away from her, riding out alone? She had not expected him to spend a great deal of his time with her even during this honeymoon week. Even her father, who had loved her more dearly than his own life, she had sometimes thought, had not spent much of his time with her. It was too dull to sit for long hours with a crippled woman. Often she felt sorry for Harriet and invented errands for her to run.

"What are you thinking?" Frederick asked, setting down his cup and saucer and coming to sit close to her so that he could take one of her hands in his. "You want to ride, don't you?"

"Oh, Freddie," she said in a rush, "I want it more than anything." She bit her lip, alarmed by the rush of tears to her eyes. Perhaps it had not been a good idea after all to try to add a little bit of life to her existence. Perhaps she would come to crave more and more and would no longer be satisfied with what she was and what she had.

But then she had never been satisfied. She had cultivated patience, but she had never been happy. Never. Not really happy.

"Then you shall ride, my love," he said. "And we shall have an open barouche for you to drive in. And you shall sit out in the fresh air whenever you wish, even when the wind is blowing. Whenever you take a chill, or whenever I do, well then, we will summon a physician."

"Oh, Freddie," she said, laughing, "that is such a careless attitude to life. It sounds wonderful."

He got to his feet, leaned over her, and kissed her. "I love you," he said. "Are you ready for bed? Shall I carry you up to your room?"

She nodded. "Yes, please, Freddie." But she wished he would not spoil the amity between them by speaking falsehoods. They were quite unnecessary.

"May I join you there later?" He was doing that with his eyes that she knew was deliberate and must surely have most women weak at the knees. It made even her breath catch in her throat. "Or would you rather be left alone after such a long journey?"

There was a throbbing deep in her womb just at the thought of what might be happening between them in a short while. She touched a hand to his cheek. "I would rather not be alone, Freddie," she said.

72

His eyes smiled into hers. "My feeling exactly," he said, stooping down to pick her up.

She set an arm about his neck and laid her cheek on her upper arm. She wondered how strongly he had hoped for a different answer. And yet his eyes had deliberately wooed her. And he had stayed with her all last night and made love to her a second time. It was not so easy after all, she thought, to understand Freddie. She had expected it to be, but it was not. And why did he want to take her riding with him tomorrow?

He took the stairs much more quickly than Robin ever did.

Frederick was not quite sure himself why he had persuaded his wife to ride the following day. It would be difficult for her. Perhaps painful. And it would certainly be more convenient for him to ride alone, to be free to explore the park and the surrounding countryside at his leisure.

He felt sorry for her, he supposed. He was beginning to have glimpses into a life that had been unbearably restricted and dull and lonely. Her father, he suspected, had made her life worse by being over-protective. And her love and respect for her father had prevented her from rebelling or asserting herself while he lived or even after he died. And so she had developed a quiet and patient self-discipline, an armor about her feelings.

She needed a little happiness in her life. A little adventure. And fresh air. He was beginning to understand why she was always so very pale. It was the least he could do to take her out occasionally, to coax her into doing things that she had always wanted to do.

Besides, he had something to prove to his parents. And to himself. He had always contended that he could put his wildness behind him and settle down whenever he chose. Now was the time, it seemed – to a certain extent anyway. Clara might not be the wife he would have chosen for himself if he could have made a free

73

choice, but the deed was done now and he must make the best of it.

And really she was not as much an antidote as he had expected her to be on first acquaintance and even when he had made her his offer. She was an interesting, even amusing, companion. And surprisingly satisfying in bed. He had spent the whole night with her again and had had her twice again. Perhaps the very stillness of her body as he made love to her and yet her responsiveness to his caresses was a novelty. His women were almost always energetic and experienced at faking sexual ecstasy.

He had rather enjoyed the first two nights with his new wife.

He selected a powerful black stallion at the stables with the assistance of the head groom and saddled it himself with a sidesaddle before leading it up onto the terrace before the marble steps. Clara was nervous, he knew. She had made another excuse at breakfast. Her neighbors would begin to call once they knew she was at home. In the morning? he had asked her and she had not been able to think of a reply. He ran into the house now and up the stairs to fetch her.

It took two of them. Her manservant, Robin, held her while Frederick mounted to the bare back of the horse behind the saddle and then stooped down and lifted her up to the saddle. He settled her there, keeping an arm firmly about her and smiling at the look of stark terror in her eyes.

"I'll not let you fall, my love," he said after nodding his dismissal to Robin. "I shall keep my arm about you like this. You may lean sideways against me whenever you wish."

"It is such a long way to the ground," she said.

He took the reins in his hand and nudged the horse into motion with his knees. He felt her tense.

"Relax," he said, "and enjoy the ride." He turned the horse's head so that they would leave the terrace to cross the park.

"Oh," she said. "Oh."

It was like giving a child a treat, he thought over the next several minutes. She sat very still and very stiff at first, and very silent, afraid even to turn her head. And then she gradually relaxed and he could see her begin to look about her at lawns and trees that she had only ever seen from the terrace or her window or the window of a closed carriage on the driveway. He could feel and hear her drawing in deep lungfuls of the verdant air. Once, when they rode close to a tree, she reached out a hand to let the leaves brush against it, but she drew the hand in sharply again, realizing perhaps that balance could very easily be lost when one was on horseback.

And then he became aware that she was crying. Silently, her head turned sharply away from him to face front. She made no sound, but he could see the glisten of tears on one half-turned cheek. He said nothing but let her cope with the rush of emotion in her own way. She reached into a pocket, withdrew a small handkerchief, and blew her nose into it after a few minutes.

God, he thought, holding her and pretending that he had not seen the tears, she was a woman brimming over with repressed feelings. She was a person. Someone he had married for the basest of reasons.

They had ridden almost the length of the park. Very slowly. He had not taken the horse even to a canter.

"Are you tired, my love?" he asked, bending toward her. "I shall take you back now."

"Oh, Freddie." She turned her head to look at him. Her eyes, slightly red-rimmed, were glowing. "I wish we never had to go back. I wish this could go on forever. How foolish you will think me. This is the most mundane thing in the world to you, is it not? And it must seem to you that we are moving at a snail's pace."

"We will come again," he said. "And again and again, Clara. You are no longer going to be housebound. You are going to go out and breathe in fresh air. That is an order. I will demand obedience of you, you see."

There was perhaps wistfulness in her eyes for a moment before she lowered them and then looked away. "I hope I will never be disobedient to you, Freddie," she said. "I never was to Papa."

He turned the horse's head and began the ride back to the house. He hoped she was not in love with him. God, he hoped it. He meant kindly to her and he was going to bring some happiness and some activity into her life. But he did not believe he could live up to the expectations of love. Indeed, he knew he could not.

She was tired though she would not admit it. After a couple of minutes she leaned sideways to rest a shoulder against his chest. When he tightened his arm about her, she undid the ribbons of her bonnet and took it off so that she could nestle her head against his shoulder.

"The outdoor world is a magical place," she said. "I wonder if people who have always had their health realize that fully."

"Probably not," he said, resting his cheek against the top of her head. "We take a great deal for granted."

He was, he realized suddenly and quite unexpectedly, feeling happy. It was a beautiful day and the surroundings were rather idyllic and the house magnificent. It was his home and the woman in his arms, still looking quietly about her at the wonders of nature, was his wife. Perhaps after all it would be possible to settle down. Perhaps after all he would not have to start looking for snow in July as evidence that the impossible did sometimes happen.

Clara found herself wishing sometimes over the next week that Harriet and Lord and Lady Bellamy were not coming quite so soon. And yet she caught herself up on the thought whenever it became conscious. Harriet had proved herself to be a dear and steady friend more than a paid companion, and her parents-in-law had been very kind to her in Bath. She should be looking forward to seeing them all again. She *was* looking forward to it.

But she did not want the honeymoon to end. She had a feeling that it would, abruptly and completely, as soon

76

as the others came. It could not possibly last. It was too wonderfully and unexpectedly perfect.

Her husband spent all day and every day with her. He sat with her through the numerous visits paid by neighbors when they heard she had returned and especially when news began to spread that she was newly married. She had cultivated friendships over the years since they had always been one of the few real pleasures of her life. Freddie showed no signs of boredom but set himself to be agreeable to the gentlemen and charming to the ladies. He won over all the latter, without exception. One could almost watch them being awed by his good looks at first, flattered by his attention after a short while, and warmed by his charm at last. One could almost watch them all fall a little in love with him during their very first visit.

Once he took her visiting, carrying her to the carriage and into the three homes they called at, and sitting cheerfully through three sessions of tea-drinking. It was an afternoon she enjoyed immensely. She was used to being visited. She did not often visit. Soon, Freddie had promised, they would go into London and choose an open barouche. In the meantime they drove with the windows wide open, a novelty in itself. Her father had always shielded her from any possibility of drafts.

They went riding once more.

She was even taken to church on Sunday and made much of by parishioners who had already called upon her at home and by the vicar and his wife, who expressed their intention of calling within the coming few days.

"That must be the first time I have been inside a church since last Christmas," Frederick said when they were driving home again. "Do you think my soul is saved again, Clara?"

"Oh, Freddie," she said, laughing, "how foolishly you talk. At least you did not sleep through the sermon as Mr. Soames did. Did you see Mrs. Soames dig him with her elbow when he snored?"

"It is amazing he did not scream," he said. "It looked to be a sharp enough elbow."

They both laughed. Something they seemed to do a great deal of that week.

On the Sunday afternoon he took her out onto the terrace in her chair and refused to allow her to take a shawl, warning that she would melt in the heat if she did so. She sighed with contentment as he wheeled her along the terrace, turning up her face to the light and warmth of the sun.

"Autumn is going to be here any day," she said. "Are we not fortunate to be having such lovely summer weather at this stage of August, Freddie?"

"That summerhouse we have seen when riding is not far off," he said. "Let's go there."

She had known the summerhouse was there. It had been described to her before. But she had seen it for the first time during her second ride with Freddie. It was an octagonal stone structure with a dome and large glass windows on all eight sides. Her father had liked to go there to read on sunny days, even when the weather was quite cold. The glass trapped the heat, he had explained to her.

My chair will not move on grass," she said rather sadly. "You go, Freddie. I shall sit here and relax. Or you can take me back inside first if you wish. I shall read."

But he grinned at her and leaned down to scoop her up into his arms. "My feet will move on grass," he said, striding away with her in the direction of the trees that hid the summerhouse from view from the terrace.

"But it is too far," she said. "I am too heavy."

"A feather would weigh more," he said. "Though you have been eating more in the last couple of days, I have noticed, Clara. Enough for yourself and a horse."

"Horrid!" she said. "I think it is the fresh air that has given me appetite, Freddie. I am too thin, aren't I?" She was not fishing for a compliment. She had always been aware of her ugliness. She just wished sometimes that she could be at least passably pretty. Especially now. She wished she could be beautiful for him. A foolish, foolish thought.

"You are as you are," he said. "Beautiful to me, my love. But I like to see you with more appetite and will not frown at a few more pounds of weight. Though I may puff and blow at having to carry them around to summerhouses and the Lord knows where."

"It is your own fault if you are out of breath," she said. "I did not ask to be brought."

The summerhouse was too hot. It felt like an oven inside. They looked at each other and laughed after he had set her down on the seat that circled the outer wall of the interior.

"Baked flesh for dinner tonight?" he asked. "Do you fancy it?"

"Not particularly," she said. "My increased appetite does not extend quite so far."

And so he carried her outside, set her down on the grass, and sat beside her. Grass felt wonderful, she discovered, soft and cool and sweet-smelling.

"Papa would never let me sit on the grass," she said, lying back and closing her eyes and setting her hands palm down on either side of her. She brushed them lightly over the surface of the grass. "He was always afraid of dampness."

"It has not rained for days," he said, propping himself on one elbow and looking down at her. "Or is it weeks? Dr. Frederick Sullivan prescribes plenty of grass and fresh air and sunshine and food. It will all do you the world of good. My reputation as a man of medicine on it."

She laughed and then laughed again as she wrinkled her nose against a tickle there and opened her eyes to find him stroking a blade of grass across it.

"This is lovely," she said. "So very lovely." She lay still and could hear birds singing. And insects droning. And an unfelt breeze rustling through the upper branches of the trees. She could feel the sun hot on her face. She could smell the grass.

It was all alive, she thought. That was what was so very different about the outdoors. Everything was alive, even the grass beneath her. She was surrounded by life. And she was alive. She breathed in life and felt it fill her lungs and her body. She felt almost as if she would be able to get up and walk or even run if she tried. She tried to flex her feet at the ankles. Her legs were not without feeling. Just weak and useless. Her ankles would not respond to the urging of her will.

She opened her eyes and gazed upward at the few clouds that were floating by. "A kitten," she said. "Look at it, Freddie. That cloud there."

He looked, a blade of grass between his teeth. "A kitten?" he said. "A sailing ship."

"No, that one there," she said. "And oh, look. A rose in full bloom next to it."

"A rearing horse," he said.

She closed her eyes again and smiled. "It pleases you to make fun of me," she said.

The sun was blocked out suddenly and his mouth covered hers. "Clouds can be whatever one wants them to be, my love," he said. "That is the wonder of clouds."

"I have never looked at them before," she said, opening her eyes again. "What a vast and wonderful universe this is, Freddie. And we are a part of it. The earth is spinning beneath us."

"I feel dizzy," he said, kissing her again, sliding his tongue into her mouth. "You will have to hold me to steady me, Clara."

"Oh, silly," she said, but she set her arms about him anyway and they kissed warmly and lazily for several minutes. It was one of the mysteries of Freddie that she was accepting gratefully for this week. Why did he feel compelled to keep up the charade? Did he get any enjoyment out of this? Why had he brought her here when he could have come alone or gone somewhere else? Why

80

had he slept in her bed every night since their wedding and made love to her twice on each of those nights?

She was afraid that she was going to become dependent on having him there next to her whenever she woke during the nights. She was afraid she was going to become dependent on his lovemaking. She had no one with whom to compare him, but she knew that he was an expert and that he was using his expertise on her at night. She loved making love even more than she had expected to do. With Freddie. Perhaps it would not be as good with another man. She could not even imagine doing those very intimate things with another man.

"If you fall asleep," he said, and she felt the blade of grass feathering across her nose again, "you are going to wake up with a face like a lobster, Clara. And a nose like a beacon. I am going to have to take you out of the sunshine pretty soon."

She sighed. She was too sleepy to answer.

"Who is your physician?" he asked. "Did your father consult more than one?"

"He called them all fools and quacks," she said. "He never did meet Dr. Frederick Sullivan, of course. I think he would have disapproved of your methods, though, Freddie."

"Was there one in particular?" he asked.

"Dr. Graham," she said. "He used to be Papa's friend. But they had a loud quarrel when he came out here to see me a few years ago. We never saw him again."

"What was the quarrel about?" he asked.

She shook her head. "I don't know," she said. "Papa would not say. All he would say was that no one was going to take his little girl from him as Mama was taken or cause her pain and suffering. I was always a little girl to Papa. Silly, was it not?"

"No," he said. "It must be hard to lose one's woman and to see the child that one has begotten and she has borne fall sick and lie near to death too."

She opened her eyes and smiled at him. Could Freddie

81

imagine what love and fatherhood were like, then? She wondered, as she had done from the start, if she was capable of bearing his child. She would like that – more than anything. But she would not hope too hard. She had learned never to hope too much.

But she was growing too happy. And too reluctant to see the honeymoon at an end. Perhaps, she thought, a little happiness for one brief week of her life was better than none at all. Or perhaps it was worse than anything. Perhaps all it would do was give her a brief and tantalizing glimpse of what life could be like.

She felt his lips on hers again. "Come on," he said. "Time to go back before I get ideas about making love to you out here on the grass. The gardeners do not work on Sundays, do they?"

"No," she said, chuckling and raising her arms to set about his neck as he got to his feet and bent to pick her up. "But the birds would see and the insects."

It would be a wonderful and heady experience, she thought as he began to stride back through the trees in the direction of the terrace and the house, to make love on the grass. In the outdoors. Surrounded by life.

She was going to have to very careful, she thought with sudden clarity, not to fall in love. Perhaps it was as well after all that Harriet and her parents-in-law would be there within a few days.

Time could not, after all, stand still. Though she wished it could. How she wished it could!

# 7

Frederick was surprised to find that he was almost sorry when the honeymoon came to an end. He had deliberately devoted a week of his life to bringing his wife some happiness and found that he had brought himself a small measure too. There was something rather pleasant and relaxing and – comfortable, he found, about having both a sexual relationship and a companionship with a woman. He had had plenty of the former, though even they could hardly be termed relationships, he supposed. He had had almost none of the latter. Except perhaps with Julia, though they had never revealed their inner selves to each other.

He and Clara had not done that either yet. But perhaps it would come in time. They found it easy to talk to each other, and they were interested in each other's lives. If he did not reveal all of himself to her during that week it was because all of himself was not a particularly attractive person. And he was not sure that he even knew himself entirely.

What did he want from life? Pleasure, he would have said a mere week or so before without any hesitation at all. He wanted his debts paid so that he could show his face in town again and carry on where he had left off. His clubs, the races, gaming, women – he had always loved them all. He still did. But for all the rest of his life? Would those pleasures never bring boredom? Did they now? Did he want more from life? A family of his own, perhaps? A home where he spent most of his days? A wife to replace all the women of his past and with whom to share a friendship?

Did he? The thought made him shudder and brought to mind all the old clichés to which he had long subscribed – a leg shackle, parson's mousetrap, a tenant for life, and so on. He had no wish to lose his freedom, to take on responsibilities.

And yet there was Clara. And the fact that she was his wife, that already a large part of his freedom was gone, that already he had responsibilities. He even began to wonder after a few days if she was capable of bearing children and could see no reason why not. If she could, then he was certainly going the right way about seeing to it that she did so.

A child! The very thought was enough to make him feel panic. And a not altogether unpleasant curiosity to know what it would be like to know himself a father. A father. Papa.

He wanted to escape. He wanted to be back in London in the familiar haunts and about the familiar tasks. He wanted to be safe. And yet he was reluctant to see the week come to an end. It had been a pleasant interlude in his life. He would not dread coming back to her occasionally, showing her the occasional kindness.

His parents came after eight days, bringing Harriet Pope with them. There was a great deal of hugging and kissing and handshaking, and there were some tears – mainly from his mother. They were both looking so very well, his mother said. And what a magnificent place Ebury Court was. She had not seen it before.

The honeymoon was over. Frederick spent most of the next two days with his father – riding, walking, inspecting the stables, playing billiards. The ladies sat together in the drawing room, nattering together, stitching away at their embroidery, entertaining neighbors. On the second afternoon they took the carriage out to call on the Soameses. The newly married couple spent little time alone together except at night. Frederick found himself somewhat nostalgic for the week of their honeymoon.

His mother was delighted with him and told him so on

the first evening, when the two of them were strolling along the terrace after dinner. "You must be doing something right, Freddie," she said. "Dear Clara is quite transformed."

Was she? The idea both alarmed and intrigued him. He looked at her with new eyes when he and his mother went back inside. Had she changed? He tried to compare her appearance now with the way she had looked when he first met her. Was she different?

No, of course she was not. Except perhaps her face. There was a tinge of color in it, caused perhaps by the fresh air he had insisted on every day since their arrival at Ebury Court. He could almost imagine that her face was not quite as thin, but that must be imagination. Although her appetite had improved, she could not possibly have put on weight yet. Her eyes were large and luminous. But then he had always conceded that her eyes were her best feature.

Of course she was no different. She was still the plain, thin woman he had decided with the greatest reluctance to woo. It was just that after one had known a person for a while, one could no longer see that person objectively. He looked at Clara now and saw – Clara. His wife. The woman he had been getting to know during the past week. The woman with whom he had been pleasantly contented. His bedfellow for the past week. The thinness, the plainness, the too-heavy dark hair no longer repelled him. They were just Clara.

Perhaps Harriet Pope saw a difference in her mistress too. Tight-lipped when she arrived, she seemed to have relaxed by the evening. She kept her distance from him, though. She probably expected him to pounce on her if he ever saw her in a dark corner, he thought with something bordering on amusement. Under different circumstances he would undoubtedly flirt with her since she was excessively pretty. But he had never been one whit interested in seducing innocents. He impatiently thrust aside the thought of Julia.

"You are going to spend the autumn here, Freddie?" his father asked with studied casualness when they were playing billiards one morning. "Your mother wants you to come to us for Christmas. Will Clara be able to travel? You had better come if you can. Les is determined to be off to Italy within the month and your mother will be lonely without either of you."

"We will come," Frederick said. "I haven't decided about the autumn. I'll probably stay here."

And he would too, he decided quite on the spur of the moment. There was nothing really to go back to in London. He would only start gambling again if he went there, and he had sworn off gambling after the recent crisis. Besides, it would be interesting to work on his marriage and see what came of it. He was growing fond of Clara, he had to admit. Perhaps he was even a little bit in love with her, though the idea seemed absurd when verbalized in his mind. He was fond of her. He would stay for a while at least, see how things went.

And yet within a few days his plans changed abruptly. His parents had left. Harriet was in the way, always sitting beside his wife, making his presence awkward. And yet he did not like to suggest that they get rid of the woman. She and Clara were friends and she was doubtless impoverished and would have nowhere else to go if she were dismissed. Besides she would be needed if and when he decided to take himself off to town for a few weeks or months.

He contrived private meetings with his wife. He took her riding one cloudy and chill afternoon. It was unwise though they both enjoyed the outing. Rain began to drip and then pelt down on them before they could get back to the stables. He turned the horse toward the summerhouse, lifted Clara down hastily, and nudged the horse sharply on the rump to send it galloping home. He rushed inside the summerhouse.

They were both laughing.

"Papa would not have allowed me to have even a window open on a day like this," she said.

"In some ways," he said, sitting down on the seat and holding her on his lap, "I am beginning to realize that Papa was a wise man."

"Your shoulder is damp," she said, brushing at the rain drops with one hand before settling her cheek there. "I thought we would fall for sure, Freddie. We were moving very fast. Don't laugh."

He had taken the horse to a canter in order to avoid the rain.

He kissed her. "It is warm in here at least," he said. "This morning's sunshine is still trapped inside."

"Mmm," she said. "It is cozy."

Several minutes passed in warm, lazy kissing.

"I have been missing you," he said, "with my parents here. And with Harriet here all the time."

"You will not feel obliged to spend so much time with me now," she said. "You will have greater freedom."

"Who says I want greater freedom?" he asked.

She did not answer and he kissed her again.

"Happy, my love?" he asked her after several more minutes.

"Mmm," she said.

"Which I can interpret any way I want, I suppose," he said, chuckling. "Well, I am happy."

"It was a lovely ride," she said, "despite the rain."

"Because of the rain," he said. "Without it I would not have thought of bringing you here and being cozy with you." He nipped her earlobe with his teeth and spoke into her ear. "Are you glad it rained too?"

He felt her swallow. "Yes, Freddie," she said.

"Have you missed me too?" he asked.

There was a long pause. "Yes," she said.

"*Yes* this time, not just *mmm*?" he said, shrugging his shoulder so that he could smile down into her eyes. "We are getting close to a serious declaration here, my love."

"Don't, Freddie," she said.

"Don't what?" He touched his forehead to hers and kissed the end of her nose. "Don't fish? I would like to hear you say the words. I can say them. *I love you.* There. They are quite easy to say. A great deal easier than one expects. I love you, Clara."

"Don't." She turned her face in to his neck. "It is so unnecessary. Don't spoil things."

He frowned and touched a hand to the back of her head. "Spoil things?" he said. "By telling my own wife that I love her? Don't you want me to love you, Clara? Or is it that you cannot return my feelings? That is all right. I can wait."

She raised her head and he could see that she was both upset and angry. "There is no need for the charade, Freddie," she said. "I think we are dealing surprisingly well together. Can we not be contented with that? Must there be all the lies?"

"Lies?" The heat seemed to be disappearing from the summerhouse. He felt rather cold.

"This claiming to love me," she said. "Calling me your love and sometimes even your darling. You do not need to do it, Freddie. Do you think I am a fool just because I am a cripple? Do you think I do not know the truth and have not known it all along? The only thing I do not know is the extent of your debts. Did the dowry cover them?"

If she had been capable of walking, he would have left her and gone out into the rain. He did not want to have to look into her eyes. But he would be damned if he would drop his own before hers.

"Yes," he said. "If you knew, Clara, why did you marry me?"

"I am twenty-six years old," she said, "and crippled and ugly. Need I say more?"

"You are not ugly." His lips felt as if they did not quite belong to him.

"It is kinder to use the word plain?" she said. "I am plain, then. We both married to satisfy a need, Freddie. And it has not been quite disastrous so far, has it? Let us

88

be satisfied with that. I do not need to be told that you love me when I know the words to be lies. I am not a child."

"My apologies, ma'am," he said.

She looked at him, the anger gone from her face suddenly, and sighed. "And I have just done an unpardonably foolish thing," she said. "It was a minor annoyance. I should have continued to say nothing. It would have been better so. I have embarrassed you, have I not?"

"On the contrary," he said. "It is always better for two people to have the truth in the open between them. Yes, my debts are paid, ma'am. There will be no others to be a drain on your fortune."

She looked at him for a few silent moments before sighing again and returning her head to his shoulder.

"I am a fool," she said. "Forgive me."

"There is nothing to forgive," he said.

He held her stiffly and silently for longer than half an hour until the rain stopped and then picked her up and walked in silence back to the house with her through sodden grass. Embarrassment, humiliation, he found, were a heavier burden than the woman he carried in his arms. She knew the truth. Of course she knew. He had never really believed that she did not. She must have had earlier experiences with fortune hunters. But having accepted him, decency dictated that they both keep up the charade.

Perhaps the words he had spoken to her were false. But he had acted on them. Everything he had done with her and to her in the past two weeks had been designed to show her a love he did not fully feel. He had tried to be kind to her and grateful to her.

He carried her into the house and straight upstairs to her dressing room. He reached a hand to the bell pull after setting her down on a chair.

"I shall order a hot bath," he said. "I don't want you catching a chill. And a hot drink afterward and at least an hour in bed."

She attempted a smile and a light tone. But it was

too late to play charades. "Is that an order, sir?" she asked.

"That is an order, ma'am," he said, turning to her maid, who had answered the summons with admirable speed. After sending her to the kitchens to arrange for hot water to be sent up, he left his wife's room without a backward glance.

He did not enter it again – or her bedchamber – before leaving for London the following morning. He took a formal leave of his wife after breakfast – her companion was with her – and told her that he would be away for a month. He fully expected that it would be considerably longer than that.

She did a great deal of crying, all of it in private, though there was no hiding the telltale signs about her eyes and in her face. Not at least from a close friend. Harriet was tightlipped about it at first.

"You have forbidden me to say anything against him," she blurted after luncheon one afternoon, several days after Frederick had left. "But I cannot bear this any longer, Clara. I hate to see you unhappy like this. I hate him."

"It is entirely my own fault," Clara said. "I'll not have Freddie blamed, Harriet." And the whole story of that wretched afternoon came pouring out. For a few days before that she had been planning to say something to him. Something quite calm and rational. They had known each other long enough, she had thought, and liked each other well enough that they could speak the truth. It would be better if the pretense was dropped. They would be able to concentrate on building a friendship.

"There was a possibility of friendship," she said to her skeptical friend. "We talked and talked during that week after our wedding, Harriet. And laughed. I have never laughed so much over such a short period of time. I wanted to get rid of the awkwardness of the other. It did not seem to matter that we did not love each other.

90

I thought we could be agreed to that. But I made a mistake."

"That man would not have enjoyed having his little game exposed," Harriet said bitterly.

"Perhaps not," Clara said sadly. "But it was the way I said it that ruined everything. I was irritated because we were in the summerhouse sheltering from the rain and it was so lovely and so comfortable just being together there. But he kept saying those foolish things and spoiling everything. I was not able to talk sensibly to him, as I had planned. I was angry and spoke unwisely."

"Just being together," Harriet said, looking at her closely. "Why were you angry, Clara? Because he was continuing to lie to you when it was unnecessary? Or because you were hurt?"

"Hurt?" Clara looked blankly at her friend. She wanted to put her hands up defensively before her face. She knew what Harriet was going to say, but she did not want to hear it.

"Because he did not mean the words," Harriet said. "Were you hurt because he did not love you but said he did?"

Clara drew a slow breath. "I did not marry him for love," she said. "You know that, Harriet. I have had everything I wanted from the marriage. Respectability and . . . Respectability."

But she continued to cry when alone. She could not seem to stop doing so or to pull herself together to resume a life with which she was long familiar. A life that had been interrupted for only a brief spell. She had known, after all, that the honeymoon could not last. She had not even expected a honeymoon when she had agreed to the marriage. She had not expected even that much.

She blamed herself for everything. For even if his words had been lies, he had been good to her. And life for those two weeks had become almost unbearably alive. She ached for the sound of his voice and his laughter, for the sight of his eyes. She ached at night

91

for the touch of his body, for the warmth of his mouth on hers.

She had humiliated him. She knew that. Her anger had made her lash out to hurt as she had been hurt. Oh, yes, Harriet had been right, she thought in some despair. She had been hurt by his words, which had been lies. And so she had hurt him. Not only had she told him that she knew the truth, but she had even specifically mentioned his debts and asked him if her dowry had been sufficient to pay them off.

How could she have done that to him? She had seen shame in his eyes and then a blank mask. A blank impenetrable mask that had stayed for the rest of the day and had still been there after breakfast the next morning when he came to take his leave of her. He had not used her name after what she had said or any of the endearments he had used in the previous two weeks. He had addressed her formally as "ma'am". He had not slept with her during what had turned out to be his last night at home although she had lain awake through most of the night, expecting him and knowing he would not come.

Clara cried for what she had done to him and for what had happened to her. For of course it had been foolish to think she could marry a man for his beauty and strength and virility and be satisfied with those things. She had been as dishonest with herself as Freddie had been with her. She surely must have known that she was incapable of possessing and enjoying those things without wanting more.

She wanted more. She wanted Freddie. Oh, not to love, perhaps. They were too different from each other ever to love. But there had been something between them during those brief days of their marriage. There had been. She was sure of it. Some friendship. More than that. Some tenderness.

Yes, tenderness, even if not love. There had been that. And it might have remained if she had not been so unutterably foolish and thrown it all away in a matter of moments.

A letter came from him after a week, a short, formal little note that she opened with trembling fingers and read with anxious eyes while Harriet looked gravely on.

He hoped she was in good health. He was going to stay in town for a while. He had business to conduct there. She paused over the second and last paragraph and read it twice.

"An open barouche is to be delivered here within the next day or two," she told Harriet. "I am to ride in it every day, weather permitting. I am to have you push me out on the terrace every day when it does not rain. I am to have at least half an hour of fresh air and sunshine each day."

"Well, that at least is sensible," Harriet said grudgingly. "With all due respect, Clara, I always thought that your father protected you too much and perhaps undermined the very health he thought to preserve. Are you going to follow Mr. Sullivan's advice?"

"Yes," Clara said, folding her letter and keeping it clasped in her hands. "Starting now. I have been missing the fresh air. I have not been outside for a week. Not since . . . Not since the day I was caught out in the rain."

She did not tell Harriet what Freddie had written in the last two sentences. There was no question of following his advice, good or otherwise. "And yes, ma'am," he had written, "this is a command. I expect to be obeyed."

She would obey him as she had always obeyed her father. She had obeyed her father because she had loved him and respected him and wanted to please him. She would obey Freddie because – because he was her husband.

The tears dried up in the coming weeks and life continued more or less as it had always been with a few changes. There were the outings, some of which she timed conscientiously so that they would not fall short of half an hour. Most of the time, though, except on especially raw autumn days, she stayed out a good deal longer than the prescribed time, from personal inclination. Once she had Robin carry her all the way to the summerhouse, and

Harriet sat with her there for an hour. But she did not repeat the experiment. The tears returned when she was back at the house and alone.

She began to visit almost as much as she was visited and even went to a few evening parties and one assembly. She watched the charades and the dancing with some wonder and a little wistfulness.

Her appetite continued to improve after a lapse of a couple of weeks following her husband's departure. She looked at herself critically in the looking glass one night and concluded that it was no longer her imagination. Her face was definitely fuller and far less pale than it always had been. She looked almost passably plain instead of ugly-plain, she thought with a private smile for the glass.

And she lived for the weekly letters that came from Freddie. Notes more than letters, all of them mere inquiries after her health and reminders of the one command he had seen fit to give her. She always answered the letters, as formally, almost as briefly, assuring him that she was in the best of health, hoping that he was too, and listing for him all the outings she had had in the previous week. Her barouche, she told him, was one of the most wonderful gifts she had ever been given. She felt a twinge of guilt, thinking of all the costly jewels her father had showered on her. But what she told Freddie was true.

Almost two months after he had left, the usual letter arrived. Clara read it with the usual eagerness, and then reread it, and read it again. She waited for Harriet to return from a short ride.

"We are going to London," Clara said when her friend came into the drawing room.

Harriet raised her eyebrows.

"Freddie is coming home next week," she said. "For one night only. He is taking us back to town with him the next day."

"To London?" Harriet's eyes lit up for a moment. Then she sobered and sat down. "You go, Clara. If you are to be with Mr. Sullivan, I will be in the way. I shall stay here or go on a visit to my mother if you would prefer."

"No," Clara said. "You must come too, Harriet. Please? I don't want to be alone. And I probably will be alone even more there than I am here. I don't know anyone in London. Except Freddie, of course. But he will have his own interests to pursue."

"Very well, then," Harriet said quietly. She was excited by the news, Clara thought. Poor Harriet. So young and so pretty and caught in a life of dreariness and poverty. Perhaps . . . She wished . . . But she had no way of bringing her friend to anyone's attention. She knew no one.

"Thank you," she said, smiling at Harriet.

She lay in bed later that night, staring upward, her letter held flat against her bosom. She did not want him to come home. She did not want to go to London. If he was coming home, he would go away again. If she was taken to London, she would be brought home again. She had not been made for excitement and novelty, she thought belatedly. She was made for dull monotony.

She did not want her emotions all churned up again.

She did not want to see Freddie again. And she would not cry, she told herself as she felt the ache in her throat and the sting in her eyes. She was not going to cry.

Why was she crying? She despised herself heartily.

# 8

Frederick immersed himself in the pleasures of town as soon as he arrived there, picking up his old life exactly where he had left it. Except that it had lost some of its luster. There was something missing but he did not know what. It was the rather grand town house, he thought, instead of the usual cramped bachelor rooms. And yet the house only added to his comfort. It was the fact that it was late summer and not the fashionable time to be in town. But he had always spent most of his time in London, regardless of the season. It had never made any difference to him before.

He became an enthusiastic contributor to the betting books at the clubs, as he had always been. He found out all the more interesting card games – at the clubs and in private homes. An interesting card game to Frederick meant that the stakes were high. And he bedded a few willing women of *ton* and a far larger number of willing courtesans. He even took to frequenting a brothel of high repute once or twice a week. He discarded the idea of employing a regular mistress after spending a second night with one particularly luscious courtesan only to find that she wanted to talk. As if her second time with him gave her the right to probe his soul. The last thing he wanted to do with women was talk.

The magic was no longer there. It was eluding him, no matter how frantically he tried to pile one pleasure on another. And he was losing at the tables and in the books. Not drastically so. Sometimes he won and sometimes he lost as one expected when one was an experienced gamer.

But the losses were always higher and a little more frequent than the gains. After a few weeks he became uneasily aware that he owed a substantial sum. Nothing he could not handle. His income was quite sufficient to cover his losses.

He began to drink in order to counter the flat feeling his days and his nights were bringing him. Never too much. He knew his limits and had always worked sensibly within them. He had done so ever since a drunken orgy when he was eighteen had left him sick for days and wishing he were dead. He had learned a lesson then. Never again would he drink more than two drinks on one occasion, he had resolved. Surprisingly, considering his other excesses, he had kept the resolve – until now. He started taking three and four drinks each night, just enough to brighten his mood but not enough to make him drunk. But he began to wake in the mornings, as often as not in a strange bed with the nauseating smell of some perfume in his nostrils, with a headache and a foul taste in his mouth.

He thought of Clara almost constantly. He had done a shameful thing and she had known about it and confronted him with it just at a time when he was making an ass of himself, telling her that he loved her, almost meaning it. He hated her. He wished in his heart that he had not taken the mad step of marrying her. Debtors' prison would have been better. Not that his father would have allowed him to languish long there. Debtors' prison would have been better than his father's sorrow too.

He never wanted to see his wife again. He would avoid doing so if he possibly could. He would have to think of some excuse to give his mother about Christmas. He did not need to look into Clara's eyes and see the contempt there. He had a looking glass that served the same purpose quite adequately.

And yet he worried about her. He had felt the essential tedium and loneliness of her life and felt almost vicious with anger against a father who had smothered her with love and made her life almost unbearably dull. She had

97

enjoyed their short rides more than another woman would have enjoyed a tour of the gayest European capitals. She had been happier sitting and lying on the grass outside the summerhouse than she would have been if he had presented her with a bed of priceless jewels and laid her down on it. Her open barouche, she had written to tell him, was the most wonderful gift she had ever been given.

She needed air and sunshine and company. She had Harriet Pope for company and a good number of attentive neighbors. He took to writing to her, commanding her to take the air and the sunshine. And he read her weekly letters and noted with satisfaction that she was obeying him. *Obeying* him! Someone like Clara was obeying someone like him? Because he was her husband. She had always obeyed her father too, and the man had let her live in a hothouse atmosphere. Her letters were always short and formal. He looked for something even remotely personal in them but found nothing, except that remark she had made about the barouche.

He tried not to think about her. They had their separate lives to lead, happily apart. He had got the money he had so desperately needed while she had got the respectability she had wanted. They owed each other nothing now.

Lord Archibald Vinney returned to London at the end of September and called on his friend the day after his return.

"Come up in the world, haven't you, Freddie, my boy?" he said in the languid voice he liked sometimes to affect. He looked about the salon, his quizzing glass to his eye. "It pays to marry a rich wife, I see."

"The house is a wedding present from my father," Frederick said.

Lord Archibald chuckled and lowered himself gracefully into a chair. "And how is the blissful bridegroom?" he asked. "Living apart from the bonnie bride? Marital bliss was too sweet, Freddie?"

"I had business in town," Frederick said, "and Clara is more comfortable in the country."

His friend threw back his head and laughed. "Business!" he said. "Making money, old chap? Are you?"

"I have had some luck," Frederick said.

He found Lord Archibald's quizzing glass trained on him. "Those words always mean that there has also been a great deal of bad luck," he said. "Another occasion when a rich wife comes in handy, Freddie. I envy you."

Lord Archibald was as rich as Croesus and the heir to a dukedom to boot. Rumor had it that his grandfather had been teetering on the brink of death for a year or more.

Frederick poured his friend a brandy and himself a glass of water.

"Ah, silence," Lord Archibald said, raising his brandy glass to his eye before sipping from it. "Are my remarks tasteless, Freddie, my boy? Do you consider yourself a married man?"

"I *am* a married man," Frederick said.

"Then my lips are forever sealed on the subject," his friend said. "Have you had at the delectable companion at all?"

"Had? Miss Pope?" Frederick frowned. "Of course I have not, Archie. What do you think I am?"

The quizzing glass was directed his way again. "Don't tell me," Lord Archibald said. "A married man. Never tell me you have been celibate since returning to London, Freddie. The very thought is excruciatingly horrible." He shuddered.

Frederick grinned for the first time. "Not exactly," he said. "Have you tried the girls at Annette's, Archie? They are something superior."

"You must recommend the loveliest and liveliest," his friend said, "and I shall sample her charms and see if I agree."

They resumed their friendship and Lord Archibald was as good as his word. He did not refer to the marriage again. But Frederick had been annoyed. His friend had seemed to take for granted the fact that there was nothing in the marriage to hold Frederick at home. It was a veiled and perhaps quite unintentional insult to Clara.

He did not like her to be insulted, indirectly or not. She deserved better than she had got. Ten times better.

He got drunk one night when luck was with him but even the pleasure of winning a small fortune could bring with it no great exhilaration. He got rowdily and finally morosely drunk and had to be carried home. He did not even know until well into the next day that he had lost the fortune and more besides. He felt so vilely sick all day that he got drunk again during the evening. And the next. He found that the only way to keep feeling marginally well was to continue drinking. Finally he drank himself into total oblivion.

Three days of hell followed and then a depression so deep that it seemed pointless to drag himself from bed in the morning. The thought of liquor or cards – or women – nauseated him. There seemed no pleasure in life worth going after any longer.

Lord Archibald dragged him out for a ride in the park one raw and gray day that perfectly matched Frederick's mood. There was almost no one else in sight.

"Everyone else is wise enough to stay indoors by a fire," he grumbled.

"Trouble with the marriage, Freddie?" his friend asked after a minute or two of silence, a note of unusual sympathy in his voice. "You are regretting it?"

Frederick laughed shortly.

"You cannot just pretend it does not exist?" his friend asked.

"It exists," Frederick said. "Be warned, Archie. Not one word about my wife. I am not in the mood to answer in any other way than with my fists."

"Hm," his friend said. "It exists but it does not exist. If it cannot be ignored, Freddie, my boy, perhaps it should be confronted. That is the only alternative, is it not?"

"Since when have you turned wise man and counsellor?" Frederick asked.

His friend lifted his quizzing glass to his eye and watched a shapely and self-conscious maid walking a dog as she passed close to them. He pursed his lips with appreciation and touched his hat to her though she peeped up only once, briefly. "Since feeling a hankering to see a certain little blond companion again," he said. "If you decide to make a visit into Kent, Freddie, I will come with you. As moral support."

"All I would need," Frederick said, "is to have a lecherous aristocrat seducing my wife's companion under my very nose. She is a virtuous woman if you had not noticed, Archie, and does not have the highest of opinions of our class."

"All the better," his friend said. "The pleasure of bedding willing wenches sometimes palls, Freddie. Not that one would contemplate bedding unwilling ones, of course. But there is a certain challenge in melting virtue and softening opinions. *Are* you going into Kent?"

"No," Frederick said.

"A pity." His friend sighed and turned his attention and his quizzing glass to a female rider who was approaching from a distance, a groom a short way behind her. "A beauty or an antidote do you think, Freddie? Five pounds on it that she is a beauty."

"Done," Frederick said. "My five pounds say she is an antidote. Who is to be the judge?"

"Honor," his friend said. "I will not pretend to see beauty as you will not pretend to see ugliness."

Frederick lost five pounds and Lord Archibald won a dark frown from the elderly groom for touching his hat and holding the girl's eyes rather too long with his own.

No, Frederick thought, he would not go back to Ebury Court. He had no reason to go. He did not wish to see her again. And she certainly would not wish to see him. And how would he behave if he went? As autocratic husband? Contrite husband? He grimaced at the thought. Charming

101

husband? She had seen through his charm. He could not use it on her again. No, he was not going back there.

And yet his friend's words kept coming back to him over the following days. He could not ignore the marriage, it seemed. Was the only alternative, then, to confront it? And something else kept running through his head too. A name. Dr. Graham. The physician who had been Sir Douglas Danford's friend and had been taken out to Ebury Court to examine Clara. And had left after a loud quarrel.

Frederick had never heard of Dr. Graham. But then he was not much in the habit of consulting physicians. When he made inquiries he found out very quickly that Dr. Henry Graham was one of London's most prominent and expensive physicians. But then, of course, nothing but the best would have been good enough for Sir Douglas Danford. Frederick made an appointment to see the man in his rooms.

Dr. Graham was reluctant at first to discuss a former patient with someone who was not involved.

"I should have explained," Frederick said. "Miss Danford is now Mrs. Sullivan. My wife."

That made all the difference, of course. Frederick was offered a chair and a drink. He accepted the former and declined the latter. "I had not heard that she was married," Dr. Graham said. "I am glad for her." Though his eyes, passing over his visitor, indicated that he was not quite sure that he was.

"You examined my wife once at Ebury Court?" Frederick said. "I would be interested to know what your findings were."

"It was a long time ago," the doctor said.

"Even so," Frederick said, "I would like to know. Exactly what is her condition?"

The doctor's lips tightened with remembered anger. "You did not know Danford?" he said. "He was a stubborn fool, Sullivan, even though he was once my friend. I felt sorry for his daughter, poor girl."

"Why?" Frederick asked.

"Pale and thin and frail," the doctor said. "Is she still the same? Danford would have breathed for her too if he could. He did everything else for her."

"From what she has said," Frederick said, "I gather that he loved her, sir."

"There is a certain type of love," the doctor said, "that kills, Mr. Sullivan. It is amazing that Mrs. Sullivan is still alive. She must have a remarkably strong constitution."

"Are you telling me that there is nothing wrong with her?" Frederick asked.

"I have not seen her for several years," Dr. Graham said. "She was undoubtedly ill when in India. Gravely ill, I believe. The months and even years she was forced to spend in bed weakened her. It would have taken time and considerable effort and some discomfort and even pain to get her back on her feet by the time she was brought back to England. It was criminal that she was not sent home a great deal sooner but I gather that Danford could not bear to be without her."

"She might have walked again?" Frederick asked.

The doctor shrugged. "If she had wanted to," he said. "If her will had been strong enough. There was no paralysis, Mr. Sullivan. Only the weakness of having been an invalid for most of her life."

"And now?" Frederick looked intently at the physician. "Might she still walk?"

"She has lost more years to the weakness," the doctor said. "She must be closer to thirty than twenty in age."

"Twenty-six," Frederick said.

"Who is to say?" the doctor said. "I cannot make a diagnosis from a patient I have not seen in years."

"Will you see her?" Frederick asked.

"At Ebury Court?" Dr. Graham frowned. "I am a busy man, Mr. Sullivan, and I do not have happy memories of that place. I was insulted. I was told that I wanted to kill my friend's daughter, that I wanted to cause her

103

unnecessary pain and suffering. A doctor does not like to be told such things."

"I will bring her to town," Frederick said. "Will you see her, sir?"

The doctor shrugged. "If it is your wish," he said. "Provided you do not already know what you wish me to say, Mr. Sullivan. I get mortally tired of fashionable patients wanting me to tell them how fashionably weak their health is. Ladies mostly, wanting an excuse to lie about on sofas looking delicate."

"I want you to tell me that my wife can walk again," Frederick said. "I will accept whatever you say. If she cannot walk, then so be it. She has learned to live patiently and courageously with her handicap."

"Oh, yes," the doctor said. "I can remember that, Mr. Sullivan. I thought it a pity that there was not also some spirit of rebellion in the poor girl."

"There is none," Frederick said. "She was an obedient daughter and is an obedient wife, sir. You will see her?"

Dr. Graham got to his feet and extended his right hand. "Let me know when she is in town," he said. "It is gratifying to know that she has a husband who seems more concerned for her wellbeing than his own comfort."

Frederick did not feel particularly pleased by the compliment. It seemed sometimes that his life was one great deceit. He deceived even when he did not try to do so.

He wrote a letter to his wife the same afternoon, announcing his intention of returning to Ebury Court the following week and bringing her and her companion back to town the following day.

He looked almost unbearably handsome and virile. She had remembered that he was handsome, of course. She had thought she remembered him perfectly. But there was something of a shock to notice again the dark intensity of his eyes, the lock of dark hair that would fall across his forehead, the breadth of his shoulders and chest, the length of his legs. And a certain breathless disbelief to know that this was the man with whom she had enjoyed such intimacies both in the flesh and in her dreams.

He was unsmiling, abrupt, courteous. Charmingly and quite formally courteous after bowing over her hand and raising it to his lips, bowing to Harriet, taking a seat, and accepting a cup of tea. He talked about London and the dismal autumn weather they had been having there. He talked about his journey and the accident of a farmer's cart overturning and sending the driver of a mail coach into paroxysms of wrath and frustration. It was an amusing account. Both Clara and Harriet laughed at it.

The old charming Freddie. But not trying to impress this time, only to fill in the silence. He had not once looked into her eyes. He glanced at Harriet more than he did at her. He was still angry with her, then. Or still shamed and embarrassed.

She wished that after all she had allowed Harriet to leave the room when her companion had observed his arrival from the drawing room window. Perhaps it would be easier if they were alone. Or perhaps not. She had not been able to bear the thought of being alone with him and had begged Harriet to stay.

"We were fortunate enough to have a drive in the barouche this morning before the rain came down again," she said. "We were out for almost a whole hour. Weren't we, Harriet?"

Harriet dutifully attested to the fact that it must have been very close to an hour.

Clara looked at him to find his eyes focused on her mouth or perhaps her chin. "I am glad to hear it, ma'am," he said.

He had not forgiven her. He had not come back from inclination. Why, then?

"You are looking well," he said.

"Yes," she agreed. "I am feeling well." She wondered if he had noticed the greater fullness of her face, the lesser

105

paleness. She wondered if she looked one whit less plain to him than she had. As if it mattered.

"I am taking you back to town to consult a physician," he said. "Dr. Graham."

"Dr. Graham?" she said. "But I feel well, Freddie. And last time all he could tell Papa was that I must be kept quiet, away from all chills and exertion. I don't want him telling you the same thing once more. I enjoy going outside every day."

"Nevertheless," he said, "you will see him, ma'am. As soon as possible. You are ready to leave tomorrow?"

"Yes, of course," she said. "You wrote to say that we should be."

"Perhaps you would prefer it if I did not go, sir," Harriet said. Clara knew that she wanted to go above all things.

"On the contrary, Miss Pope," he said. "My wife will need your companionship there as much as she does here."

Harriet nodded a quiet acquiescence. Clara was wrestling with a new realization that had just come to her. Of course. He wanted Dr. Graham to examine her to see if she could bear a child. Freddie was, after all, to be a baron one day and would want to have a son of his own to succeed. Perhaps she could not give him one. She had been bitterly disappointed, even though she had not known that she was hoping, when she had discovered that she had not conceived in almost two weeks of marital relations after her wedding.

She did not think she would be able to bear being told in cold words that there never could be hope. She could not bear the thought of Freddie knowing it.

"Harriet," she said, "would you pull the bell rope, if you please? I shall have Robin take me up to my room. It is time to be changing for dinner unless you would like it set back for half an hour or so, Freddie."

He got to his feet. "No," he said. "Leave the bell pull alone, Miss Pope." And he stooped down and lifted his wife up into his arms.

106

She had not expected it, though he had always carried her from place to place when he was at Ebury Court before. She had not expected it and had not steeled herself for the sensations caused by his arms and the touch of his body. She set an arm about his neck. His hair was longer than it had been. It looked even more attractive this way.

He said nothing and did not look at her as he climbed the stairs with her, quickly as he had used to do. She wanted to set her cheek on her arm, as she had used to do, but she did not do so. She kept her head away from him, as she always did with Robin.

He set her down on a chair in her dressing room and rang the bell for her maid. He hesitated, perhaps feeling that it would be too abrupt to leave the room without a word.

"Freddie," she said. *Welcome home*, she wanted to say. *It is good to see you. Forgive me. You have not forgiven me yet, have you?* She wanted some sort of peace and ease between them. But she could not find just the right words.

His eyes touched on hers for a moment. Then he bent his head and kissed her firmly and briefly and with closed lips on the mouth. He left the room without waiting for her maid to arrive.

Dinner and the couple of hours in the drawing room afterward passed with greater ease than Clara had feared. He set himself to be entertaining and charming and succeeded admirably. Even Harriet responded. And yet it was all so very impersonal. Clara thought back with some nostalgia to the week of their honeymoon when he had entertained her in very similar manner but with her hand in his or with an arm about her shoulders. And there had been smiles and kisses and the endearments she had found so irritating.

If only she had swallowed her irritation and said nothing. But perhaps nothing would have been different. He would have tired of charming her after a few weeks anyway and taken himself off to London just as he had. A little later than it had actually happened, perhaps. But it would have come. Nothing would be different. Except that perhaps he would be able to look into her eyes and call her by name.

He carried her to her room at bedtime and summoned her maid. He said nothing about returning later. But she stayed awake waiting for him, hoping that he would come, doubting that he would. She wanted him with a terrible ache. She wanted him next to her. She wanted to feel his weight, the warmth of his mouth, the deep and intimate joining of his body to hers.

After a few long and lonely hours she fell asleep.

Frederick paced his room for more than an hour before lying down and remaining awake for another one or two.

She was his wife. He had a right to go to her, to take her. It was not as if she had ever shown reluctance about receiving him. Quite the contrary. Even on their wedding night she had been eager. Her enjoyment of their couplings had only grown after that. She had never failed to come to climax, even during those middle of the night encounters when she had sometimes lain sleepy and only gradually awaking as he had mounted her.

It was easy to bring pleasure to Clara because she anticipated pleasure and never showed anything but delight no matter where he chose to put his hands or his mouth. She was totally without the ladylike shrinking from sexual titillation that he would have expected of her or of any other lady he had chosen to marry.

There was nothing to stop him from going to her. He wanted her surprisingly enough. Even looking back on the experienced girls he had had in the past two months did not dim the fact that tonight he wanted his wife.

And yet the very thought of all those girls and women he had enjoyed with such vigorous enthusiasm gave him pause. He was not diseased. He chose his women with far too great a care to risk that. But even so he had only

108

a sullied body to take to his wife. He would be putting inside her what had been in another woman just two nights before. And another the night before that. And so on back over two months.

Clara deserved better.

Besides, she despised him. She knew him for the fortune hunter that he was and the deceiver that he was. She must hate him even while she treated him with quiet courtesy – so quiet and so courteous and so impersonal since his return just that afternoon. And even while she obeyed his every command without question.

She must hate him. How could she not? He hated himself badly enough, heaven knew.

He fought desire, something he was not accustomed to doing and did not do easily at all. He fought it and won. At the expense of several hours of sleep.

# 9

Clara had passed through London a few times, but she had never been there to stay. It was a city she had always yearned to see but had never really seen. Or perhaps it was just a life she had yearned to live but never could, she thought as their carriage drove through the streets on its way to their town house. Everywhere was teeming with life and motion and noise.

"Oh, how wonderful it all is," she said, craning her neck to see all there was to be seen out of the window. "Look at it, Harriet. Have you ever seen anything like it?"

"No," Harriet said quietly, though Clara knew that she was excited too. "I always thought that Bath was crowded and busy, but it is nothing compared to this."

"Neither of you has been to London before?" Frederick asked.

"Only to pass through," Clara said. "Years ago when we had just returned from India and I was still feeling sickly. Harriet has not been at all."

"Then I shall have to make sure that you see everything that is to be seen," he said.

It was the first time there had been any real friendliness in his voice. Were they to stay longer than a day or two, then? Was this not just a brief visit to consult Dr. Graham? Was there to be some sightseeing too? Some sort of holiday? Clara looked at her husband and smiled tentatively.

"Everything?" she said. "Not one thing is to be omitted, Freddie?"

110

"Not one." There was a suggestion of a smile in his eyes for a moment before he looked away.

What had he been doing alone in London for two months? she wondered. But she did not like to let her thoughts dwell too long on the question. Her father too had sometimes come to town for weeks at a time, on "business". She had guessed what that business was, just as she had known, even as a girl, why the beautiful young Indian girl, who had no definable function as a servant in their home, had continued to live there.

She did not care to think of Freddie with other women. She had known from the start that he would not be faithful to her. She had accepted the knowledge quite calmly. It was a little more difficult now that she was his wife and had known him herself. It was not pleasant to think of him doing those things to another woman. To other women.

"Is the house attractive?" she asked him.

"You can see for yourself in a moment," he said. "You will find it considerably smaller than Ebury Court, but I like it."

The house, four stories high, fronted on the street on one side of a pleasant, quiet square. Frederick carried his wife inside to a high tiled hallway from which an oak staircase rose straight to the first floor. He presented her to the housekeeper, who was smiling and curtsying, and to the butler, who was bowing stiffly from the waist.

"Do you want to see some of the downstairs apartments?" he asked her.

"My chair is with the baggage coach," she said. "I am too heavy to carry, Freddie."

For answer he carried her into the first room on his left after instructing the housekeeper to show Miss Pope to her room.

"A receiving salon," he said. "My mother supervised the furnishing of the entire house, Clara. If you wish to change anything, then you must do so."

But she did not live there. It would make no difference to her how it was furnished. Would it? Did he intend that

111

she spend some time living there? Living in London? Being able to attend the theater and some concerts. How wonderful it would be.

"What are you thinking?" he asked. "You do not like it?"

"Very well," she said. "I am thinking that I am too heavy for you, Freddie."

"A mere feather," he said. "Perhaps a feather and a half. You have put on some weight."

"Spending time outdoors makes me hungry," she said. "I will have to be careful not to grow fat."

"You have a long way to go before there is any danger of that," he said. "You look good."

The compliment warmed her. Two months ago he would have told her that she looked beautiful and he would have said that he loved her. She would not have been warmed at all. This muted praise sounded far more sincere.

"And your face has some color," he said.

"I have never felt more healthy," she said. "Are you sure we should bother Dr. Graham, Freddie? I find it embarrassing to be poked and prodded and pulled."

"Nevertheless," he said, leaving the salon and carrying her into a study and library, "you will see him, Clara."

He was calling her by name, she noticed, looking about her. It was a room of masculine comfort, all wood and leather, it seemed. And very few books.

"A library," she said, "with almost no books."

He grinned. "Books are not quite my forte," he said. "You will have to stock the shelves, Clara. You are the reader, the one with impeccable reading taste."

But if she was to buy books and have time to read them, she would have to live here for awhile.

He showed her a formal dining room before taking her upstairs and setting her down finally on a chair in the drawing room. She looked about her. It was all green and golden.

"We will have a cup of tea," he said, "before I take you up to your room. You will be ready for a rest."

Harriet did not come downstairs. They sat alone, glancing at each other, looking away again. They talked about the room, about the house, about the quality of the tea they drank and the currant cakes they ate.

"Freddie," she said at last, raising her eyes resolutely and looking into his, "have you forgiven me?"

"Forgiven?" His eyes were deliberately blank. "There is nothing to forgive, Clara. The truth was spoken between us finally. The truth is always better than falsehood."

She nodded and looked down into her cup. "You went away," she said. "I thought you were angry."

"Our marriage is no different from thousands of others, Clara," he said. "It was a marriage of convenience for both of us. There need not be hostility just because there is no love. An enforced closeness might lead to hostility and that would be a pity. We each need room to live our own lives. What we had together was a honeymoon. Honeymoons do not last. We would have been foolish to expect it to and equally foolish to believe that our marriage has failed merely because it did not."

Calm and sensible words. He did not sound like Freddie the charmer. He had just said exactly what she had thought before her marriage. And since too. *Because there is no love.* It would be foolish in the extreme to let the words hurt. They were the simple truth. There was no love. They needed room to live their own lives, she at Ebury Court, he in London. Yes, it was what she had expected at the start. If she could have him just occasionally, she had told herself then, she would be content.

Nothing had changed. Had it?

"You do not agree with me?" he asked. "You find me too contemptible even for a marriage of convenience?"

"No." She looked up at him again. "You are my husband, Freddie. And yes, I agree with you. It is what

113

I expected and wanted of our marriage. I did not need what you seemed to think I needed."

"Well, then," he said, setting down his cup and saucer and getting to his feet. There was a note of finality in his voice. "That point is cleared up to our mutual satisfaction. We might as well deal with the remaining point, I suppose. Is it to be a real marriage again on those occasions when we are occupying the same house? Or would you rather not? What is your preference?"

"It is a marriage, Freddie," she said. "I am your wife."

He leaned over her to pick her up. "Very well, then," he said. "That is my preference too."

She leaned her head on the arm that was about his neck and closed her eyes. She was chilled and comforted all at the same time. Their marriage, then, was to be exactly as she had always wanted it to be. There would be times when they would be together, together in every way a husband and wife were meant to be. And there would be times, long dreary stretches of time, when they would be apart. When perhaps they would continue to communicate with each other through brief and impersonal weekly letters.

It would be enough. It would have to be enough.

"Tired?" he asked.

"Mmm, a little," she admitted, opening her eyes again.

"You must rest for a while, then," he said, opening a door that led directly into her bedchamber, a cozy room decorated in varying shades of blue. He set her down on the bed, removed her slippers, and doubled the comforter back over her. "I shall leave instructions that you are not to be disturbed for an hour."

"I will be late for dinner," she said, smiling at him.

"Dinner can wait," he said.

She was fond of him, she realized suddenly, reaching up a hand toward him. And she had missed him far more than she had admitted to herself – his company and his concern for her wellbeing. It was good to be with him again. She hoped it would be for longer than just a day or two. "Thank you, Freddie," she said.

He raised her hand to his lips, kissed the palm, and closed her fingers over it, a gesture she found strangely touching. He set her arm down at her side and covered her to the chin with the comforter.

"Sleep well, my l –" He smiled ruefully. "Sleep well, Clara."

He was gone, leaving her smiling as she closed her eyes. And swallowing against an ache in her throat.

Dr. Graham came promptly the following afternoon, far sooner than Frederick had expected of such a prominent physician. Frederick sent word to Lord Archibald Vinney that he would not be able to join him for an afternoon ride, as planned.

Clara was rather upset at having to see the doctor, he knew, though she said very little about it. He supposed it was not easy for a woman of virtue to allow herself to be touched and examined by a male doctor. He kept her company in her private sitting room until the doctor arrived, telling both her and Miss Pope about the sights of London he intended to show them over the coming days. But his wife did not smile much. He guessed that she did not hear a great deal of what he said.

He carried her through to her bedchamber when the doctor's arrival was announced and left her there, looking tense and unhappy, attended by her companion.

"I'll be downstairs in the library," he said before he left, bending over her and grinning. "At least it will not take me a great long time to choose a book."

She half smiled and turned to look anxiously at Dr. Graham, who was opening his black leather bag on the table beside the bed.

Poor Clara, Frederick thought when he reached the library and seated himself behind the desk without even attempting to choose a book. She had looked as pale as she had ever looked. He was strangely pleased to be back with her again. She was not lovely by any stretch of the imagination. Even with the improvements of a few pounds of extra weight and a slight flush of color in her cheeks she had not been suddenly transformed into a beauty. He had tried to look at her objectively in the last day or so and had seen that. And there was no great vitality in her to mask her lack of beauty. Just a quiet good sense and a quiet cheerfulness.

He did not know quite why it was good to be with her again. Even being in bed with her the night before had been good, though why it should have been so he did not know either. He compared it rather unwillingly in his mind with some of the more satisfactory of the beddings he had enjoyed during the past two months. The slow, careful lovemakings with Clara should have been far inferior but were not. Perhaps it was, he thought, that with Clara he always made sure that he gave her maximum pleasure whereas with other women he concentrated more on his own.

Freddie the unselfish giver? He chuckled at the unfamiliar and surely inaccurate image of himself. He was merely trying to assuage his guilt. Please her in bed and perhaps she would forget the great injustice he had done her. He was glad at least that they had had a chance for that private talk the day before and that there was some peace between them again. Everything was thoroughly satisfactory, in fact. They would live apart most of the time but come together for brief amicable interludes. What more could he ask of a marriage?

This particular interlude he would prolong for a while. It pleased him to show his wife something of London. Taking her about would make something of a change from the tedium of the past two months. Though when he thought of it that way, he frowned. Tedium? His chosen way of life? Anyway, he would enjoy driving Clara about, showing her the sights. And he would enjoy sharing her bed again for a short while. One could grow mortally tired of strange rooms and strong perfumes

116

and practiced sexual arts. There was some appeal about virtuous innocence.

He had expected to be summoned back upstairs as soon as the doctor had finished his examination. He was surprised when the physician appeared in the library. He got to his feet and raised his eyebrows.

"Mrs. Sullivan seems not to be a great lover of physicians," Dr. Graham said. "I had the distinct impression that she wished me in Hades. Most ladies of fashion adore me especially if I can diagnose some non-fatal ailment and prescribe some impressive-sounding medicine."

"Could you make such a diagnosis for my wife?" Frederick asked.

"Not at all," the doctor said, taking a seat and accepting the offered drink. Frederick poured water for himself. "I can find no more wrong with her now than I could the last time I saw her. She must be a remarkably strong woman. She appears to have recovered completely from a childhood sickness that would have killed most women or permanently damaged their health. Indeed it did kill her mother."

Frederick found himself feeling almost breathless. "And her legs?" he asked. "Is there any possibility that she can walk?"

"Oh, absolutely," the doctor said. "It will be a long and slow process after so many years. Possibly painful. Definitely frustrating. But in short, Mr. Sullivan, if your wife wishes strongly enough to walk, then there is nothing except her will to stop her."

"How did she react to that news?" Frederick asked.

The doctor raised his eyebrows. "I told her nothing," he said. "The decision of what to tell her is yours, sir. Is she to be told that she is of delicate health as her father decided? Or is she to be told that she can fight for normal health if she wishes?"

"The choice is mine?" Frederick said, frowning, his glass of water stranded halfway to his mouth. "Devil

117

take it, man, is it possible that we can have such power over women?"

"In short, yes," Dr. Graham said. "Danford chose his course and his daughter is as she is as a consequence."

"Perhaps," Frederick said, "women should be given more control over their own destiny. Or perhaps at least the woman under my absolute control should. I shall tell my wife exactly what you have told me."

Dr. Graham drained his glass and got to his feet. "If there were more men like you, Mr. Sullivan," he said, "perhaps women would find it less fashionable to be of delicate health and perhaps men like me could devote our time and skill to those who are indisputably sick. I do not know of anyone who is an expert at teaching someone who has not walked since childhood to walk again. I am afraid that if your wife decides that she wishes to do so, common sense and determination will have to be her teachers."

Frederick nodded and showed the doctor on his way. "I appreciate your coming," he said, "especially to a woman who is in perfect health. I hope I will not have cause to summon you to her ever again."

The doctor shook his hand and smiled. "Fortunes are not made in that way," he said.

Frederick grinned back at him.

Clara took a glass of water from Harriet's hand, her own slightly shaking. "Thank heaven that is over," she said. "What a strange, silent man. I remember thinking so when he came to Ebury Court and Papa quarreled with him. Will Freddie be satisfied now? I wonder. And I wonder what put such an idea into his head anyway?"

It was the thought that had been circling her brain for a few days. Did he believe her ill just because she could not walk? Did he think perhaps that she faked her crippled state? Her favorite theory that he had wanted to know if she was capable of bearing him an heir could not have been the right one after all. The doctor had made no examination that might have determined that.

Was he ashamed of the fact that she could not walk?

118

she wondered. Was he ashamed to have a crippled wife? But it was a foolish idea. There was nothing in her to inspire pride in her husband anyway. It could make no difference to him that she was unable to walk.

The doctor had said nothing and she had asked nothing. "Do you think there is something wrong with me after all?" she asked Harriet. "I mean, apart from the obvious."

Harriet clucked her tongue. "Dr. Graham will merely look grave and report to Mr. Sullivan what you already know and draw his fat fee," she said. "Don't go making yourself ill over such goings-on, Clara."

Clara laughed. "What would I do without your common sense?" she said.

But the door opened at that moment and her smile disappeared to be replaced by a look of anxiety. Freddie's face was very serious.

"You may go down to the drawing room if you wish, Miss Pope," he said, "and relax for a while. We will join you for tea shortly."

Harriet left and Clara's anxiety grew. She watched her husband with wary eyes as he seated himself on the side of the bed and took one of her hands in his.

"What is it?" she asked. "Is something left over from that long illness, Freddie? Is it going to come back? But I have been feeling so well."

"And no wonder," he said, squeezing her hand. "Dr. Graham reports that you are in perfect health, Clara."

"I could have told you that free of charge if you had asked," she said.

"I mean *perfect*," he said, emphasizing the word. "There is a great weakness in your legs, Clara, because you have not used them since childhood. There is no other reason why you cannot walk again."

Oh, no. She had taught herself a long time ago to give up hope. She had learned to live with her disability, to accept it, to adjust her life to it. She did not need this. Not from Freddie who knew nothing about her, nothing

119

about her hopes and dreams and the ones she had had to abandon for the sake of common sense and sanity.

"Don't," she whispered.

"You can walk again," he said, possessing himself of her other hand and squeezing both. "It will be a long and slow and difficult process, but it can be done. If you want it."

"Papa said I was never to exert myself," she said. "He said I would weaken myself and bring the sickness back if I did. Dr. Graham said those things, Freddie. Why has he changed his mind now?"

He hesitated before answering. "That was a few years ago," he said. "The doctor has seen since then that your health has improved to the point at which a relapse is not even a realistic danger. You can walk if you really want to do so."

She closed her eyes. And dance. That was the first absurd thought that leapt to mind. She had watched her neighbors dancing at the assembly a few weeks before and had wished it were possible to step outside her body just for a few minutes and dance too. It must be the most wonderful feeling in the world to dance.

"Don't cry," he said softly.

Was she crying? Her eyes were wet when she opened them. "I can't, Freddie," she said. "I cannot even move my legs."

"It will take time," he said, "and effort."

"And perhaps all be in vain," she said. "Is this why you brought me here, Freddie? Is this what you hoped to discover?"

"Yes," he said.

"But why?" she asked. "What difference does it make to you whether I walk or not?" She listened to herself in some surprise. Why had she not simply said thank you? She should be grateful. Without him she might never have discovered that her condition had changed and improved since her father's time.

"You are my wife," he said.

And less than whole? Less than a real person? An affront to his own beauty and strength? Beauty and the beast in reverse? She knew she was being unfair. But she was panicking.

"Is it to salve your conscience?" she asked. "Does it make you feel better to do me a favor that might not turn out to be a favor after all?"

She could have bitten out her tongue. She could hear the echo of her words in the silent room long after they were spoken. Why had she said them? She had not thought them. They seemed to have issued from her mouth without first passing through her brain. Could she do this to him a second time but without cause this time?

He got to his feet. "The decision is yours, ma'am," he said. "The doctor was quite adamant on the fact that only your will can make it happen. Not mine. This is something I cannot command. It is up to you. It is all the same to me. My life will not change either way."

Well. So he had hurt her back. They were even. *Thank you for caring enough to arrange for the doctor to see me*, she wanted to say to him. But she could not force the words out.

"Time to go down for tea," he said, bending over her.

"I am a little tired," she said. "I think I will stay here, Freddie."

But he scooped her up into his arms. "The decision of whether you try to walk or not is yours, ma'am," he said. "The decision of whether you retain your health or not is mine. You will not become an invalid. That I will not allow."

It was like a declaration of war, she thought, setting an arm about his neck. Could she ever walk? Could it really be possible? Could she one day walk beside him? Ride beside him? Dance with him? It was too enticing a possibility to be believed in. She sighed and watched his lips tighten into a stubborn line.

Perhaps one day too she would learn to curb the tendency she had not known she possessed to lash out at someone in self-defense when she herself felt hurt or bewildered or threatened. And yet it had only ever happened with Freddie. Perhaps because she felt so very inferior to him.

She sighed again as he opened the drawing room door and then forced a smile at the sight of a visitor.

# 10

Harriet was alone in the drawing room when the visitor was announced. She hesitated as the butler waited for a response. There was no telling how long Mr. Sullivan would be before bringing Clara downstairs. But both at Ebury Court and in Bath she often received visitors herself. Besides, she knew Lord Archibald Vinney. He had been at Clara's wedding – the tall, aristocratic-looking gentleman who had made free use of his quizzing glass in order to intimidate and had stared at her when Mr. Lesley Sullivan had presented him to her with such a direct gaze that she had been quite convinced that from the front he could see the hair on the back of her head. From silver eyes. She would swear his eyes were silver.

"Show his lordship in, please," she told the butler now, getting to her feet and trying to look as regal as a young girl of impoverished family, who was forced to work for a living as a lady's companion, possibly could.

Lord Archibald Vinney was an extremely attractive man, she remembered. She could remember feeling wistful at the interest he had shown in her. But Harriet's feet were ever planted firmly on the ground. She understood the nature of that interest very well. Hence the wistfulness. If she were Miss Pope of Something Park in Something-shire, with ten thousand a year, it would be a different matter perhaps. But she was not.

He strode into the drawing room now, stopped with studied surprise, fingered the handle of his quizzing glass, and bowed with great elegance. "Ah, Miss Pope," he said. "What an unexpected pleasure."

123

She curtsied. She had been right to remember him as attractive, she thought. He was not as obviously handsome as Mr. Sullivan, but he was ten times more attractive. In Harriet's opinion, anyway. He was dressed with fashionable elegance in green coat, buff pantaloons and shining, white-topped Hessians, and yet there was an air of carelessness about his appearance, as if he had thrown his clothes on with little care and they had just happened to fall into perfect place.

"Mr. and Mrs. Sullivan will be down soon, my lord," she said. "They have been detained abovestairs."

"Really?" he said, raising both eyebrows and lifting his quizzing glass almost to his eye. "How delightful for them. I can almost envy my friend."

"Will you have a seat, my lord?" Harriet said, indicating a chair. The meaning of his words struck her only when she had seated herself too and had raised her eyes to his, ready to make polite conversation. She felt her cheeks grow hot and could not for the moment remember what the weather was like in order to comment on it.

Lord Archibald raised his glass all the way to his eye. "How delightfully you blush, Miss Pope," he said. "Some ladies cannot do so without also displaying red patches on their necks and, ah, bosoms. You are not one of their number. I congratulate you."

She caught herself only just in time before saying thank you. "Is it not a pleasant day, my lord?" she said. "The air is fresh and invigorating."

"The wind is chill," he said.

"Yes, it is," she said earnestly. "But the sunshine is pleasant."

"Except when the clouds are overhead," he said.

"Yes," she agreed. "It is not so pleasant a day then."

She raised her eyes from his cravat to his to find them observing the hair at the back of her head again. Oh, dear, she thought, she had fallen into that trap very easily. He was making fun of her. The little provincial nobody. She straightened her back.

"I trust you left your aunt well in Bath, my lord?" she said.

"She is too bad-tempered to fall ill," he said, "and far too stubborn to die even though she is eighty. Or is it ninety? I am never quite sure. She will outlive her whole generation and mine, Miss Pope, and survive to plague the next generation but one or two."

"Oh," Harriet said. It seemed a very disrespectful way of talking about an aunt. She did not know quite what to say. "I am glad she is well."

When his eyes bored through to the back of her skull, she thought suddenly, he was hiding amusement. She amused him. He was playing with her as with a toy. She raised her chin.

"We have exhausted the weather," he said, "and touched upon the subject of health. What is left, Miss Pope? Fashion?"

"I am afraid I know little about it," she said, "having lived all my life far from town." And never having had the money to allow her to be fashionable.

His silver eyes moved down her body though he did not, she was relieved to find, raise his quizzing glass. "I think it an unarguable fact, Miss Pope," he said, "that beauty supersedes fashion. Some ladies do not need to be fashionable."

Harriet blushed again. The compliment had not been a direct one, but his eyes both laughed at and caressed her. She needed a chaperon, she thought suddenly. She ought not to have admitted him on the assumption that Clara and Mr. Sullivan would be there soon. Of course, she was a mere companion and companions did not need chaperons.

"And so you are to play odd man out to a couple about to resume their honeymoon," Lord Archibald said. "An awkward third in a *pas de deux*."

"I will be no such thing, my lord," she said indignantly. "My job is to give Mrs. Sullivan my company when she needs it."

125

"As she does not at the moment," he said, "while she is, ah, delayed abovestairs with her husband. She has poor taste, Miss Pope. You are far prettier than Freddie."

Certain comments were not conducive to conversation. They were unanswerable. Harriet did not answer.

"Four is a far more felicitous number," he said. "I shall have to offer myself as a fourth on occasion, Miss Pope, to save you from being an ignominious third."

Sometimes it was hard to know what he was talking about. Was he offering himself as her escort in London? The thought had its definite appeal even though she did not like the way he laughed at her secretly and made her feel like a gauche provincial. But she longed to see something of London, something of the fashionable life she had only been able to dream of until now. To be able to see it with such an escort . . . A lord, no less. The heir to a duke, no less.

Harriet got to her feet. "I shall ring for tea, my lord," she said. "Would you like me to go up and inform Mr. Sullivan of your arrival?" She took a few steps toward the door.

He got to his feet too and raised his quizzing glass to his eye. "Perhaps you had better, Miss Pope," he said. "I have a reputation for devouring unattended females after ten minutes alone with them, you know. Especially pretty ones."

What a strange man, she thought, blushing yet again. What he undoubtedly did have a reputation for was causing unattended ladies to blush at regular five-minute intervals. He was not really a perfect gentleman. She turned to the door again and was vastly relieved when it opened from the other side and her employers came into the room.

She rang the bell for tea while greetings were being exchanged and took a seat a little farther away from their visitor than the one she had occupied before.

Frederick left the house with Lord Archibald after tea.

They dined at White's with a group of acquaintances and sat on for several hours, conversing and drinking – Frederick drank water and coffee. It was thoroughly pleasant, he thought, to be with male companions again, to be able to relax in the sort of atmosphere he was familiar with and enjoyed. One could be stifled by female company. Though he had been only two days in his wife's, he realized when he thought about it.

It had been a mistake. He should have left things as they were. Clara had obviously been happy with her seemingly dull life at Ebury Court, and he had been happy with the bachelor life that had always suited him. It had been a mistake to think that perhaps he could do her a kindness. She wanted no such kindness. He had done it to ease his guilt, she had said, infuriating him. He did not believe he had done it for that reason, but how was he to know? Perhaps she was right.

To hell with it, he thought, joining in the uproarious laughter that followed a bawdy joke told by one of their number and launching into one of his own. To hell with it, whatever "it" was, and to hell with her.

He took Lord Archibald to Annette's much later. They walked there.

"You are scowling, Freddie," Lord Archibald commented. "You have been scowling all evening."

"What am I supposed to do?" Frederick asked irritably. "Wear a beatific and asinine smile wherever I go, Archie?"

Lord Archibald laughed. "It appears that confrontation is having no greater success than denial," he said. "How long are you planning to keep her here, Freddie? Long enough for me to improve my acquaintance with the little companion, it is to be hoped. She is the most charming blusher it has ever been my delight to provoke into blushes. Is she ripe for the picking, do you think?"

"Over my dead body," Frederick said.

Lord Archibald toyed with the handle of his quizzing

glass but did not raise it. "Interested yourself, old boy?" he asked.

Frederick stopped abruptly. "If you want a poke in the nose, Archie," he said, "you are going the right way about it. I thought I had made myself clear on that point before."

"Ah, but opinions do sometimes change," Lord Archibald said. "If you want my opinion, Freddie, my lad, as I am certain you do not, I would have to say that you are developing some unwilling feelings for Mrs. Sullivan. I believe we happy bachelors are about to lose –"

"You are right," Frederick said, his voice testy. "I do not want your opinion, Archie. Ask for Caroline when we reach Annette's. She is the best. Though they are all good. Carefully chosen and thoroughly well trained, you know."

"You would sacrifice the best to me?" Lord Archibald asked. "You are a true friend, Freddie."

Truth to tell, Frederick was not in the mood for visiting a brothel, even one with such skilled girls as Annette's. But he did not want to go home either just in order to pace his room wondering if he should spend the rest of the night in his wife's. There was something distinctly humiliating about thinking of asserting one's conjugal rights with a woman who despised one. Even if she enjoyed it. It made him think uncomfortably of gigolos.

Caroline had a free hour and was borne off by Lord Archibald. So did Lizzie. She was well-endowed in every way, Frederick thought, escorting her to her room. In five years' time, if she did not watch herself, or if Annette did not do the watching, she was going to be fat. He often asked for her. She was marvelously skilled in a languorous sort of way.

He sat at the foot of the bed and scowled while Lizzie looked at him a little uncertainly, waiting for instructions that did not come, and then began to undress, one enticing garment at a time. Frederick's scowl deepened. He spoke finally when she came to her *pièce de résistance*, the removal of a flimsy chemise, her last remaining garment.

"You had better get dressed again, Liz," he said. "I seem to have caught something and would hate to infect you."

She dressed with a little more speed than she had undressed and came to sit beside him on the bed and run her fingers through his hair. "Never mind, love," she said soothingly. "A doctor can fix you up in no time and you can come back."

He had burned his bridges in this particular establishment, he thought gloomily. Lizzie would dutifully pass along the very pertinent information to Annette and he would be politely but firmly denied admittance for the rest of his natural lifetime. He sighed.

She kissed his jaw. "It's a pity," she said. "I was looking forward to an hour of fun. You are my favorite."

"Yes, well, Liz," he said, "I couldn't do that to you, could I? You would lose your place here and suffer into the bargain."

"You are a kind gentleman, sir," she said, kissing his cheek. "You have paid your fee. Can I please you in any way?"

"Talk to me," he said. There was almost an hour to be filled in before he could expect Archie to emerge from Caroline's clutches. "Tell me about your home and your family, Liz. How did you come to this particular point in your life?"

"Oh, my," she said. "It is forbidden, sir."

He turned his head, kissed her on the lips, and looked at her steadily from beneath lowered lids. It was a look that never failed with women.

"But you will break the rules for me, Liz," he said.

And so he spent his last expensive hour at Annette's listening and learning that a whore could also be a person, that she had had a childhood and a girlhood, complete with hopes and dreams, just like anyone else. It was an interesting and somewhat disturbing lesson. It was easier to think of them merely as bodies whose sole function in life was to provide pleasure for men.

It was a day of disasters, he thought, thoroughly out of sorts, when his hour was finally over. He had not felt so depressed since he did not know when. And to crown it all, when Archie joined him downstairs, he was wearing that beatific and asinine smile Frederick had described earlier.

"Divine," he said as they walked away from the brothel. "It must have been a sacrifice beyond the call of duty and friendship to leave her to me, Freddie. My heartfelt thanks, old chap."

"Lizzie is better," Frederick said, his voice a growl.

Lord Archibald was ready to go home. An hour at Annette's could do that to a man, Frederick thought irritably. He was not ready to go home. He would go and see if there were any interesting games in progress at any of his clubs, he decided. He was not going to play. He had sworn off gambling with the last round of debts, fortunately more modest than the ones that had precipitated him into marriage. He would just watch, fill in the tedious hours of a night that he wanted over.

He watched for an hour and played for two, going home only when everyone else decided to play no longer. His pockets were slightly better lined than they had been when he had arrived, but his mood had not improved. He had said he was not going to play, had he not? What if he had lost badly?

Sometimes it seemed that he was not in full control of his own actions. As if his mind and will had become divorced from his body. A foolish thought, of course. Once he had spent a week or so taking Clara dutifully about London as he had promised, he would be able to take her back to Ebury Court, where she would be happier again, and he would be able to take up his bachelor existence once more, his conscience clear. He had tried to be kind to her. He had shown her the way to a better life of greater freedom, and she had rejected it. So be it. It was up to her, as the doctor had said and as he had explained to her.

If she wished to wallow in an unnecessary misery, then she would be left free to wallow. To hell with her. He fell into bed finally when dawn was already graying the windows of his bedchamber.

"And so that is how it is," Clara said. "Can you believe it, Harriet? I could have been walking all these years back in England instead of sitting forever in chairs and having to be wheeled or carried from place to place. I could walk for the rest of my life." She and her companion were in her private sitting room.

"But it is wonderful news." Harriet had her hands clasped to her bosom. "Clara? It is glorious."

"But I don't believe it," Clara said. "I can't. When I fell out of bed this morning –" Fortunately a maid had been in her dressing room, bringing a jug of steaming water, and had heard the thump and come running. Clara, though hurt and frightened, had pretended to be waking up from sleep. "I did not fall out. I tried to stand. My legs were quite, quite useless."

"But of course they were," Harriet said. "Gracious, you might have hurt yourself badly. You cannot expect just to get up and walk because you have been told that it is possible for you to do so, Clara. You have not walked for years."

"For twenty," Clara said.

Harriet tutted. "And you thought to step out of bed this morning and walk down to breakfast," she said. "How foolish."

"It was rather, was it not?" Clara felt sheepish. "Though I do not think I was quite so unrealistic, Harriet. I would have been happy just to stand there for a few moments."

"Did you not just say that Mr. Sullivan told you it would be a slow, frustrating process?" Harriet asked.

"Yes," Clara said, sighing. "I have always been renowned for my patience, Harriet. People tell me how wonderfully

131

patient I am in adversity. I am not sure I have enough for this. I want to walk now. I want to run yesterday. I want to dance the day before. I just don't think I can do it. How can I begin to hope now when I have developed this legendary patience, and perhaps have my hopes dashed? Better not to have hoped at all."

"But you are doing just that," Harriet said. "And I know you well enough, Clara, to feel sure that you will be quite unable just to close your eyes to this chance."

Clara sighed again. Of course Harriet was right. She had lain in bed the night before trying to move her toes. She could feel them. She could even feel them moving, though she doubted that their movement would be perceptible to the eye. They were so very weak, and so far from her brain that the message she was trying desperately to send seemed not to be reaching them. Frustration? Oh, yes, she had wept with it just the night before. If her toes would not obey her will, how was she to command her whole legs?

"How is it to be done, Harriet?" she asked. "To know that it can be done is one thing. To know how it can be done is another. If I cannot just get up and walk, what am I to do?"

Harriet sat down, clasped her hands in her lap, and thought. "Exercises," she said after a while. "We will have to devise exercises for each part of your legs and feet to strengthen them and teach them to move. That will have to be accomplished before you try putting any weight on them. Starting with your toes, I think. And then your ankles and then your knees."

"It sounds like a long, long process," Clara said. "Toes by the time I am thirty, ankles by forty, knees by fifty, stand by sixty, walk by seventy. Dance on my eightieth birthday."

She laughed without humour at first until Harriet joined her. Suddenly, they were both rocking with uncontrolled mirth.

"At least," Harriet said, "we can see the funny side."

"Oh, dear," Clara said, wiping the tears from her eyes

with a handkerchief, "*is* there a funny side, Harriet? Do you suppose I should start with the toes now? Two hours a day? Instead of embroidery?"

They were laughing again when a tap sounded at the door and Frederick opened it. Clara sobered instantly. It seemed that her reaction to his words the afternoon before had amounted to a quarrel. He had left with Lord Archibald after tea and not returned for dinner, though she had had it held back half an hour. Nor had he returned all night. She had lain awake until almost dawn but had not heard either his footsteps or the click of his bedchamber door. She had lain awake wanting him and imagining all the places he might be and despising herself as a jealous wife. She had never expected him to be either a devoted or a faithful husband. She had tried to imagine what the woman looked like, what type of woman he most favored. She had wondered if it was a casual encounter or if she was a mistress of long standing. Perhaps there was a home and a woman and family of his somewhere in town.

"You are both sounding very merry," he said, bowing to each of them. "How would you like to see Westminster Abbey and perhaps St. Paul's too today?"

If he had come from a night of debauchery, Clara thought, it did not show. As usual he was dressed with impeccable good taste and looked quite impossibly handsome. She would accept their relationship for what it was, she decided, as she had always intended. When he was not there, she would live her own life and make the most of it. Perhaps she would even learn to walk.

"That would be wonderful, Freddie," she said, smiling at him.

"I shall stay here," Harriet said. "I shall be quite happy."

"I don't believe Lord Archibald Vinney would enjoy an afternoon spent with me and my wife," Frederick said. "You must come to make up numbers, Miss Pope, if you will."

Harriet blushed deeply, Clara noticed with interest

and some alarm. She would hate to see her friend get hurt. Although she was a gentlewoman, Harriet was impoverished and her family was of no great social significance. She had only beauty and good nature and practicality to recommend her to the heir to a dukedom. Especially one as suave and worldly as Lord Archibald Vinney appeared to be.

"Very well, then, sir," Harriet said quietly. "Thank you."

They were to have an early luncheon and then be on their way. The sun was shining, Clara saw, looking toward the window. It was a lovely day, though probably chilly. She loved the crisp air of autumn, something she had scarcely experienced before since she had never been allowed out in it. She hoped they would be taking an open carriage to Westminister Abbey. She felt as excited as a child expecting a treat.

"I feel as excited as a child," she said to Harriet after Frederick had left the room. "Is that not foolish in the extreme?"

"I would be jumping up and down if it were not quite undignified to do so," Harriet said.

"Shall we dance?" Clara said. And they both dissolved into laughter again.

A pair of children, Clara thought, starved of treats and now having a plum dangled before their eyes and mouths.

# 11

Westminster Abbey and Gunter's that first afternoon, St. Paul's another day, the Tower on a third, visits to Madame Tussaud's and to various galleries, several drives in Hyde Park, though it was nowhere near as busy as it always was during the spring – there always seemed to be somewhere to go. Occasionally they went alone. Often Harriet accompanied them. Sometimes Lord Archibald joined them.

His wife and Miss Pope were enjoying it all with such undisguised wonder, Frederick found, that he had not the heart to cut short their visit. Besides, he enjoyed it all too, his jaded eyes seeing the nation's capital with fresh vision.

He always ordered around an open barouche instead of a closed carriage unless it was actually raining, even though the weather had turned cold and crisp. He did not know how his companions felt about this spartan treatment. None of them complained. Archie seemed even to enjoy it.

"Have you noticed, Freddie," he asked one day when they were alone together, "how roses in female cheeks can rouse fires in a quite different part of the male anatomy?"

Archie was talking about Miss Pope, of course. But Frederick liked to see the flush of bright color in his wife's cheeks and even on her nose, and the sparkle in her eyes.

He had decided to take his marriage as it came, a day at a time, not looking for too much, not rejecting what little there was. At present they seemed reasonably and cautiously contented with their life together. He had not said anything more to her about walking, and she had not referred to it either. It would be left at that. He had explained matters to her and told her that the choice was hers. He would now respect her decision. Or lack thereof. He was a little disappointed to find that she was not of such strong character as he had thought. But then, of course, he could not put himself in her place. He could not quite imagine what it must be like.

He spent time with her and took her about. He spent some nights with her. Not every night. Sometimes he was not at home. And some days he kept to himself. He was exercising and sparring at Jackson's Boxing Saloon. He was enjoying male company at his clubs. He was gambling, alternately winning and losing, salving his conscience when he won by telling himself that there was no harm in it, mortally depressed when he lost, always convincing himself that he could give it up entirely whenever he wished, just as he had given up women and drinking. Clara was the only woman he was currently bedding.

He had never taken her out in the evening. He had made no effort to introduce her to society. But then the autumn was not a good time in which to do that. However, the season was growing late and more and more people were coming back to town. Evening activities were resuming.

"Would you like to go to the theater one evening?" he asked his wife early one morning after he had finished making love to her and they were lying close together, drowsy but still awake.

"Oh, Freddie." She turned her head and even in the near darkness of the room he could see the glow in her eyes. "Could we? Could we really? Papa would never allow me out in the evenings though I did go out a few times at Ebury Court after you left while the weather was still quite warm. Papa was afraid of the chill night air."

"We will wrap you up warm," he said, "so that the chills will not be able to find you."

136

"The theater!" she said. "Is it very wonderful, Freddie? Oh, it must be." Her tone changed suddenly. "But I have nothing to wear. Only the dresses I wear at home in the evenings."

"An easily solved problem," he said. "I shall have a modiste summoned to the house tomorrow. You must have a whole range of new clothes made, Clara. Now that winter is coming on and everyone is returning to town, there will be evening entertainments for us to attend."

There was a short silence. "I am to stay for a while, then?" she asked.

Was she? He had intended to keep her with him for only a week or two before taking her back home and resuming a life of greater freedom. More than two weeks had passed already.

"We will see how things go," he said. "Shall we?"

She nodded and nestled her cheek against his shoulder, and he settled for sleep. But she spoke again.

"Freddie," she whispered, "when will we go to the theater? Soon?"

He turned onto his side, wriggled an arm beneath her neck so that her head could lie on his shoulder, and kissed her mouth. "Soon," he said. "Or sooner. Satisfied?"

She chuckled. "As long as there is time for my dress to be made," she said. "How am I supposed to sleep now?"

"By closing your eyes and relaxing," he said. Good Lord, she was excited. Too excited to sleep. All because he had suggested taking her to the theater. He felt curiously like crying. He turned her onto her side, drew her against him, rubbed a soothing hand up and down her back, and kissed her warmly again.

She sighed, almost a purr of sound.

She could clench her toes. "Which is a dreadful whopper," she told Harriet, "when I compare it with clenching my fist. There is no power in my toes." With a great deal of concentrated effort she could move each foot from side to side. "Almost enough for the human eye to detect," she said. She could even lift her foot an inch or so toward her leg, though the movement could hardly be called flexing the foot. Her knees would not obey her will at all.

"Did I say toes by the age of thirty?" she said to Harriet once morning, falling back against the pillows of her bed in a show of exhaustion that was only partly faked. "I believe I was over-optimistic. This will never do, Harriet. How can I hope ever to walk?"

"Perhaps if I massage your legs the blood will flow more vigorously and help them grow stronger," Harriet said. "I used to massage Mama's shoulders and back. She suffers from the rheumaticks. She always said I have powerful hands."

They were indeed powerful, rubbing and massaging with a firmness that was both painful and soothing.

"Ouch!" Clara said, wishing at one point that she could jerk her leg away from Harriet's hands. "At least we know there is feeling there, Harriet. What an unpleasant task for you. Ugh, my legs are like sticks. How can I ever think of walking on them?"

The words struck them both as funny and they were off into gusts of laughter again. They had been doing a great deal of laughing, even giggling, since Clara had begun her "exercises". Laughter was better than acknowledging pain and frustration and even despair, Clara had decided. And perhaps Harriet found it better than giving in to the pity she must be feeling.

Clara did her crying alone. Far too much of it for her own self-respect. She cried particularly during the nights when Freddie did not come home. Despicable tears of self-pity. For as long as she had thought she could never walk again, she had accepted her crippled state with a studied cheerfulness. Now she knew there was a chance, she was in despair. Progress was so very slow as to be almost non-existent. It would never happen. No matter how hard she tried, it would not happen. And in the meantime there was effort, concentrated, bone-wearying effort for infinitesimal results. And pain.

She had not told Freddie. She was working in secret. If she failed, then he would never know that she had even tried. If she succeeded – but sometimes she thought she would never succeed – well, then, she would surprise him. She had a pleasant dream of herself walking into the library one day while he was busy at the desk at some task. She would watch his jaw drop to his chest and then hear the crash of his chair as he rose hastily and came around the desk to clasp her in his arms.

What a ridiculous dream, she thought, sniffing and drying her eyes and trying to laugh aloud at herself. As if it would matter that much to Freddie. Even if she could walk, she would still be thin and ugly. She hated her ugliness. She wanted beauty. Only the moon and the stars, that was all. She would be content to leave the sun where it was. She blew her nose.

No, she would not. She wanted the sun too. And she saw something in a blinding flash, just as if she were looking into the heart of the sun. Oh, dear God, she thought. Oh, God. Oh, God. But she could repeat the phrase to kingdom come and not mask the other thought, which did not need the medium of words. She wanted his love too. All of it. Why? Because she loved him, of course. Foolish, stupid, ridiculous woman.

It was a truth not to be dwelled upon. He had not come home again on that particular night. He would be with *her* again. If there were one "her", that was, and not a different one each time. Either way, he was with her rather than with his wife. She wondered, not even trying to shake the thought from her mind as she usually did, what they were doing. Sleeping? Or –

No, she would not tell him that she was trying to learn to walk. If she succeeded, then she would have greater freedom to make a life for herself independent of a faithless husband. Whom she just happened to love. It was an incidental point, not relevant to anything.

The sun would grow rather too bright on the eyes if one

139

possessed it, anyway. It was as well to be philosophical about these things.

Sometimes she and Harriet talked about London, about what they had seen and what there was still to see. They could talk endlessly and with mutual enjoyment on the topic.

"Freddie is going to take us to the theater soon," Clara said the morning after he had told her so, while Harriet was massaging her legs.

Harriet looked up, the sort of longing in her eyes that must have been in her own much earlier that morning, Clara thought. "The two of you?" she said. "How wonderful for you, Clara. You must tell me all about it afterward."

"No, silly goose," Clara said. "I said 'us', did I not? He is going to invite Lord Archibald too."

"Oh, Clara." Harriet's hands had stilled. "It would be altogether too wonderful. But I have nothing to wear."

Clara laughed. "That was my objection too," she said. "Freddie is sending a modiste here this afternoon, before our drive. He wants me to have several dresses made. You are going to be measured for one too." She held up a staying hand when her friend would have interrupted her. "As a thank-you for all the help you have been giving me for the last couple of weeks, Harriet. No, don't say no. It will give me such pleasure."

"Thank you," Harriet said softly, looking down sharply to resume her task, but not soon enough to hide the fact that tears were glistening in her eyes.

"Do you like Lord Archibald?" Clara asked. They had not spoken about him before, though he had been quite attentive.

"He likes to laugh at me," Harriet said. "He likes to make me blush. He treats me like an amusing child."

"Hardly that," Clara said, frowning. "Has he made any improper advances, Harriet?"

"Of course not." Harriet looked up, startled. "Do you think I would allow it?"

"No," Clara said. "But I think he is a dangerous man. He is used to getting his own way, I would guess. I believe he fancies you."

Harriet blushed. "How foolish," she said.

"You are very sensible," Clara said. "Far more so than I am, Harriet. But I cannot resist one word of maternal advice. Be careful. Will you?"

"I am not sure about being sensible," Harriet said, "but I am a realist. I know that to Lord Archibald Vinney I am merely an amusing interlude. If I take your foot in my hand and flex it forward, do you think you can push it back against my hand? Perhaps we should try it that way first since you are not making great progress at flexing it yourself. Shall we try?"

Clara sighed. "Slave driver," she said. "Yes, let's try it, then."

She fortified her spirits with thoughts of theaters and new evening gowns that would transform her into a beauty as she exerted every ounce of strength and willpower over the coming half hour.

The theater was unexpectedly crowded for the time of year. It seemed almost full when Frederick carried his wife into Lord Archibald's private box and looked about him before lowering her into a chair. A large number of quizzing glasses and lorgnettes were undoubtedly trained their way. Perhaps many people had not heard either that he was married or that his wife was unable to walk, he thought.

He smiled reassuringly at her as he set her down. Her new blue gown really became her well, as he had told her earlier in her dressing room, when he had given her the gold chain with its sapphire pendant that she now wore about her neck – bought with his winnings of two nights previous. But she did not need reassurance, he saw. Like Miss Pope, she was gazing about her with wonder and awe, quite unaware of the fact that she was drawing a great deal of attention.

141

"There will be a play to watch too, you know," he said, settling himself beside her and grinning at her. "Save some of your admiration for that, Clara."

She laughed. "I am enjoying every single moment of the evening as it happens," she said. "Don't make fun of me and make me feel like a little child."

He took her hand in his and squeezed it – and kept it in his. That feeling was creeping up on him again, the one that had so surprised him at the end of his honeymoon just before their first quarrel. The feeling that it would be altogether possible to fall in love with her. He liked to please her. He was always catching himself in the act of thinking up new ways of doing so. He liked making her happy.

"Happy?" he asked.

"Silly," she said. "How could anyone be here and be anything but happy, Freddie? Go ahead, laugh at me."

He laughed. Archie, he could see, was saying something to make Miss Pope blush. There was nothing particularly unusual about that. Archie had asked him if he could possibly delay carrying Clara out to the carriage after the play was over until everyone else had left.

"And leave you alone with Miss Pope?" Frederick had said. "Forget it, Archie."

"For five, maybe ten minutes," Lord Archibald had said. "Sometimes I can make haste and thereby deny myself a great deal of pleasure, Freddie, my boy, but I don't believe even a marginally satisfying ravishment could be accomplished in five minutes, could it? It would seem hardly worth the expenditure of energy. I merely want to talk to my little blushing beauty."

"Merely talk?" Frederick had raised his eyebrows.

"Well, almost merely," his friend had said, smiling engagingly. "You and Mrs. Sullivan make quite oppressive chaperons usually, my lad."

"Well," Frederick had said, "I will see what can be arranged, Archie. But I will not have the girl frightened or compromised."

"You sound like a grandfather who has raised fifteen daughters and is now starting on his granddaughters, Freddie," Lord Archibald had said. "It is most disconcerting."

He hoped he had not agreed to something that would cause his wife's companion any embarrassment or suffering. Damn Archie. Couldn't he restrict his attentions to those women who were available or at least to those who understood the game of dalliance? Miss Pope was a babe in the woods.

Clara gripped his hand with unconscious excitement when the play began and watched it with rapt wonder until the interval. If the theater had burned down around her, she would not have noticed, Frederick thought with a sort of tender amusement. He watched her more than he watched the play. He had never been much of a one for drama. He had always attended the theater in order to sit in the pit with the other unattached men and ogle the ladies. His wife was the only one he was ogling tonight, though he was not really doing that. He was merely watching her. A great deal of inner beauty came shining from her eyes, he thought.

Lord Archibald persuaded Harriet to step out into the corridor for some air and exercise during the interval after having convinced her that it would be so crowded with people out there that they would scarcely be able to move. Frederick stayed to keep his wife company, still holding her hand and listening with a smile to her enthusiastic analysis of the play and the acting.

"Don't you agree?" she asked, pausing at last.

"I agree, my l – I agree," he said. "Everything you say is true and wise, Clara."

She looked suspicious. "You are laughing at me," she said. "I suppose it is not fashionable to show such enthusiasm for the theater, is it? I don't care a fig for fashion."

"And yet," he said, "you chose a dress design that is the very height of fashion, Clara."

"Merely because the modiste recommended it," she said. "If it had been last decade's design I would not have known the difference."

He chuckled and turned his head to see who had opened the door and was coming into their box. Then he scrambled to his feet.

"Freddie," his cousin, Camilla Wilkes, said, stretching out both hands to him and turning her cheek for his kiss. "One would think you were totally blind. We have been nodding and winking and doing everything to attract your attention but standing on our seats and waving our arms above our heads. All to no effect. Have we not, Malcolm?"

Malcolm Stacey, his sort-of cousin, Camilla's betrothed, was standing behind her, tall and thin and blond, smiling. "Hello, Freddie," he said, extending a hand. "We did not know you were in town. We arrived ourselves just last week."

"We are marrying here just before Christmas," Camilla said. "At St. George's of all places. Can you imagine, Freddie? Both Malcolm and I are quiet people and would have liked nothing better than a quiet country wedding. But families can become monsters. The least important people, it seems, when it comes to a wedding, are the bride and groom."

Frederick felt acutely embarrassed. They had sought him out and they were being perfectly friendly, but they knew exactly what had happened at Primrose Park during the early summer. They and Dan and Jule and himself, of course. Just the five of them.

"Come and meet my wife," he said. "Did you know I was married?"

Camilla flushed. "Yes, we had heard, Freddie," she said, her voice subdued. It was perfectly obvious what family opinion about his marriage must be.

Clara smiled, quite at her ease while he made the introductions. "Forgive me for not rising," she said. "I am unable to walk."

144

It was unclear from their expressions if they had known that too. Camilla took Clara's hand in hers and seated herself beside her. Malcolm stood looking gravely down at them, his hands clasped behind his back. Whatever they might think of him, Frederick thought in some relief, at least they were going to be civil to his wife.

"I know you," Clara was saying, a slow smile of delight spreading across her face. "You are Freddie's cousins who always spent the summers at Primrose Park with the rest of the family. He has told me about all the games you used to play and the mischief you always used to get into."

"With himself as villain," Camilla said with a laugh. "If ever there was a pirate or a bandit or a highwayman to be played, Freddie was always first to volunteer. The next family gathering will be for our wedding. You and Freddie will be there, of course, Clara. You will be able to meet the rest of us."

Frederick's discomfort grew. "I am going to go out in search of a drink for Clara," he said, "if you will excuse me. I shall be only a few minutes."

The devil, he thought when he was in the corridor and hurrying along in search of a drink. Of all the rotten luck. A family wedding – again – and in London of all places. He and Clara would have to be gone. They would have to return to Ebury Court and make some excuse not to attend. Devil take it, Dan was Camilla's brother. Julia was her sister-in-law.

He was walking too fast for the crowds. He collided with three separate people and had to stop each time to mutter apologies. The third time the words stuck in his throat. And the lady whose upper arms he had clasped appeared dumbfounded too.

"Jule," he said at last, his voice sounding almost like a croak. Good Lord, of course, he might have expected that they would be at the theater with Camilla and Malcolm. But they would have rejected the pleasure of calling at his box.

145

"Hello, Freddie," Julia Wilkes, Countess of Beacons-wood, said. Her pretty, normally goodnatured face, did not smile.

He swallowed, released his hold of her arms, and looked over her shoulder. Of course. "Dan?" he said, inclining his head.

"Hello, Freddie," the earl said. "Camilla and Malcolm called at your box? They have been trying to attract your attention all evening."

"They are talking with my wife," Frederick said. "You knew I was married?"

"Yes," the earl said. His countess seemed to have become mute, a fact that was more than unusual with Julia.

"Well." Frederick smiled and tried to look jovial. "I have not had a chance to congratulate the two of you, have I? I am sorry I was unable to attend your wedding. It was most annoying."

The countess, he saw when he glanced at her, was gazing downward at the floor.

"We understood," the earl said. He had one arm about Julia's waist, Frederick noticed, as if he thought his cousin might be about to abduct her. A painful thought.

"May I present my wife to you?" he asked.

The earl hesitated. It was the countess who answered.

"Yes, please, Freddie," she said, looking up to his neckcloth and taking her husband's arm. "May we please, Daniel?"

And so he had landed himself with the painful task of escorting the two of them into his box and making the introductions. Dan made a formal bow to Clara, he noticed. Julia surprised him by taking one of Clara's hands in both of hers and bending to kiss her cheek.

"Freddie has been telling Clara all about us," Camilla said, laughing. "She knows all our sins in advance. Is not that a disconcerting thought?"

Clara laughed and looked up at the countess. "Did your

146

husband tell you all about them too?" she asked. "They had a wonderfully wild childhood. I envy them more than I can say."

"But I was one of them," the countess said, chuckling. "And in many ways the worst of the lot. Ask Daniel. He spent his boyhood frowning at me and telling me that Grandpapa should have spanked me a few times when I was a child."

"I am sorry." Clara looked bewildered while Frederick wished he had some excuse for slipping from the box. "I don't think Freddie mentioned you. Julia? No, I do not remember that name. Were you always there?"

"Yes," the countess said quietly. She was biting her lower lip, Frederick could see. "From the time I was five. I was not strictly speaking a member of the family. Only the stepdaughter of the former earl's daughter. A rather obscure relationship."

Clara smiled. "Are you enjoying the play?" she asked. "I think it is wonderful though Freddie has been laughing at my enthusiasm. It is my first visit to a theater, you see, so I am easily pleased."

Conversation moved into safe channels for a few minutes until it was time for their visitors to return to their box and Harriet and Lord Archibald returned to theirs. The play was about to resume.

Clara turned her head to smile at Frederick. "How delightful that some of your family are in town," she said. "Now I can put a face to some of the cousins you have been telling me about."

He smiled at her and took her hand again.

"Freddie," she said, "did I make a dreadful blunder? Had I forgotten about Julia? I felt so foolish when she said that she had always been with the rest of you at Primrose Park. She had even lived there. But I have no memory of your ever mentioning her."

"I never did, Clara," he said quietly. He looked up from their hands to gaze into her eyes, which were wide with inquiry. He hesitated. "I was there – at Primrose Park –

earlier this summer, before I went to Bath. I asked her to marry me, but she chose Dan instead."

"Oh," she said.

But the play was beginning again. There was no time to say more. He had certainly bungled that, he thought. What would she make of that explanation? But he could hardly tell her the whole story. He hated even to think of the whole story.

The rapt look had gone from his wife's face, though she looked steadily at the stage for the rest of the performance. He wondered if she saw as little of the action as he did.

# 12

When Lord Archibald Vinney rose immediately on the conclusion of the play and ushered Harriet from the box and down the stairs to the waiting carriage, she assumed that her employers were not far behind them. Yet they did not immediately follow into the carriage.

"I daresay Freddie saw the crush of bodies," Lord Archibald said, closing the door, "and decided it would be wiser to wait with Mrs. Sullivan until the crowds thinned."

"Perhaps I should go back upstairs," Harriet said. "Perhaps Clara will need my assistance."

But Lord Archibald set one long-fingered, well-manicured hand on her arm. "Swimming against the current can be an exhausting business," he said. "They will be here in a few minutes, Miss Pope. I do not believe I have time to devour you between now and then. Though it must be confessed that you look quite delicious enough this evening."

Harriet felt herself blush. She had never owned a dress as frivolous and magnificent as the one she now wore, the one Clara had paid for as a gift.

"You must be finding your duties as companion less arduous now that your employer is married," he said.

"My duties never were arduous, my lord," she said.

"Ah." He smiled. "The voice of the truly dutiful and loyal employee. Pretty clothes become you. And being out in society animates you."

Harriet said nothing. She was wondering if she should remove her arm, on which his hand still rested.

"Perhaps it is time you embraced such a life full time,"

149

he said. "Instead of always being somewhat on the outside looking in and living for most of the time in extreme dullness."

His silver eyes, Harriet saw when she darted a glance at him, were regarding her lazily. But keenly too. She felt a shiver of excitement despite her good sense and her ability always to keep her feet firmly on the ground. Was it possible? Did the Cinderella story sometimes become reality?

"I know of someone," he said, "who could offer you a life of greater comfort and ease and greater wealth. You would have a home of your own and your own carriage and servants. You could go about as you pleased and be to all intents and purposes your own mistress."

Harriet's heart was beating right up into her throat. "There could not be any such employment," she said. But in truth it was not employment she was thinking of. She looked up into his eyes again. "Who would offer me such an easy life, my lord?"

"Me, of course," he said, taking her hand in his and raising it to his lips. "You could have all these things and more, Harriet. Clothes, jewels, outings. You have enslaved me, you see." His eyes were smiling lazily at her.

"Oh," she said. Her heart was fit to thump right out of her chest. She wanted to shout and jump for joy, but she held onto her dignity.

He leaned forward suddenly and kissed her on the mouth, a light kiss but with parted lips. Harriet had never been kissed before. After the first shock of contact, she jerked back her head. Spirals of excitement had whirled downward to her very toes.

"You may have whatever your heart desires while we are together," he said. "And I will make a settlement on you and any children of our liaison before we begin it, so that you will know yourself secure for life. Now kiss me, my little blushing charmer, before we are interrupted. We will talk again tomorrow."

150

Harriet's feet had never been more firmly planted on the ground. Her heart was there too – beneath her feet. "No," she said. "I mean no to everything, my lord. I have employment that I find pleasant and secure, I thank you."

"Ah." His silver eyes laughed at her. "A prim little charmer too. You will enjoy it, Harriet, I promise. I am reputed to have some little skill with women, I believe. You were made for a life of greater ease and more diverse pleasures than you can achieve as a lady's companion."

"I would rather be a lady's companion than a gentleman's, thank you, my lord," she said. She had thought herself immune to foolishness. Well, she had fallen into it once now – painfully – but she would learn from the experience. One learned more in life from pain than from pleasure, her father had always said. She had thought she was listening to a marriage proposal. It was pathetically laughable. Perhaps tomorrow she would be able to laugh at her naivete.

He regarded her quietly for a few moments. "Think about it," he said. "Perhaps the prospect of being my mistress will not seem so horrifying when you have done so. You would be able to live like a duchess, Harriet, both while we are together and afterward."

She leaned away from the backs of two of his fingers, which were trying to caress her cheek, and drew breath to speak. But the carriage door opened from the outside and she closed her mouth again.

Clara began talking with great enthusiasm about the play even before she was set down on the seat opposite Harriet. She continued to do so most of the way home. Though to Harriet, who knew her, her voice sounded falsely bright and her remarks lacked the depth of intelligence that was more usual with her. And it was unlike Clara to prattle.

And yet, Harriet thought, none of the rest of them seemed eager for her to stop talking. No one else seemed wishful of making conversation. She wondered what had

151

happened between Clara and Mr. Sullivan. She focused her mind on the question, trying to ignore the silent man at her side, trying not to think about the particular proposal he had just made to her, trying not to admit that she was tempted. Horrifyingly, sinfully tempted.

He was heavy on her and deep in her, moving with the slow rhythm that her body recognized and responded to. She had her arms wrapped about his waist, her head turned against his shoulder, and tried to concentrate on the pleasure he was undoubtedly arousing in her body, as he always did. She tried to anticipate the growing pleasure to come over the next several minutes, the near-frenzy that would seem more like pain than pleasure until it burst into glory. It never failed. Freddie was always good to her in bed.

He had come into her without kisses and caresses tonight and was working longer at the slow part of the rhythm. It felt good. It undoubtedly felt good. Sometimes she wished that this part could last on and on and on, that the greater pleasure – and also the end – could be held back and savored in anticipation. Sometimes she thought that being close to him, being joined with him, was more pleasurable than sexual release. No, not more so, perhaps. But equally pleasurable in a totally different way.

But tonight her brain could not be stilled as it normally was so that her body was free to enjoy. Tonight she could not stop thinking. She closed her eyes tightly and concentrated on the hard thrust of his body.

She was pretty. Slender and lithe and very, very pretty. And in love with Freddie. It had been clear from the way she had not looked at him, from the almost tangible tension that had hung in the air between them. Clara did not know why she had married the Earl of Beaconswood. Perhaps just because he was an earl and could offer her status and wealth and security. She must know Freddie well, after all. She would have been well aware of the fact earlier in the summer that he was deeply in debt. She would have known that he was a habitual gamer and womanizer. And so she had done what was sensible.

But she loved Freddie. And he loved her. That fact had almost shouted itself aloud in the box at the theater. *I asked her to marry me, but she chose Dan instead.* Clara turned her head sharply inward and clipped off the sound of what might have been a moan or a sob.

Frederick lifted his head and looked down at her with dreamy, heavy-lidded eyes. "Am I hurting you?" he asked.

She shook her head.

"I am too heavy?"

She shook her head again.

He kissed her open-mouthed. Lingeringly. "Does it feel good, my love?" he whispered into her mouth.

"Yes." Oh, God, he was calling her that again. She wondered if he was trying as hard as she to put the evening's events from his mind. She wondered if he was pretending that he was making love to Julia.

He had talked about all his cousins and uncles and aunts during the week of their honeymoon. She had felt almost as if she knew them all. But not a whisper of Julia, though she had been there every summer when the family gathered at Primrose Park. She had lived there with the old earl, her step-grandfather. But not a mention of her in all the stories he had told. Because he loved her. Because he had asked her to marry him and she had rejected him and married his cousin instead. Because it would have been painful to talk about her.

"Mmm," he said, unclasping her arms from about his waist, setting his palms against hers on the mattress, lacing his fingers with hers, and raising her hands above her head. He was licking into her mouth and increasing the pace of his loving.

He had come to Bath directly from Primrose Park and his rejection. And he had seen Clara, discovered that she was wealthy, and begun his wooing with even greater

153

cynicism than she had realized. He had married her when he must still have been bruised and aching from the loss of the woman he loved. The woman who loved him.

Her body was aching into response. She could feel the familiar building of tension and clenching of muscles. She clutched his hands tightly and buried her face against his shoulder again. Perhaps she had always been Julia to him in bed. A dream substitute. Whereas to her he had always, always been Freddie.

"Ahh," she said. And blessedly she lost her thoughts while all the tension in her body and all the love in her soul shattered about him and he murmured something soothing into her ear and she called his name.

He turned her and held her close, drawing the blankets up about her, and stroked the fingers of one hand through her hair. He knew she was unhappy, wondering about Julia and why he had carefully omitted all mention of her from his stories about Primrose Park. *I asked her to marry me, but she chose Dan instead.* Had he really said those words? It was about the worst explanation he could possibly have given, though it was true. But then a small part of the truth could sometimes be worse than a complete lie. Goodness only knew what interpretation Clara had put on his words. And the trouble was he could not give any further explanation without making the matter even worse.

He kissed her softly. He had tried to love her with some tenderness, having rejected the idea of going out again as soon as he had escorted her home from the theater. God, if she knew the full truth, she would turn away from him in disgust, more than she had done at the end of their honeymoon when she had objected to the deception of his endearments. He *felt* a tenderness for her too, an affection. It was not that he was falling in love with her, he thought. It was just that he was getting to know her and like her. He felt protective of her.

He cared.

She moved her head with sudden impatience so that his fingers became entangled in the thickness of her hair.

"I hate my hair!" she said with a vehemence that took him completely by surprise. He had thought her on the verge of sleep. "It is so dreadfully ugly. Just like the rest of me. I hate it."

"Clara?" He drew back from her a little way so that he could look into her face in the darkness. "It is not ugly. It is thick and shining and healthy. And you are not ugly."

"It is horrible," she said, her voice shaking with emotion. "It looks always like a dark ugly turban on my head. Other women have pretty hair."

"Short hair is fashionable," he said. "Yours has a natural wave, I believe, Clara. Why don't you try it short?"

"It would look ugly anyway," she said. She sounded rather like a petulant child, but he did not smile. She was very obviously upset, and by more than her hair.

"I think it would look very pretty," he said.

"You are just saying that," she said. "I wish I had not spoken. I cannot imagine why I did. I did not mean to."

"I shall have someone come to the house tomorrow to cut it for you in the latest style," he said.

The burst of passion seemed to have left her. "Papa would never allow me to cut my hair," she said.

If only he could have her father alive before him for half an hour, Frederick thought, he would cheerfully run him through with a sword. After first blackening both his eyes and ramming all his teeth down his throat.

"Your husband says that you must have it cut if you wish," he said. "Do you?"

"Yes," she said. "Yes, please, Freddie. Will you arrange it?"

"Tomorrow at first light," he said, drawing her close against him again. "Perhaps even sooner."

She chuckled.

"Go to sleep," he said. "I need my beauty rest."

"Yes, Freddie," she said.

If he had married Julia, he thought, he would never have met Clara. He would have missed something precious in his life.


Clara spent a busy morning. She had to keep busy so that she would not think. There was no point in thinking. She had known from the very start what she could expect, or not expect, from her marriage. It was certainly no worse than she had expected. Indeed, in many ways it was better. She had not really expected Freddie to be kind, but he was.

She almost decided to forgo her exercises since someone was coming to cut her hair before luncheon and she was tired from the night before. And of course she hated the exercises, which drained her of energy and often caused her pain and filled her with a daily dose of despair. But if she did not fill in those hours somehow, then she would brood. And she did not want to do that.

They did all the usual exercises, she and the faithful Harriet, and a few new ones. Harriet bent her legs so that her feet rested flat on the bed, and she tried pushing them down into the mattress. She even tried lifting her bottom from the bed. That, of course, proved an impossibility, but surely the mattress was depressed a little from the pressure of her feet.

"Maybe I should just swing my legs over the side of the bed," she said, "and take off running. Perhaps I would take them so by surprise that they would bear me at a trot all about the room."

It was the sort of daily silly remark that usually set them off laughing and gave a welcome break from the painful exercises.

"Yes," Harriet said.

Clara looked at her closely, not for the first time. "What happened last night?" she asked. "You were alone with

Lord Archibald for a while because Freddie was afraid to take me out into the crush. Did he try anything improper, Harriet?"

"He proposed to me," Harriet said.

"Harriet!"

"He proposed to make me his mistress," Harriet said. "He promised me a house, carriage, clothes, jewels, outings – anything my heart could desire. It was a very attractive offer."

"Harriet!" Clara was horror-struck. "I shall have him forbidden the house. I shall tell Freddie that he is not to be admitted here again."

"It was a very attractive offer." Harriet smiled bleakly. "I was very tempted. All night I lay awake, tempted."

"Harriet!" Clara said again.

"Oh, don't worry," Harriet said. "I am too much my father's daughter to give in to temptation. I shall probably look back on this in twenty or thirty years' time and be sorry that I did not. He is a wonderfully attractive man." Her face was very pale.

"You will never be subjected to the pain of seeing him again," Clara said. "We will cut the acquaintance."

"No," Harriet said. "It really is of little importance. He was not impolite. And it really was a flattering offer. I am sure he meant no disrespect. I am of a class of woman that must seem mistress material, after all. He did not cut up nasty when I said no."

"I wish he were not Freddie's friend," Clara cried passionately. "I wish Freddie could challenge him to a duel. Nasty, horrid man."

Harriet smiled and then giggled rather bleakly. "Perhaps," she said, "we can set your feet to the ground and you can run after him so that he will die of astonishment."

"With my hair uncut and billowing out behind me like a heavy thundercloud," Clara added.

"Both fists flailing," Harriet said.

"And a rolling pin brandished in one."

They both collapsed in laughter. Harriet briskly wiped away tears of mirth and grief when they were finally recovered. By then it was time to finish with the exercises and prepare for the haircut.

"About which I feel as nervous as if I were planning to have my head cut off," Clara confided to Harriet. "Do you think I will suddenly be transformed into a beauty?"

She was not, she discovered well over an hour later, when Monsieur Paul finally allowed her to look at her image in a glass. Nothing could make her into a beauty. Her face was too thin, her features too plain. But even so she stared at herself in stupefied wonder.

"Oh," she said, raising a hand and touching the wavy tendrils that trailed along her neck. Her hand was trembling. The rest of her hair, in soft short waves, hugged her head and curled around her temples and over her forehead.

"Madame is 'appy?" Monsieur Paul asked, brandishing his comb and waving his fingers elegantly a few inches from her head.

"Yes," she said, raising her eyes from her own image to his. "Oh, yes. Thank you." It was hard to believe that that was herself. She was no beauty, but she looked – normal. Like a normal woman.

"Monsieur Sullivan will be wanting to see madame," Monsieur Paul said, moving to her dressing room door to open it.

Freddie? She had not known he was at home. What would he think? Would he think she looked even more dreadful? She peered anxiously into the looking glass at the doorway behind her.

He stood in the doorway for a while, gazing at her. Then he came across the room to set his hands on her shoulders and meet her eyes in the glass. She waited for his comment, trying to tell herself that it really did not matter a great deal what he thought. And then he came around in front of her, reached for her hands, and went down on his haunches in front of her. His dark, hooded

158

eyes smiled at her, and the smile gradually spread to his mouth. She found herself smiling back.

"Well?" he said.

"I am bald," she said.

"You are beautiful." He raised one of her hands to his lips.

It was gross flattery. And as grossly untrue. It warmed her from her new short curls to her toenails. She laughed, and he leaned forward to kiss her briefly on the lips before straightening up and turning to talk to Monsieur Paul.

Frederick spent a few hours of the afternoon riding in the park with Lord Archibald Vinney. His mind was preoccupied. He had not used the right word, he thought, though he had not used it to flatter. He had called her beautiful. She was not. Nor was she pretty. But all the unbecoming weight had gone with the bulk of her hair, leaving it wavy and pretty and bringing out classical lines in her oval face with its now healthy coloring. The short waves made her eyes seem larger and more alluring.

*Handsome* was the word he should have used. His wife looked handsome.

"Winter furs," Lord Archibald said, nodding in the direction of an approaching landau, in which a young lady, warmly wrapped in furs, was seated beside an older woman. "They ruin the view, don't they, Freddie? Beddable or not, would you say?"

"Not," Frederick said. "The dragon would not allow you within half a league, Archie."

"Ah, but I have perfected the art of charming dragons," Lord Archibald said, illustrating his point by bowing from his horse's back as the landau passed and sweeping off his hat, staring almost reverently the whole while at the older lady. She inclined her head regally. "Beddable, Freddie. Definitely beddable if the face is any indication. Sweet and all of eighteen, at a guess. Not a day older."

"I did not think you were interested in robbing cradles," Frederick said.

159

Lord Archibald threw back his head and laughed. "Nor am I," he said. "Only in ogling them and making them blush. I brought color to the cheeks of that delectable infant. She knew that I was looking at the dragon and seeing only her. Freddie, my lad, you become boring. Not so long ago you would have been in competition with me. I have to sharpen all my skills when competing against those eyes of yours. I have seen them slay women by the dozen."

Frederick answered only with a chuckle. They indulged in a short gallop, the park being almost empty of either traffic or pedestrains.

"You see me with a broken heart today," Lord Archibald said when they slowed their horses to a walk again. "I even contemplated setting a pistol to my temple and blowing my brains out last night. But I thought of that wretched dukedom passing to that pompous ass of a cousin of mine, Percival Weems, and decided to make the sacrifice of staying alive. I was rejected last night, Freddie, my lad. Did you have hysterics to contend with when you arrived home?"

"Rejected?" Frederick looked closely at his friend. "Miss Pope? You offered her marriage, Archie?"

"Marriage?" Lord Archibald's eyebrows shot up and he reached for his quizzing glass, which he was not wearing. "Do you have marriage on the brain, Freddie? Like some strange tropical fever? I shall marry when it becomes imperative that I set up my nursery. I have three or four years of living to enjoy yet before I have to contemplate that particular horror. And when the time comes I shall doubtless feel obliged to choose some young thing with ice flowing in her veins along with very blue blood. I was rejected as a lover, my boy, with a very pretty, 'No, thank you, my lord.' "

"I could have told you what she would say," Frederick said. "Miss Pope has a great deal of good sense."

"Good sense?" Lord Archibald said. "To choose a life of single dreariness and drudgery – with no offense meant to your wife, old chap, when she might have one of excitement and luxury and security?"

"And daily and nightly mounts without benefit of clergy," Frederick said. "There is a certain type of female who considers it too high a price, Archie."

His friend laughed. "You missed your calling, Freddie," he said. "You should have been one of the aforementioned clergy. Is this what marriage does to you? One shudders at the very idea. Dinner at White's? A visit to Annette's later? And perhaps find out a game somewhere after that? If Annette's girls do not prove too thorough, that is."

It was tempting. The thought of dinner at White's anyway. The thought of not returning home to face his own memories and secrets and inferiority. But if he dined with Archie, he might feel obliged to accompany him to Annette's and then find it too embarrassing to sit downstairs awaiting his return. Unless Lizzie had talked and Annette kicked him out, he might find himself upstairs with one of the girls, doing to her what he had done with his wife the night before with some tenderness. And if that happened – or even if it did not, perhaps – self-hatred would send him in search of a game with high stakes to see him through the rest of the night.

And if he won, would he buy Clara another jewel with which to salve his conscience? And if he lost?

"I am taking Clara out for some air at five," he said. "Some other time, Archie. I'll not invite you. I don't imagine that Miss Pope would be over-delighted."

"I would not wager on it," Lord Archibald said with a grin. "Behind the simple no, thank you, I distinctly heard the words 'But I wish I had the courage to say yes and perhaps will if you persist, my lord.' But I shall not come with you this afternoon, Freddie. The little blusher must be left to languish for a few days. She must be led to believe that I have accepted her rejection."

"I rather believe you will have nothing but rejection from the lady, Archie," Frederick said.

161

"A wager," Lord Archibald said, brightening. "Fifty guineas say she will be mine before Christmas, Freddie, my boy. Better still, a hundred. Not only an acceptance but on the mount already."

"Done," Frederick said. "One hundred guineas."

They shook hands on it before parting, the one to ride to White's, the other to return home.

There were visitors in the house, Frederick sensed as soon as he entered it, though there was no evidence of their presence in the hallway.

"Visitors?" he asked his butler.

"Her ladyship, the Countess of Beaconswood, and the Honorable Miss Wilkes to call upon Mrs. Sullivan, sir," the butler said with obvious relish, bowing to his master.

Frederick grimaced. He had known that last night was not the end of it, of course. They were in London for a wedding just before Christmas. He had known that he would be forced to make a courtesy call on his aunt now that he knew she was in town. He had not expected Julia and Camilla to come calling on his wife, though. Not so soon, anyway.

He considered leaving the house again. Or going up to his room, tiptoeing past the drawing room. But there was no point in avoiding the issue. He supposed he had realized all along that the summer's embarrassment – masterly euphemism – would have to be faced sooner or later. They were family, after all, he and Dan and Julia, and they had always been a close family. He drew a deep breath and climbed the stairs with measured tread.

"Ah," he said, opening the drawing room door and stepping inside. "How pleasant. Hello, Camilla. Jule." He nodded to Harriet and crossed the room to Clara's side. He set a hand on her shoulder and squeezed it. He raised two knuckles to brush against her jaw. "Hello, my love."

Julia was watching his hand, he noticed. Clara's shoulder had stiffened. He wished profoundly that he could change those last words he had spoken.

162

# 13

Clara had been intending to take a short drive with Harriet since Freddie had not mentioned any outing for the day. But their plans were disrupted by the unexpected arrival of visitors. Unexpected because the only people who had called on her since she had come to London were Mr. and Mrs. Whitehead. Freddie had made no attempt to enlarge her circle of acquaintances, perhaps because he thought her crippled state would make it difficult for her to visit or to attend social functions.

She was surprised and a little disconcerted when she discovered who the callers were. She had liked Camilla Wilkes the evening before. But she did not particularly wish to see the Countess of Beaconswood again. There had been too much pain during the night and morning. But she smiled graciously. There was something to be said for having visitors at all.

The Countess of Beaconswood was even more lovely than she had appeared the night before, Clara thought with a sinking of the heart. She was wearing a dark blue velvet carriage dress and pelisse. Her face was not only very pretty but sparkling with animation too today. Her short dark hair was curlier than Clara's own. Clara scarcely noticed Camilla.

"You look different," the countess said after greetings had been exchanged and Harriet had been presented. She sat down and set her head to one side, studying her hostess.

"I had my hair cut off this morning, my lady," Clara said, flushing. She still felt bald.

The countess went off into peals of laughter. "I almost looked over my shoulder," she said. "I am still not used to being the possessor of such a grand title. I believe I shall have to start wearing a purple satin turban and carrying a lorgnette. You must call me Julia, please, Clara. We are cousins by marriage, after all. Your hair does look lovely. The style suits you. Does it not, Camilla?"

Camilla smiled with quiet charm. "It must have been a dreadful feeling to have all that length cut off," she said. "It must have taken many years to grow it so long. But yes, this is very becoming. You do not regret being so rash, Clara?"

"No," Clara said. "But it does make me nervous to be such a focus of attention."

"Ah, the weather, then," the countess said with a light laugh. "It is an obligatory topic. Who wishes to begin?"

Clara found herself relaxing with unexpected speed. Freddie's cousins were very different from each other, but they were equally charming and unaffected in manner. They were treating her as family rather than as a newly made acquaintance, she thought, nodding at Harriet to ring for tea. Even Julia. Whatever her feeings were for Freddie, at least she was making an effort to be civil to his wife.

"You will be coming, of course, Clara," Camilla said when the conversation moved inevitably to her approaching wedding. "You will persuade Freddie that he must? It is time that small rift was healed."

Clara glanced at the countess, who was looking down at her hands in her lap, the animation gone from her face for the moment. She looked up and caught Clara's eye.

"Freddie had not mentioned me to you," she said. "What did he tell you about me last night or this morning? Anything?"

Clara hesitated. "Only that he had offered for you earlier this year but you had married the earl instead," she said.

"Ah," the countess said, her lips moving into what

might have been intended to be a smile. She glanced at Camilla. "We decided that we should tell you everything, did we not, Camilla? We both suspected last night that you must have noticed a slightly strained atmosphere, and we both agreed that Freddie would probably not tell you the whole story. But you are our cousin now and we wish you to be our friend. Don't we, Camilla?" Her voice had gained brightness as she spoke.

"Yes," Camilla said smiling, "We want you as a friend, Clara. It was very naughty of Freddie to marry you in such secrecy without inviting any of the family."

"Lord and Lady Bellamy were there," Clara said. "And Lesley."

"Oh, dear Les," the countess said. "I will not ask you if you loved him, Clara. No one could not love Les. I am so glad he went to Italy. It was his great dream. But I am procrastinating. My grandfather died in the spring, Clara – and forbade us to wear mourning if you wonder why none of us are wearing black. He was not my grandfather actually. He was my stepmother's father, but he had brought me up as his own after my father's death and my stepmother's. But when he died I was in an awkward position. I had no claim to any of his property or fortune, you see. Although he had taken care of me very well as it turned out, it seemed at the time that I was to be destitute. Everyone rallied around, offering me a home. Everyone was very sweet."

Clara smiled. She remembered the dreadful feeling of loneliness that had followed her father's death. And yet she had not also had to contend with the fear of destitution.

"Well, you were our cousin, Julia," Camilla said. "Of course we were not going to turn you out."

The countess flashed her a smile. "Anyway," she said, glancing down at her hands before looking up directly at Clara again, "the male cousins started offering me marriage. Was not that the most foolish and endearing thing you have heard in your life? Lesley asked me and

165

Gussie – you have not met Gussie, have you? – and Freddie. And Daniel, of course. It was excessively kind of them all. But of course I could marry only one. I chose Daniel. He made me a wedding present of Primrose Park. Can you believe that?"

Clara smiled again. Julia had married the wealthiest of them. It was understandable when she had nothing herself. She had reached out for the greatest security.

"We believe Freddie was embarrassed," Camilla said. "He left Primrose Park directly after the betrothal was announced and did not stay as the rest of us did for the wedding. I suppose it would be embarrassing to attend the wedding of the woman you had offered for yourself, would it not?"

"Yes," Clara said. "I suppose it would." And yet Lesley and the cousin they called Gussie seemed to have overcome their embarrassment and stayed. And why should something done purely out of kindness cause embarrassment?

"Not hurt," the countess said quickly, her eyes bright, a glow of color in her cheeks. "We do not believe he was hurt, Clara. He would have had to be in love with me or something foolish like that to have been hurt, would he not? Freddie and I were always pals, partners in mischief and crime. I was a dreadful hoyden when I was growing up and still am sometimes. I think Daniel is always afraid when we are in the park that I am going to suddenly start climbing trees and throwing acorns down on passers-by." She laughed merrily. Too merrily. Her manner was too bright.

It was a story they had decided together to tell her. It seemed almost rehearsed. They were both smiling. It was she they were trying to protect from hurt, Clara realized with a rush of gratitude. They were afraid that she had divined the truth the night before and had felt sorry for her. And so they had come to discover what Freddie had told her and to tell her a plausible story if it turned out that he had not himself told her the

166

full truth. She had a part to play now just as they did.

"I am glad everything turned out well for you, Julia," she said. "It must be wonderful to belong to such a close and loving family." Her smile matched theirs.

"Oh, it is," the countess said in a rush.

"As you will discover for yourself," Camilla said. "My mother wanted to come with us to call, but we wished to talk to you about this ridiculous awkwardness with Freddie so we made an excuse. But you must come and call on us. Are you able to get about?" She smiled up at Harriet, who was pouring the tea and handing around the cups and saucers. "Thank you, Harriet."

"Freddie carries me to places where my wheeled chair will not go," Clara said. "I also have a servant I employed for just that task before my marriage."

"And so," the countess said, sipping on her tea and smiling brightly, "you met Freddie in Bath, married him after a whirlwind courtship, and are living happily ever after. It all sounds very romantic."

They knew, Clara thought. Of course they knew. They had both been well acquainted with Freddie from infancy. They pitied her and had come to befriend her. And yet Julia must be aching with jealousy too. Her smile was brittle. This visit must be very difficult for her. And she was so very lovely.

How was she to answer? Join in the charade, which they all knew to be ridiculous? Offer some explanation that was a little closer to the truth? Say nothing?

She was saved from her dilemma – if saved was the right word – by the opening of the drawing room door and the appearance of Freddie. Looking as cheerful and hearty as her visitors. Greeting them and Harriet with practiced ease. Crossing the room to her and setting a hand on her shoulder and caressing her jaw with the backs of his fingers.

"Hello, my love," he said.

Her heart plummeted. If she had wanted any further

167

proof that she had heard nothing approaching the true story of what had happened earlier in the spring between Freddie and Julia – not that she needed further proof – it was there in his greeting.

"Hello, Freddie," she said. She wanted to turn her face in against his hand and bawl her heart out. "Did you have a pleasant ride?"

He accepted a cup of tea from Harriet and they all sat and conversed for ten minutes longer with great amiability. Harriet was perhaps the only one of them who allowed her smile to slip even for a moment. Yet Clara would have sworn at the end of the visit that Julia and her husband had not once allowed their eyes to meet. And she had the fanciful notion that if only she could have got to her feet, a sharp knife in her hand, she would have been able to cut the air between the two of them. It was thick with tension.

All because Freddie had been embarrassed at being one of the three cousins to have offered for Julia and been rejected? Clara wished it could have been just that. How she wished it. But unfortunately she had not been born yesterday.

The ladies finally rose to leave and Freddie rose with them. They both bent over Clara's chair to kiss her cheek and beg her to call on them. Freddie was waiting to accompany them downstairs. But at the last moment Camilla turned back.

"Perhaps you will join us for an afternoon drive one day when the weather is suitable, Clara," she said. "I would like it of all things and I know Mama and Julia would too. I can make sure that the carriage is warm for you with a heavy robe to cover your lap."

Clara laughed. "I am not an invalid," she said, "although I cannot walk. Freddie insists that I take a drive in an open carriage every day except when it is actually raining. But, yes, I would love to drive out with you, Camilla. Thank you."

"You must call on Mama first, then," Camilla said.

"Perhaps within the next day or two? We can make further arrangements then. Oh, it is such a novelty to have a new cousin. The rest of us have intermarried, Daniel with Julia, me with Malcolm, though that is not as unhealthy as it may sound. Actually there is no blood relationship within either couple. But I am not going to launch into an explanation of that now." She laughed softly.

They talked for a minute or two longer before Camilla left. Clara was very aware that the other two had proceeded on their way when Camilla had turned back.

She smiled brightly at Harriet.

There was a feeling of near panic when he realized that Camilla had not followed them from the room but had turned back to say something else to Clara. Julia would not take his arm to walk downstairs, though he offered it.

"I told you at the time that I would never forgive you, Freddie," she said quietly, her voice shaking with emotion. "I have not and I will not. I hate you."

"I don't blame you, Jule," he said. "I am only sorry that we had to run into each other like this. I shall do my best to stay out of your way. I shall take Clara back to Ebury Court."

"Oh, no, you won't," she said vehemently. "We want her here for Camilla's wedding. We want to make her welcome in the family. How could you do it, Freddie? Poor Clara."

He swallowed. "I don't think my marriage is any of your concern, Jule," he said.

But that had never stopped Julia, of course. "She is very wealthy," she said. "Perhaps the wealthiest woman in England, according to Daniel. She is also a person, Freddie. She is sweet and gentle. Have you even bothered to discover that?"

"Yes," he said.

"I suppose you rushed with great glee to pay off your

debts," she said. "And rushed even faster and more gleefully to run up new and even higher ones. I suppose you did. You could not change even if you wanted to, Freddie. But I'll never forgive you for this. Never. And don't you dare take her back to the country. Do you hear me? Don't you dare."

They were standing facing each other at the foot of the stairs. She was almost hissing at him.

"I will have to consult my wife's wishes," he said.

"Oh." She looked at him with utter contempt. "Is that supposed to impress me, Freddie? Since when did you consult anyone's wishes except your own? I like her. And it is not just pity because she is crippled and because she is not quite the beauty one might have expected you to wed. Or because she was deceived into marriage by a rake and a wastrel. I like her for herself and I want to be her friend. I am going to *be* her friend. And if you take her back to the country, I shall get Daniel to take me there too."

"That would be very uncomfortable for three of us," he said. "Listen, Jule. I can't change the past. I wish I could. And I cannot do more than apologize for what happened. I wish I could." He tried smiling at her. "Can't we at least call a truce?"

"Don't try using those bedroom eyes on me, Freddie," she said. "And, no, I hate you. I escaped from you and am happier with Daniel than I could have ever dreamed of being with anyone. But Clara did not escape. I'll never forgive you for rushing straight from me to her, when you were supposed to be so sorry for what you had done, and for achieving instant success with someone who did not know you. I suppose she fell in love with you. It would be strange if she did not since all other women seem to crumble before your charm. Is her heart quite broken yet? Or does it take a little longer for hope to die and a heart to break?"

"Jule." He was becoming angry. "You are out of line. My marriage is none of your business."

She would have argued further. Being Julia, she would

170

have ploughed in where she did not belong, tongue wagging, both fists flying. But Camilla was at the top of the stairs and coming down and smiling with her usual calm sweetness and apologizing for keeping them waiting.

"Freddie," she said, taking his hands and stretching up to kiss him on the cheek, "Clara is quite delightful. I am very happy for you. She is to call on Mama within the next day or two. Will you bring her?"

"I'll have to see," he said vaguely, squeezing her hands. Camilla at least was willing to give him a second chance, to give him the benefit of what he admitted must seem a very large doubt. "Thank you for calling. I know it will mean a great deal to Clara."

And they were gone, Julia without another word or look. The trouble was, he thought, staring at the front door after it had closed behind them, he could not even fan his anger with righteous indignation. She was so damned right about him. About everything. Except for the fact that he did know that Clara was sweet and gentle. And he did care for her.

*You could not change even if you wanted to, Freddie.* He paused with one foot on the bottom stair. He winced. But she was wrong about that too. She was wrong about a lot of things. She thought she knew him, but she did not really.

The park was almost deserted. Anyone seeing them there in an open barouche on such a chilly, blustery day would have thought them mad, Clara thought. But they were dressed warmly, and she did not really care what anyone might think. She had years' worth of fresh air to catch up on and loved the feel of cold air against her face and the knowledge that her complexion was probably gleaming as red as a ripe apple.

She was beginning to feel more than just not an invalid. She was beginning to feel healthy. She was beginning to feel that she had energy – physical energy – to spare. Under cover of her heavy laprobe she flexed her feet at the ankles secretly and experimentally and even succeeded in drawing them inward, a little closer to the seat. It felt like a major victory.

Frederick took her gloved hand in his. They were alone, Harriet having excused herself from joining them on their late afternoon drive. They had been silent for a few minutes, since running out of trivialities to talk about.

"Well," he asked her, his tone just a little too casual, "have you enjoyed making the acquaintance of new cousins, Clara?"

"Yes," she said. "It is very exciting when one has no family of one's own."

She knew him well enough to recognize the tension in both his body and his voice.

"Camilla and Jule had arrived only just before me?" he asked.

"No," she said. "They had been there for a while."

"Ah," he said. She could have asked the question for him, but she waited for him to ask it. "What did they have to say?"

"They liked my hair," she said, laughing and wishing they could turn back from this course they were taking. She wished there were not this terrible mystery. She wished she could treat it with unconcern. "We talked about the weather and about last night's play and about Bath and about Camilla's wedding." She paused. "And about what happened at Primrose Park earlier this year."

"Ah," he said.

She could not help him. Would he tell her the rest? Did she want to hear it? She wished she could just put it all from her mind and forget about it.

"Did they tell you everything?" he asked.

"Yes," she said.

"Ah." There was another silence while he lifted her laprobe, placed her hand beneath it, and covered it up. Now they were not touching at all. "You always did know me for the blackguard I am, Clara. Now any last doubts

172

you may have had have been put to rest. You must depise me heartily."

For running from the woman he loved and charming into marriage a wealthy, crippled, ugly, and lonely spinster? She had not heard the full story from anyone, and she was not going to ask. She was not at all sure she wanted the full truth. Had Freddie and Julia been lovers? It seemed altogether possible in light of the very strong tensions between them. She did not know the truth. Perhaps she was completely misinterpreting everything that she had heard and observed. Perhaps Camilla and Julia had told the full truth after all. But she did not think so. And she thought that her interpretation must be the right one. Everything fit.

Frederick laughed rather harshly. "The incurably honest Clara," he said. "You do not like to lie and so you say nothing."

"You are my husband, Freddie," she said.

"To be meekly honored and obeyed," he said. "You are good at those things, are you not, Clara? It would not fit your notion of a good wife to tell me that you despise me. Well, I know that you do. And if you do not, you should. Someone called me a rake and a wastrel very recently. Both terms are quite accurate."

She did not want to hear this. She did not want the fragile peace between them destroyed. She had so little. She did not want to lose even the little she had. If he continued in this vein, there would be too much in the open between them. There would be no possibility of holding together a viable marriage.

"Freddie," she said, "you are my husband. That is all that matters to me."

"Your property and fortune are not in trust, are they?" he said. "I worked that out for myself some time ago, Clara. You just did not want me to get my hands on all your wealth. You were very wise. Almost the whole of your very generous dowry has gone already in the expected way. My own income will doubtless go the

173

same road. But don't worry. I can't get my hands on your fortune, can I? And I would not take any of it if you were to offer it. Would you, Clara? Like the dutiful wife you are? That is why I married you after all, isn't it? You can come and visit me in debtors' prison some day. Have Robin carry you in there."

"Freddie, please don't." But it was too late already. Everything was ruined.

"I have been unfaithful to you with a dozen women since our marriage," he said. "More. But then you knew that, didn't you, Clara? You knew when you married me that I was a rake. And you knew that a woman never reforms a man after marriage. You have been wise enough never to have tried."

God. Oh, God. Oh, God. Oh, God. She bit her lip and stared fixedly ahead.

"I suppose you have partly blamed yourself," he said. "I believe that is usual with virtuous women. You have blamed yourself because you are crippled and because you perceive yourself as ugly. If only you could walk and were beautiful you could hold my love and fidelity and keep my feet on the straight and narrow. So you think. Do yourself a favor, Clara. Learn to hate me. I am worthy of nothing less."

"Take me home," she said.

"Archie and I are a well-suited pair, aren't we?" he said. "I gather he offered your virtuous companion *carte blanche* last evening and was rejected. She has more sense than you had, Clara."

"I shall go back to Ebury Court tomorrow," she said.

"It is a shame," he said, "that you cannot obtain a bill of divorcement for simple adultery, is it not? You would have me cold, Clara. And of course annulment is unfortunately out of the question. I have planted my seed in you rather too many times."

She closed her eyes and willed them to be home soon. They had left the park behind them several minutes before.

174

"You must wish," he said, "that you could open those eyes and find yourself back in Bath, the last few months all a bad dream."

"Yes," she said.

He laughed. "You must blame yet another weakness in my character," he said. "If only I had been a little firmer of purpose, Jule would have married me and you would have been saved, Clara. You would never have met me. But I was not firm of purpose at all. I let her get away, and she married Dan."

Oh, God. Oh, God.

The barouche stopped in front of their house at last. Frederick jumped out and reached for her. His face was set into a cynical, devil-may-care type of half smile. Clara stared straight ahead again after one glance at it.

"I want Robin to carry me inside," she said.

Frederick made an impatient sound, grabbed her none too gently, and slid her across the seat toward him, preparatory to picking her up.

She spoke with icy distinctness. "I want Robin to carry me inside."

There was a pause before his hands left her and he turned without another word to enter the house. Robin appeared within a minute and carried her up to her private apartments. She did not see her husband again before leaving for Ebury Court with Harriet early the following morning.

# 14

Self-loathing could sometimes reach such depths that one plummeted frighteningly close to despair. Frederick touched very close the morning after his drive in the park with his wife. He walked home, still wearing evening clothes, feeling unclean and unkempt and unshaven. Mostly unclean.

He had joined Archie for dinner at White's after all and had drunk reckless amounts of wine with his meal and lavish glassfuls of port after it. The evening had developed along predictable lines from then on. The night rather. Lizzie had not said anything to Annette, it seemed. He had been admitted with no trouble at all and assigned a new girl, a young one who could not have been at work for any great length of time, though she had not been a virgin. But her skills had been used with conscious deliberateness and she had protested her pain when he had been rough with her. He had given her a generous gift of money before leaving her though he knew she was strictly forbidden to accept any personal payment. He still felt as he walked away with Archie as if he had deflowered innocence.

"Trouble in paradise?" Lord Archibald had asked.

"I don't want even to think about it, Arch," he had said, "much less talk about it."

Nothing more had been said.

And then the gaming and the drinking – at a private home rather than at a club. And waking up, or rather regaining consciousness, in a bed in the same house when it was already light, with a head like a lead ball and spirits even more leaden than that. He had looked about him gingerly. At least there was no naked female beside him or anywhere else in the room. It was a marginally cheering thought until he remembered the little girl at Annette's. And until he remembered the card games, at which he had lost a sizable sum as far as he could recall. And all the drinking.

Gaming, drinking, womanizing – all vices he could give up at a moment's notice. It was simply a matter of willpower. He threw an arm over his eyes to prevent the daylight from paining them further. Yes, he could give them all up. When hell froze over. Perhaps.

He walked wearily homeward feeling unclean. Knowing that he would still feel so even after having a hot bath and a shave upon arriving home. Knowing that he would probably never feel clean again. Or be clean.

At first when he had woken up and even when he had dressed and dragged himself outside, no one else in the house having been up yet to delay his leaving, he had forgotten the events of the day before. Now memory of them hammered through his temples and into his conscious mind.

Julia had had her revenge and told Clara everything. And so he, noble mortal that he was, had whipped up his guilt and his hurt and despair into cynical fury and had unleashed it all on the most precious possession that remained to him. On his wife.

He had told her, among other things, that he had bedded a dozen women or more since their marriage. She probably had known it anyway. Clara was not stupid. But it was a firm convention of society that wives were to be protected from the harsh reality of knowing without a doubt that their husbands were unfaithful. He had broken one of the strictest taboos of the *ton*. And, which was far more important and far worse, he had hurt her immeasurably too. She may not love him and she may have known the true state of affairs, but it must have been painful and humiliating to be told the bald truth by

177

her husband himself. He must have made her feel even less of a woman than she already seemed to feel.

He had done that to her. For that alone he deserved to be shot.

He was going to have to apologize to her, he thought as he approached his own house and glanced up at the blank windows. An apology was a pitifully inadequate atonement, of course, but it must be made. And with it a vow to change if she could just find it in her to overcome the disgust she must feel for him. He could change, and he would change. It was merely a matter of wanting to do it. And he wanted to. He was sick of that other life. Mortally sick. The very thought of last night was more powerfully nauseating than the headache he still carried around with him.

He went straight up to his rooms when he entered the house and ordered hot water for a bath and his shaving gear. He would clean himself up on the outside at least before going to face Clara, though he was all impatience to do it without delay. He was going to start a new life and he was all eagerness to begin it – with his wife at his side. He would be able to do it with her there. But it would be discourtesy itself to go to her now. He would wait until he was clean.

An hour later, too nervous to go along himself to her sitting room as he normally would, he sent his valet to ask if he might have the honor of waiting upon her. The formality might seem a little excessive coming from a husband and directed to his own wife, but he was very aware that she might well not want to see him. He might have to exercise a patience that would be agony to him and send regular such messages through the day until she weakened and admitted him to her presence.

His valet returned. "Mrs. Sullivan is not at home, sir," he said.

Frederick frowned. Out? This early? "Did you find out where she has gone?" he asked.

178

"To Ebury Court, I gather, sir," his valet said, wooden-faced.

*I shall go back to Ebury Court tomorrow.* Frederick could hear the words as she had spoken them in the barouche the day before. He had forgotten. She had meant them, then.

"When did she leave?" he asked.

"A little over half an hour ago, I gather, sir," the valet said.

He had been in the house already. Immersed in a bathtub of hot soapy water. Trying to make himself clean for her. Perhaps she had known he was at home. Perhaps not. Perhaps she had not been interested in knowing either way.

"Thank you, Jerrett," he said. "That will be all."

For the first two weeks there seemed to be nothing to live for. Nothing at all. It was frightening to know life to be so empty, so devoid of all meaning. It hardly seemed worth getting up in the morning. She had to do so in order to keep up appearances for Harriet and the servants. And of course her neighbors and friends started to call as soon as they knew she was at home again. Some of the visits had to be returned.

She had to go on living unless she was prepared to take the step of actively ending her life. That was the one thing she could not contemplate doing. But she did only the living she felt forced to do. She stopped going out except for the occasional visit and to attend church, when she took a closed carriage. The weather was turning from autumn chill to winter cold. It was too cold to go out in her barouche or in her chair onto the terrace. Besides, she could not be bothered to make the effort of dressing up warmly and having Robin carry her outside.

She wondered if letters would start coming from Freddie again, ordering her to take the air each day. If they did, she supposed she would obey him. He was still her husband

179

and always would be until one of them died. But no letter came.

She stopped exercising. It was troublesome and time-consuming and painful. And worthless. She was never going to be able to walk. There was no point in even trying. She spent her days indoors, embroidering, reading, talking with Harriet or with the occasional visitor, sometimes doing nothing at all.

Two weeks passed during which she tried to persuade herself that she was no worse off than she had been until just a few months before when she had been Miss Clara Danford. Life was the same as it had been then – dull and tedious, perhaps, but also comfortable and respectable. Thousands of poor souls in England would give a right arm to change places with her. If she could just blank the last few months from her mind, from the moment of her meeting with Freddie on, then she should be able to pick up the threads of her old life without any great damage having been done.

But life was not that simple, of course. The months of her marriage could not be blocked from either her mind or her emotions. Neither could Freddie.

After two weeks she glanced at herself in the looking glass one morning and saw herself. Really saw herself. She looked somewhat familiar except for the short hair. Thin face, so pale that it was almost yellow. Large, wistful eyes. She wondered if she had been eating well or even adequately and could not remember.

"How has my appetite been?" she asked Harriet at breakfast. She had had the butler put two sausages and two slices of toast on her plate and now found the prospect of having to eat everything quite formidable.

Harriet gave her a strange look. "Poor," she said. "Like it used to be."

"When was I last outside?" Clara asked.

"The day before yesterday," Harriet said, "when we called on the Goughs."

"In a closed carriage," Clara said. "When was the last time I was out in the air?"

Harriet thought. "I think that must have been in London," she said.

The afternoon when she had driven alone in the park with Freddie. An eternity ago. She looked toward the windows. Gray, heavy clouds. Trees bending in the wind. It was a wintry scene. Chill, raw winter, not the cheerful frosty winter of Christmas imaginings.

"I shall drive out in the barouche for half an hour this afternoon," she said. "You may stay inside if you wish, Harriet."

But her friend smiled. "Welcome back," she said.

Clara looked down at her plate and determinedly speared a piece of sausage. It was the closest either of them had come in two weeks to admitting that there was anything wrong. Harriet probably had no real idea of what had happened to bring them back so precipitately to the country.

Welcome back. Yes, she was back, she thought grimly, taking a slightly larger than ladylike bite out of one slice of toast. She was back to stay. She might feel regret at no longer being Miss Danford of Ebury Court. She might feel pain at the memories of the last months, which had transformed her into the Honorable Mrs. Frederick Sullivan. But she had a life to live. One God-given life not to be wasted in self-pity.

"I wonder," she said, "what Robin knows about teaching someone to walk."

Robin had been a pugilist with a promising career ahead of him until one ill-fated bout in the ring with a famed prize-fighter had put him in a coma for almost a month and he had given in to advice not to fight again. But he had trained to box for a living. He knew something about making the body fit and strong.

It was a little embarrassing having a man help her exercise her legs. Her neighbors would have been scandalized had they known. Her father would have turned over in

181

his grave. Freddie would probably be furious. Harriet was intrigued.

"I have always felt so helpless," she said. "So eager to help you, Clara, but not knowing how to go about it. There was always so little progress."

Clara had a daybed set up in her private sitting room, that setting seeming a little less intimate than her bedchamber. She always covered herself carefully from the waist down with a white cotton sheet. Harriet was always in the room, quietly sewing or knitting and smiling encouragement when it was needed.

And it turned out to be not really embarrassing at all. Robin's hands were strong and impersonal, as was his whole manner. Indeed, Clara had heard the rumblings of rumors from belowstairs, rumors occasioned by the fact that Robin, young and brawny and reasonably goodlooking despite a broken and crooked nose, seemed quite uninterested in any of the maids or in any other female of the neighborhood. But Robin's personal preferences were none of her business, Clara had decided long ago. She was grateful for the fact that he did not make her aware of him as a man.

The exercises were frightening but surprisingly free of real pain. There was to be no more gentle clenching of the toes and flexing of the ankles. Her legs were bent and straightened, bent and straightened with speed and force, both while she lay on her back and when Robin rolled her over onto her stomach. Her feet were moved in wide and swift circles about her ankles. Her legs were massaged by hands many times stronger than Harriet's – sometimes Robin reached his hands beneath the sheet without removing it – until she could feel the blood pulsing through them and the feeble muscles clenching and relaxing. Until sometimes she had to bite her lips in order not to scream. Once – only once – she began to cry almost hysterically.

"How long, Robin?" she asked him after the first week, when her progress was exciting her. "In your expert opinion, how long?"

182

"By Christmas, Mrs. Sullivan," he said, "if you have the courage and if you keep eating well."

Robin had even been giving her instructions on the food she was to eat. Wholesome, body-building food.

"If I have the courage to put up with this torture," she said, "I will surely have enough to walk when the time comes."

Robin grinned, one of the rare occasions when he lost his impassive expression. "By spring I will be looking for new employment, Mrs. Sullivan," he said.

She had not thought of that. Robin was conscientiously working himself out of a job. "What will you do?" she asked.

"Open a boxing saloon," he said. "See if I can take some business from Gentleman Jackson."

"If you need a recommendation," she said, "refer your customers to me, Robin."

She began to be able to move her legs as she sat in her chair. She could even lift them one at a time from the floor. But Robin, a strict taskmaster, would not allow her to try to stand. She would fall and perhaps hurt herself and certainly discourage herself and they would have to start all over again, he told her. She waited with forced patience for him to decide that it was time.

But she began to feel alive again. She began waking up in the mornings to find herself looking forward to a new day.

There were three unexpected visitors, one coming alone, two together. But no Freddie. And no letter from Freddie. It was better so, Clara told herself. It was better to reconstruct her life without looking back.

Clara and Harriet had returned from a drive one sunny afternoon and had only just settled in the drawing room when the butler arrived to announce visitors.

"The Earl and Countess of Beaconswood, ma'am," he said grandly.

Clara glanced quickly at Harriet. "Show them up," she

183

said. Her heart plummeted. She had liked Julia. She still did. But she did not want to see her. She wanted to look forward, not back. She smiled as the butler reappeared and bowed to the guests as they entered the room.

"Clara," the countess said, almost rushing across the room, hands extended. "How lovely it is to see you again." She took both Clara's hands in hers, squeezed them tightly, and bent to kiss her cheek. "How do you do, Harriet?"

"Clara," the earl said less effusively but in a thoroughly kindly manner. He took her right hand and raised it to his lips. He bowed to Harriet while Clara made the introductions.

"We happened to be passing and decided to call on you," the countess said brightly and then she went off into peals of laughter and seated herself on a sofa. "Actually we came here quite deliberately, did we not, Daniel?"

"Yes," he said. "Julia has been feeling cheated of the company of her new cousin, Clara, since you left town. And my sister is upsetting herself with the thought that perhaps you will not return for her wedding next month. Hence this rather long journey to call for afternoon tea."

"I am glad you dropped the hint, Daniel," the countess said, laughing again. "I am parched. And starved too, though I know it is indelicate to say so and you will frown at me ferociously when you think Clara and Harriet are not looking."

"Julia!" he said sternly as Harriet got to her feet to ring the bell.

"We were about to order tea anyway," Clara said, smiling.

"It is all Daniel's fault that I am so hungry anyway," the countess said. "All his fault. Not mine at all."

"Julia," the earl said a little more quietly.

"Clara is family," she said, smiling up at him, "And you know that I burst to tell everyone I can. I think myself

184

enormously clever as if I am the only woman in history to have accomplished such a wonderful feat. Besides, it will be obvious to the eye soon, Daniel, and everyone will know anyway. Unless you plan to be Gothic and lock me up to save the blushes of those young ladies who still believe in storks. We are going to have a child in five months' time, Clara."

Clara restrained her hand from spreading over her own abdomen. "How wonderful for you," she said.

"Do stop glowering and come and sit beside me, Daniel," the countess said, reaching up a hand for his. "You know you are fit to burst with pride. You need not pretend to be angry with me."

"Angry?" he said, shaking his head, but taking her hand and seating himself beside her. "You cannot see that it is embarrassment, Julia, having my impending paternity announced with only ladies present except for me?"

The countess laughed and gazed at him fondly.

*Fondly.* She had developed feelings for him, then? It was hardly surprising, Clara supposed. Feelings sometimes did develop after marriage even if they had not been there before. And Lord Beaconswood was a very handsome man – almost as handsome as Freddie. Clara guessed he was devoted to Julia.

Conversation was light during tea and dominated mainly by the countess, though the earl was careful to keep topics general and was even courteous enough to draw Harriet into the conversation. Harriet usually made herself invisible to visitors.

"Miss Pope," the earl said when they had finished their tea, getting to his feet, "I believe I saw a conservatory to the west of the house as we drove up. Are there many plants there? Would you care to show them to me?"

Clara looked at him, startled. Harriet was rising. The countess seemed quite unperturbed but was sitting smiling at Clara.

"It was planned, you see," she said after the other two had left. "I hope you do not mind Harriet being without a chaperon for a short while. Daniel and I thought it would be better if I spoke to you alone."

Clara looked at her warily.

"You left London the day after Camilla and I called on you," the countess said. "Perhaps there was no connection between the two events, and you must tell me to mind my own business if there was not. Or even if there was and you think me impertinent for prying. Your marriage really is none of my business, as Daniel has been telling me for weeks past. But I cannot help feeling responsible for the fact that you have been banished here."

The brightness had totally disappeared from her face. She was gazing at Clara earnestly and unhappily.

"Banished?" Clara said. "Freddie did not banish me, Julia. I came of my own free will."

"But on the spur of the moment," the countess said. "You were not planning to come, were you? Surely you would have told us if you were. You would not have led us to believe that you were going to pay a call on my mother-in-law within a day or two."

Clara clasped her hands in her lap and looked down at them. "I sometimes do things impulsively," she said. "But it was thoughtless of me not to send you a note. I am sorry, Julia. It was kind of you to call on me in town. I should have sent an explanation when I decided to leave."

"I think it was because of what I said, was it not?" the countess said unhappily. "And because of the quarrel I had with Freddie downstairs. He went back upstairs and quarreled with you too, didn't he? And made you so miserable that you came here. I am so meddlesome. I should have left well enough alone. I should not have tried to explain something that perhaps did not need to be explained. I should have left it to Freddie if he thought it necessary."

"Nothing was your fault, Julia," Clara said. "And nothing is wrong. It is just that I prefer to live here and Freddie prefers to live in town. I visited him there

186

for a few weeks and then came home. It was as simple as that."

"And you will return for the wedding?" Julia asked.

Clara hesitated.

The countess jumped to her feet. "I think we made a dreadful mess of it," she said. "Although I discussed it with Camilla ahead of time and Camilla is always marvelously sensible, I think we made a mess of it. You think that Freddie was in love with me, don't you? You think that is why he offered for me."

"It does not matter," Clara said. "What happened before my marriage is none of my concern, Julia."

"Oh, but it is." The countess had tears in her eyes. "If he was in love with me, asked me to marry him, was rejected, and then went to Bath and married you, it would be dreadful, Clara. Dreadful for you. But it was not like that. He did not love me. He was just being gallant. And I was not in love with him. Did you think perhaps I was but married Daniel because he was rich? I married Daniel because I love him. Because I adore him. There never has been anyone else and never could be."

Clara examined her hands. She did not want to ask the question. She did not want to know any more. But she asked it anyway.

"What is between you and Freddie, then?" she asked.

"Embarrassment," the countess said quickly.

"No," Clara said. "But we will leave it at that. I don't think I want to know. I am afraid to know. There is so much more than you have told me, is there not?"

The countess sat down again and was quiet for a while. "Why did you leave so abruptly?" she asked. "Camilla and I visited deliberately to try to make things easier for you. Because you are our cousin. Because we like you and wanted you to be our friend. Why did you leave?"

"I told Freddie that you had told me everything," Clara said. "You had not. I don't think you told me even a fraction of everything. But I think Freddie must have believed me."

The countess closed her eyes and bowed her head. "It was nothing, Clara," she said. "Nothing of any lasting significance. Oh, Freddie. Idiot Freddie. I could kill him. You love him, don't you?"

"Yes," Clara said.

"I suppose he made you fall in love with him within five minutes of meeting you," the countess said crossly. "Freddie is an expert at that. I could kill him."

"No," Clara said. "I was not quite a foolish innocent, Julia. You don't have to be afraid that he deceived me into marriage with protestations of love." She smiled fleetingly. "Though he did try it, I must admit. I married him for reasons of my own. I have come to love him since."

The countess leaned forward. "Forget about what happened at Primrose Park, then," she said. "Whatever it was, you do not want to know. It was utter foolishness, typical of Freddie, and harmed no one in the end. Forget it, Clara, and be happy with what you have. Freddie is not a vicious person, believe me. He is even lovable in an annoying sort of way. I always loved him – as a cousin and a friend. Almost as a brother. Forget it all, Clara. Come back to London. Be a part of the family. We all want you."

Clara smiled. "That is kind of you," she said. "But I don't think Freddie can forget, Julia. I think he was harmed. Whatever happened was all his fault, wasn't it? I think he cannot forgive himself. And I cannot forgive him and give him the absolution he needs. It did not concern me."

The countess closed her eyes.

"I think only you have that power," Clara said sadly. And yet a part of her rejoiced too. Whatever had happened – and it must have been something dreadful – it was not what she had thought. She had misinterpreted all the signs. Julia did not love him. She loved her husband. And if Julia was right – and she seemed quite certain she was – Freddie did not love her either. Never had. Oh, yes,

188

part of her rejoiced. She did not care what it was as long as it was not that.

"I told him that afternoon," the countess said, "the afternoon Camilla and I called on you, that I would never forgive him. Not because of what he had done to me. I think after all that that only helped bring Daniel and me together. But because of what he had done to you so soon after. I told him I hated him. It was such a lie. How could anyone hate Freddie?"

"He did not do anything to me," Clara said, "except marry me and give me a taste of joy."

"And a great deal of misery," the countess said.

"Yes."

"Oh, Freddie," the countess said. "I could kill him."

Clara smiled.

"I wonder if Daniel and Harriet have examined every leaf of every plant in the conservatory yet," the countess said. "I must go down to rescue them, Clara. And we must be on our way. The inn we picked out must be five miles along the road."

"But you will be staying here," Clara said. "Of course you will. I took so much for granted that you would do so that I did not even think to issue the invitation when you arrived. Forgive me."

"But we would not wish to impose," the countess said.

"Impose?" Clara laughed. "You keep telling me that we are family. Well, then."

"How delightful," the countess said, getting to her feet. "But I must still go and rescue those two downstairs. I shall come right back. Is it dreadfully annoying to be confined to one spot all the time? And is it dreadfully rude of me to refer to your disability? Daniel would be frowning fiercely at me if he were here."

Clara laughed as Julia swept from the room without waiting for a reply to either of her questions. She had been deliberately trying to lighten the atmosphere and had succeeded. Somehow Clara felt that a load

189

had been lifted from her shoulders. Though why she should feel that she did not know. Nothing really had changed.

Nothing at all.

# 15

The third visitor arrived four days later. Harriet did not have many callers of her own. But on this occasion the butler's grand announcement was all for her.

"Lord Archibald Vinney for Miss Pope, ma'am," he said to Clara from the doorway of her private sitting room.

"For me?" Harriet jumped to her feet in an uncharacteristically jerky movement. "Lord Archibald? Oh, no. There must be some mistake. He must have come for you, Clara."

"Do you wish to see him?" Clara's lips had compressed. "I shall send him away if you do not, Harriet. He has no business coming here without an invitation and without even a request to call."

Harriet stared first at Clara and then at the impassive butler. "I'll see him," she said at last. "Would you show him into the drawing room, please, Mr. Baines?"

Why had he come? she asked herself as she flew along to her own room to glance desperately into her looking glass. But there was no time to change her dress, and there were no prettier ones to be worn anyway. There was no time to comb her hair into a prettier style. She pinched her cheeks ruthlessly to bring color to them and then straightened up, frowning.

What was she doing? *What was she doing*? She was going hysterical over the arrival of Lord Archibald Vinney? Her heart was going pitter-patter over a man who had offered to make her his mistress? Harriet straightened her shoulders, drew a deep breath, and left the room.

He was standing propped against the mantel to one side of the crackling fire, in a pose of studied casualness. He was gazing at her, a look of faint amusement in his eyes.

"Ah, Miss Pope," he said. "How kind of you to do me the honor of receiving me. I half expected to be thrown out on my ear."

He had come to a respectable home to see her. He had ridden the long distance from London just for that purpose. Why? Surely it was only in the realms of fantasy that a man's intentions in such matters changed. Wasn't it? But she found painful hope coming alive again. So much for good sense.

"What may I do for you, my lord?" She was proud of the quiet calmness of her voice.

"You may come here and kiss me, Harriet," he said. "I have missed you."

She stayed where she was, just inside the door, and clasped her hands loosely in front of her.

"Have you given any more thought to my offer, my little charmer?" he asked her.

She had thought of little else. "I gave you my answer, my lord," she said.

"And it stands unchanged and unchangeable," he said. He straightened up and took a step toward her. "I will not offer greater material inducements. They will not sway you by as much as an inch, will they? If I offer you my deepest regard, Harriet? My faithful and undivided attentions until such time as we are both agreed it shall be otherwise? We would be good together, my dear."

Very good. She did not doubt it.

"I think of no one but you," he said. "I dream of you. I awaken thinking of you."

She knew just how that felt.

"Harriet." The quietness of his voice caressed her. "Admit at least that you are tempted."

She looked up at him. "It would be very strange if I

were not," she said, "and very unbelievable if I said I were not. But what you suggest is sin, my lord."

"And yet you are tempted." He smiled.

"There is no sin in temptation," she said. "Only in giving in to it. I will not give in, my lord."

There was a pause during which neither of them spoke. "No, I can see you will not," he said. "I have miscalculated, have I not? Well, Harriet, you have the distinction of being my only failure. But then I have never before chosen a mistress from the ranks of virtuous women."

Her heart was aching as she stared down at her hands and wondered if she should leave the room or wait for him to take his leave. She had no precedent to follow in such circumstances.

And then he was coming toward her and stopping in front of her and lifting her chin with one hand.

"You will be able to tell your grandchildren about the rogue who would have ruined you," he said, "and compare him very unfavorably to the stalwart respectability of their grandfather. But perhaps you will admit to them or perhaps only to the fire as you gaze into it that you lost a little corner of your heart to the rogue."

"I have not lost –" she began indignantly.

His mouth on hers prevented her from completing the sentence. The fact that it was open did not shock her quite as much this second time. It was warm and moist and seeking, and his tongue darted once, swiftly and startlingly deep, into her own opened mouth. Then his silver eyes were laughing down into hers. And yet the laughter seemed tempered with a little sadness too. Or perhaps she was seeing what she wanted to see.

"You have my permission to tell them that he lost a small corner of his own to their grandmother too," he said. "Will you now please stop haunting my dreams, Miss Harriet Pope?"

Only if he would stop haunting hers.

"Good-bye, then," he said. "I daresay we shall meet again if Freddie ever decides to bring Mrs. Sullivan back to town. Perhaps time will weaken your sense of sin. But I shall not hold my breath."

"Time will make no difference, my lord," she said.

He touched the pad of his thumb lightly to her lips before removing his hand from beneath her chin. "Good-bye, little blusher," he said.

"Good-bye, my lord."

The door closed so softly behind him that she was not even sure for a while that he had gone. She did not move. If she counted to twenty slowly – no, better, to one hundred, *very* slowly – he should be gone. Gone from the house and gone along the driveway beyond recall. If she could hold out that long, counting very slowly, then perhaps she would be able to resist the almost overpowering temptation to go racing after him, calling his name.

But she had never called his name. What would she call him? What would she have called him if she had become his mistress? "One-two-three," she counted silently, her lips moving. She had felt him from her shoulders to her knees. His body heat had enveloped her like a cloak. "Four-five-six." Her knees had almost buckled when he had darted his tongue into her mouth. Was that a mere sampling of what a man would do with a mistress? "Seven-eight." She loved him. "Nine, ten." No. No, no, no. she spread her hands over her face, shaking her head vigorously from side to side.

The last time. She would not see him again. She must not. She must see to it that she never saw him again. Sin had never seemed so attractive. It became more so every time she saw him. She had only a certain degree of inner strength. It was almost exhausted. She must be sure she never saw him again. She must never go to London again with Clara.

She had seen him for the last time. The last time ever.

The weeks following Clara's removal to Ebury Court were

194

not good ones for Frederick. His first instinct was to go after her, to make the apology that he so desperately needed to make. To try to explain to her – but explain what? To try to persuade her that he was going to turn over a new leaf? But it was such an easy cliché to mouth. Would he be able to do it? And did he want to commit himself exclusively to Clara? He had grown fond of her, he had grown to value her. But was there that extra something in his feelings for her? Did he want there to be? There was something terrifying about the thought of total commitment.

He would wait for a while, he decided. He would clean up his life, turn it around, and then try to pick up the threads of his marriage again. There would be no more drinking. That was the easy one. Drinking had never been a real problem for him. It was just something he fell into occasionally when everything else was going bad. He would give it up. And women. Apart from the momentary sensory pleasure that came from coupling, he had never gained any real enjoyment from womanizing since his marriage. He always felt dirty afterward and unpleasantly lethargic. And guilty. He would give up women entirely for a while and then make a rational decision about whether to resume his marriage – if Clara would have him back – or to employ a mistress. But no more promiscuity.

And gambling. That was the hard one. Playing cards was such good, sociable recreation, and accepting bets and placing money on the betting books were enjoyable activities that he indulged in with friends. Yet it seemed that a fiend sometimes got into him. Once into a game, he could not draw himself out. He did not know when to stop, when to cut his losses or conserve his gains. He did not know how to think cautiously or rationally once the fever of a game was in his blood. The only thing to do was to give it up altogether.

He gave up all three of his vices for the day and night his wife left and the day following that. And then, home

195

alone, loneliness gnawed at him and the wretchedness of guilt and self-loathing over what he had done to his life. All in one year. Less. Until the early spring he had been a gay and carefree bachelor about town just like dozens of other men of his acquaintance. It was the life he had lived for years, the life he loved, the life he intended to live until the time came, somewhere in the vaguely distant future, when it would be necessary to settle down and take a wife and begin a family. Life had seemed uncomplicated and very pleasant.

And then suddenly and without any real warning he was more severely dipped than he had ever been and his desperate efforts to bring himself out of the mess had plunged him farther in. His father had rescued him several times in the past from embarrassing situations. This was far worse than embarrassing. And then had come his uncle's death and all that ghastly business with Julia. And the terrible deceit of Clara. Suddenly his vices, which had seemed the harmless excesses of youth until very recently – a young man sowing his wild oats – were affecting other people. Hurting other people. Julia. Clara.

Julia had escaped from him and was happy with Dan. Clara was stuck with him. He remembered suddenly telling her during that ghastly drive in the park that she must wish she could wake up in Bath to find the past few months all a bad dream. She had replied with a simple affirmative.

Clara. He closed his eyes. Her father had hurt her all his life with a selfish, over-protective love. And now her husband, who did not even have the excuse of love.

Clara.

He could not bear to be alone. Too much crowded into his head when he was alone. He needed the company of others. The most obvious place to find that company, of course, was one of his clubs. But then there was always the danger of being drawn into a game if he went there. He would just have to use willpower, he decided, getting up. He could not stay home any longer.

He did not return home for two days and then he came back only to bath and to sleep and change his clothes. In the coming days and weeks he often forgot even to do those things but immersed himself in a frantic orgy of carousing, gaming, and doing the rounds of all the more respectable brothels and even one or two of the other type. His companions became lesser acquaintances rather than friends. His way of life became too hectic and too wild and debauched for even his closest friends, like Lord Archibald Vinney, to keep up to him.

But his pace was not frantic enough for his own peace of mind. Thought kept intruding, insinuating itself into his conscious mind whenever he relaxed his guard over it, and sometimes even when he did not. He could not even keep his own simple resolution to clean up his life, he thought sometimes. Though he could if he really wanted to, he told himself defiantly. He was married, he thought at other times. His wife was in the country, not so very far away. He should write to her. He should instruct her to look after her health, to take the air whenever the winter weather would allow. But who was he to talk about looking after health and taking the air? Who was he to send any instructions to his wife? Instructions she would almost certainly obey. Who was he to demand obedience?

He hated sleeping. He dreamed of her. He awoke reaching for her, only to find either an empty bed beside him and a foul aching inside his head, or – worse – a naked stranger at his side. He took to instructing the whores he hired not on any account and on pain of his wrath to allow him to sleep.

He lost count of the days and the weeks. He did not know how many of either had passed between Clara's leaving and the visit of the Earl and Countess of Beaconswood. They called early one afternoon when by the purest chance he was at home, immersed in a bath of hot suds.

197

"Tell them I am not at home," he told the butler, whose knock his valet had answered. "Tell them I am not expected home." He ran a hand over a jaw that was rough with three or four days' growth of beard – he could not remember exactly how many – and closed his eyes, which were stinging with weariness.

"Yes, sir," the butler said, and his valet made to close the door.

"Wait," Frederick said. Lord, he should have called on his aunt weeks ago. Doubtless more of the family would be arriving soon, or had already done so, for that infernal wedding that was coming up – how soon? Lord, he had made a mess of this. He had made a mess of everything. "Put them in the drawing room if they want to wait half an hour or so until I am decent."

"Yes, sir," the butler said.

A charming picture he would make for guests, Frederick thought ten minutes later, standing naked in front of a looking glass before reaching for his clothes. Hair that must have needed cutting even two or three weeks ago, face as pale as his wife's had used to look, eyes that were ringed with dark shadows and that were most attractively bloodshot. Even his shave, which came next, would not be able to improve the picture a great deal. He looked as if he needed to sleep without interruption for a week or so. He looked thoroughly dissipated, in fact.

Sometimes, he thought wryly, turning away from the rather painful contemplation of his own image, looks did not lie.

It did not seem quite the occasion on which to make small talk about the weather, but that was what Frederick did after greeting his guests with a heartiness that made him wince inwardly and wish that he could make a second entrance. And they responded in kind. The weather was indeed chilly, the Earl of Beaconswood agreed. But most invigorating, the countess added. Lovely for walking.

"Freddie," she said finally, sounding rather as if she

were fit to burst, the first of them to admit that the reason for this call was not purely or even in any way social. "Freddie, I cannot stand this any longer. I told Daniel so and he agreed with me and offered to bring me here. This will just not do. It is unbearable."

Frederick, who had seated his guests and then himself before beginning to talk about the weather, got to his feet and crossed to the window. He stood with his back to the room.

"I think we are even, Jule," he said. "I didn't think much worse than what I did to you could be done. But it could. I can understand your need for revenge. I can even concede the point that I needed more punishment than was meted out at the time. One poke on the chin from Dan was hardly a just chastisement. But at least your revenge could have been directed fully at me. Not at an innocent who had already done more suffering in her life than anyone should be asked to endure. You have told me that you can never forgive me, Jule. Well, I am compelled to return the favor. I can't forgive you for hurting Clara. So we are even, and I would ask you to leave."

"Freddie!" She sounded like the old Julia indignant and ready to fight. "What on earth are you talking about? What is he talking about, Daniel? But of course I know the answer. Clara made it clear when we went to Ebury Court a few days ago. You think I told her everything, don't you, Freddie? You really think I am capable of doing such a thing. You must be mad. If I wanted revenge on you, I would come and punch you in the nose. You must know that has always been my way."

Spite had never been Julia's way. He had not thought of that before. "She said you had told her everything that had happened at Primrose Park," he said.

"She believed that I had," the countess said, exasperated. "Camilla and I knew that she had sensed a certain atmosphere between us at the theater, Freddie. We liked her and wanted to make her our friend. We did not want her hurt. So we came here to tell her that you had offered for me out of gallantry after Grandpapa's death, because you thought me destitute. We told her that you were embarrassed when I married Daniel instead and that was why you rushed away to Bath and found it awkward to meet me again. That is all we told her, Freddie."

Frederick leaned forward so that his forehead was resting against the cool glass of the window. He closed his eyes.

"A partial truth can sometimes be as bad as a lie," the earl said. "I wish Camilla and Julia had discussed it with me first, Freddie, but then it is always easy to know after the event what should have been said or done. They thought they were acting for the best. They did not intend for it to lead to a misunderstanding between you and your wife."

Clara. He had lashed out at her in the park in an orgy of self-loathing turned against her.

"I knew something must have gone wrong when Clara went into the country so soon after our visit," the countess said, "when she had said she would be calling on Daniel's mama. We went out there to see her a few days ago, Freddie."

A thousand questions crowded into the forefront of his mind. How was she? How happy was she? How miserable? He kept his eyes closed.

"She realizes that she does not know everything," the countess said. "We did not add to the story at all, except to assure her yet again that you did not love me. I know that has always been her greatest fear."

Lord. Oh, good Lord, why did they not just go away?

"She is looking well, Freddie," the earl added quietly.

That was something at least. He had not destroyed her, then. And yet even now there was a horrifying selfishness, almost as if there would have been some satisfaction in hearing that she was thin and pale and desperate with unhappiness.

"Freddie." The countess touched his arm. "Forgive me for being the cause of misunderstanding."

200

Frederick laughed and kept his forehead where it was and his eyes shut. "*You* apologizing to *me*, Jule?" he said.

"Yes," she said, "and offering forgiveness. I think you need it, Freddie. I forgive you for everything. Of course I do. You were not vicious enough to carry through with your plan, anyway. You were taking me back home, if you will remember, when Daniel and Camilla and Malcolm caught up to us. No real harm was done, and you were probably a means of bringing Daniel and me together sooner than it would otherwise have happened. I forgave you as soon as my temper had cooled and would have told you so, you idiot, if you had not run away so ignominiously. I have never known you to run away from having to face the music, Freddie. I only said a few weeks ago that I could never forgive you because of your marrying Clara. But that is really none of my business as Daniel has been at pains to point out to me."

He swallowed. Twice. Lord, he wished they would go away. He was going to disgrace himself if they did not.

"It was just another foolish escapade at Primrose Park," the countess said. "Heaven knows there have been enough of them over the years, Freddie. Let's forget about it. Let's be friends again. Oh, you silly idiot, how can we not be when we have been friends forever?"

"I think we had better leave, Julia," the earl said. "We will call again, Freddie. Better still, come and see Mama. She is wondering what is going on. And Aunt Roberta and Uncle Henry have arrived with Stella to give Malcolm some support with the wedding getting closer. Come on, my love."

But Frederick turned sharply suddenly and grabbed her before she could take a step away from him. He wrapped his arms tightly about her and buried his face against the hair at the top of her head.

"Silly idiot!" she said against his neckcloth after several silent moments. "Oh, Freddie, you are so foolish. I could kill you."

201

"Keep up the words of endearment," he said a little unsteadily, "and Dan will do it for you, Jule."

"You had better not hug me much harder," she said. "There is a four-month baby squashed between us, Freddie. Aren't we clever, Daniel and I? Is he blushing? Are you?" She turned up a laughing face to peer into his. "You had better congratulate us."

He kissed her forehead. "Congratulations, Jule," he said. "I always knew you were a clever girl. Congratulations, Dan." He looked up to find his cousin standing close by, regarding him gravely and extending his right hand. Frederick took it in a firm clasp, keeping one arm about the countess's shoulders.

"You look dreadful, Freddie," she said. "When did you last sleep? I suppose you have been –"

"Hush, love," the earl said. "Freddie, we are on our way. Call on Mama, will you? And on the rest of the family? I am head of the family, after all, and I don't want any rifts. Bring Clara to the wedding?"

"I'll have to see," he said.

"Bring her," the countess said. She laughed and kissed his cheek before taking her husband's arm. "You heard Daniel. It was an order. I tremble in my shoes whenever he directs one at me."

The two men exchanged grins.

"For the record, Jule," Frederick said when they had already taken their leave and were on their way out the door, "I love her, you know."

"Idiot!" she said, smiling back over her shoulder at him. "I don't need to be told that. You have been telling me so in everything but words since we arrived here, Freddie."

God help him, he thought, despair washing over him and obliterating all the ease of mind their forgiveness had brought – God help him, it was true.

# 16

Frederick gave himself two days in which to recover enough to look human again before taking himself off to pay a call on his Aunt Sarah, Viscountess Yorke, the earl's mother. He called too on Malcolm's parents. Aunt Syliva and Uncle Paul too were due to arrive any day with Gussie and Viola. His own parents wrote to say they would be returning to town within the week, bringing Aunt Millie with them. The clan was gathering as surely as they had gathered every summer at Primrose Park for as long as Frederick could remember.

Everyone, of course, showed a great interest in his wife and wondered when they were to meet her. Was dear Freddie waiting until the very last moment to bring her up to town for the wedding, provoking boy? His wife was more comfortable in the country, he explained, due to her crippled state. He hoped he could persuade her to come to town for the wedding, of course, but he could not be sure she would agree. She was somewhat shy. That last lie was spoken within earshot of the earl and countess and made him feel uncomfortable and ashamed.

His father was certainly going to want an explanation if Clara did not come, Frederick thought. And he was conscious of a familiar sinking of the heart as he thought so. His heart did nothing but sink these days. It was amazing that it had any farther descent to make. His father would be disappointed in him – again. He had failed yet again to prove that he had grown up, that he could settle to a worthy life, that he could take a man's responsibilities.

He had failed. Oh, it was true that he could now put behind him the episode with Julia. Forgiveness could do wonders to lift heavy burdens from the conscience, he had discovered. But what had happened with her was after all just a minor sin in comparison with what he had done to Clara. He had failed with his marriage. Failed miserably. He had done irreparable harm to someone who had suddenly come to mean more to him than anyone else in his life, himself included.

It was his overwhelming sense of failure that sent him to a private party one evening, knowing very well that it was to be a card party and that the play was to be deep. There was really no point in avoiding it, he thought. If he missed this one, he would go to the next one or the next one after that. He just did not have the willpower to change his way of life. Or the sense of purpose. Perhaps that was what was missing. There seemed no particular point to anything.

He would try at least to impose some control over himself, he decided. He would limit his losses. Once he had lost a certain sum, then he would go home. Not that he could afford to lose anything. He had lost an appalling amount since his marriage. If he was not very careful, he was going to be in dun territory again before long and would have to be begging from his father or from Clara – though he would rather die than beg from either – or facing the possibility of debtors' prison again.

It was rather ironic, he thought as the evening progressed, that he had not set any limits on the winnings he would allow himself to earn before going home. It was one of those charmed evenings. He felt it from the first. He could do no wrong. Even if he had tried to lose, he would not have been able to do so. Or so it almost seemed. He was not drinking. He could enjoy his triumph to the full.

How long should he play? he wondered with an inward chuckle when he guessed that he must have won back everything he had lost since his marriage. Until his luck turned as it inevitably must? What had come easily would go even more easily, he knew. And yet the compulsion to continue when he was winning was every bit as strong as that he always felt when he was losing. One more hand, he always thought, to see if his run of luck was still with him. If it was not, then he would stop. Or if he was losing, he would tell himself one more hand to see if his luck changed. If it did, then he would play another hand again. Either way, he was always staring into a bottomless pit, or into a whirlpool that forever sucked him inexorably inward to its vortex.

Word of his extreme good fortune had spread about the two rooms in use, with the result that a silent throng gathered about his table. He wanted to laugh with exultation, but it was bad form to show any sort of emotion at all at the tables. He sat outwardly impassive. Everyone had gathered to witness his luck.

And then Lord Archibald Vinney touched him on the shoulder. An impersonal touch with no pressure and no accompanying words. Yet a message passed. And the scales fell from Frederick's eyes. The gathering was not there to witness his good fortune. Did crowds ever gather to share in someone's happiness? Always the reverse was true. They were not there to witness his winnings but to witness Hancock's losses.

Sir Peter Hancock, young, handsome, rash, of only moderate fortune was about to be stripped of it. No, there was nothing future about it. He had already been divested of his fortune and was playing on vouchers, on expectations of future winnings. Another candidate for debtors' prison. A man whose father had died two years before, leaving him with a mother and three younger sisters to care for. A responsibility too heavy for his young shoulders.

Frederick glanced at his opponent's bet, looked down at his unbeatable hand, bet everything he had on it, felt the almost silent sigh of sympathy for poor Hancock, looked at the man's inferior hand when he laid it down on the table, and tossed his own cards into the pack face-down, rising with an exclamation of disgust.

"Your win, Hancock," he said with a yawn as the spectators looked on, stunned, and his adversary gazed at him as if a noose was being lifted away from his neck. "I'll see you downstairs now before I leave, my dear fellow."

Sir Peter Hancock was looking dazed with victory when Frederick led him into a salon downstairs, a room he had found by the simple expedient of opening a few closed doors. It was a reception room, with the chairs arranged about the walls. There was a great deal of empty space in the center of the room.

"How many women depend upon you, Hancock?" Frederick asked. He had not heard of any of the sisters marrying.

"Four," Hancock replied. "Mother and three sisters."

"Only you stand between them and destitution?" Frederick asked.

Hancock shrugged. "That was bad luck, Sullivan," he said. "Betting all your winnings on one hand, I mean. Good luck for me, of course."

The last word had scarcely left his mouth before he hit the floor, hardly realizing for a moment as he stared up at the ceiling that it was a fist that had put him there. Frederick leaned over him, grabbed him by the collar of his coat, and hoisted him to his feet.

"You and I are two peas in a pod, Hancock," he said through his teeth. "Perhaps I can punish myself by pounding your face to pulp. Perhaps you can teach yourself a lesson by skinning your knuckles against my person. Now get those fists up because by God, when I fight, I like to have a worthy opponent."

Hancock, furious with the humiliation that had already been dealt out to him, put up his fists and they fought fiercely, doggedly, and almost silently for long minutes.

Hancock lay on the floor eventually, not unconscious, but winded and bruised and defeated. He held up a hand as Frederick loomed menacingly over him, fists still clenched, waiting for him to get up and put up his defenses again. Frederick reached down a hand and helped him to his feet.

"You are handy with your fives," he said, straightening his clothes, touching his fingertips gingerly to one sore cheek. "Why have I never seen you at Jackson's, Hancock?"

Sir Peter chuckled. "I promised my mother two years ago that I would never engage in anything rough or dangerous," he said. "Poor mother. She never did know what promises to extract. She always thought more of my safety than of her own. You are lucky, Sullivan. If I had been in practice, you would be watching stars whirling about your head from a position on the carpet by now. What *was* the hand you threw in, by the way?"

"Nothing at all," Frederick said. "A mere bluff in the hope that you were bluffing even more recklessly. Are you walking my way?"

Sir Peter nodded, made some adjustments to his clothing, and left the house with Frederick.

"I call it my devil within," he said. "Fortunately it has never run up against an opponent on such an incredible run of raw luck – until tonight. I wonder how long the streak would have lasted."

"It ran out in rather a spectacular manner," Frederick said. "It was most enjoyable while it lasted. The devil within, eh? Yes, an apt description. One's only hope, perhaps, is to replace it with an angel."

"An angel within." Hancock laughed. "Female, I presume?"

Except that he had spurned his angel, Frederick thought, and hurt her and wronged her in the process. And he had not even had the decency or the courtesy to face her or to apologize to her. Or to try to set her free. Angels should be free to fly.

Harriet was out riding. Clara was sitting before the fire in her sitting room, not reading or embroidering. It was

207

the sleepy time of the afternoon, and yet she did not feel like ringing the bell so that she could be carried in to her bed either. She sat and gazed into the flames, one hand spread over her abdomen as it so often was these days, a faraway look in her eyes.

She had had a vigorous session with Robin, as she had every day. Her legs were feeling strong and muscled. Deceptively so. For the second time that morning he had drawn her to her feet, one strong arm so tightly about her that he had in fact been supporting all her weight. She must not try it alone for a while yet, he had warned. Perhaps for a week or two. He did not want her falling and discouraging herself.

But it had felt wonderful beyond description. To be upright. To feel her feet on the floor, her ankles supporting her legs and her knees too, to feel her legs supporting her body. It felt wonderful even though she knew they were still very weak.

"I want to dance for Christmas, Robin," she had said. "Will you dance with me?"

"A highland fling, Mrs. Sullivan?" he had said. "It is the only dance I know."

They had chuckled together. Robin was not much given to joking or to laughing. But Clara guessed that teaching her to walk and seeing her close to a minimal success at least was giving Robin too a sense of achievement. Giving up his life's dream of becoming a prizefighter must have been hard on him. Doubtless he was looking forward to being able to leave her employment. It must be dull at best.

Clara smiled into the fire. She would not be greedy. Just to be able to walk would be wonderful. To be able to move from room to room without having to call for assistance. To be able to stroll out on the terrace. To be able to walk to the summerhouse. Ah, the summerhouse. And to be able to ride a horse the length of the park. But she would not be greedy.

She did not know that she slept. And yet there was

a feeling suddenly of not being alone and she turned her head slowly to find that the door to her room was open and he was standing in the doorway, one shoulder propped against the frame. And then she was not sure that she was awake. He had come to her silently, as he came often in her dreams. She flexed her fingers, found them still spread over her abdomen. She smiled slowly.

"I have come to set you free," he said.

They were strange words, the sort of words one heard in dreams. But she knew now that she was awake, that he was really there standing in her doorway. That he had come home.

"Hello, Freddie," she said.

"Unfortunately it cannot be done literally," he said. "You are bound to me for life. But I will do the next best thing. I am going to take you to London with me for Camilla and Malcolm's wedding. You will meet my family, every last one of them. They are warm people, Clara. They will be a family for you. They will take you to their collective bosom for the rest of your life and never let you go. You will not need to be lonely again. After the wedding I will take myself off to America or perhaps to Canada. You will not need to see me ever again."

"You can't do that, Freddie," she said, still smiling at him, though there was sadness in her eyes. "I am going to have a baby. The two of us are going to need you."

If she had ever visualized herself telling him, it had never been quite as baldly as she was doing it in actuality. She watched him, her head against the back of the chair, where it must have fallen when she fell asleep. He did not move. But he was biting on his upper lip and his eyes were filling with tears. And then he jerked his head back to look up at the ceiling, and he was crying in noisy, awkward gulps.

"Oh, Lord, Clara," he said when he could, "what have I done to you? I am so sorry. I am so very sorry."

"For what?" she asked him softly, her heart aching for him. "For making a child with me, Freddie? I am going to

209

swell with child and give birth. I am going to hold my own son or daughter to my breast. Even just a few months ago it would have seemed such an impossibility and now it is reality. You have filled me with contentment. Don't be sorry."

"How can I be a father to a child?" he asked. "I have nothing to offer. There is nothing in me for a child to look up to. It will be better if I am not here, Clara. Better if I go away as planned."

"Freddie." She stretched out a hand to him though she did not expect him to take it. "Tell me about your pain. When I met you in Bath, you were vibrant with life and charm. And with roguery too. I did not feel then that you hated yourself. That has grown since. Tell me what happened at Primrose Park."

He laughed and folded his arms. "Why not?" he said. "You might as well know it all. You will be buying my passage to America yourself before you know it, Clara. My uncle's will left Primrose Park to whichever of his five nephews could win Julia's hand. Primrose Park is a prosperous estate."

"Ah," she said quietly.

"I used all the charm I could muster to win her," he said. "But of course Jule knows me too well, and besides she was falling in love with Dan without realizing it. And he with her. When I finally realized that Jule was not going to marry me, I abducted her."

She looked at him, waiting for him to finish the story.

"I took her to Gloucester," he said, "tricking her into getting into my carriage alone with me. I thought just the fact that a day's outing would compromise her reputation would be enough to win her consent, but of course Jule is made of sterner stuff. The ultimate plan was to keep her away from home for a night and give her no choice. Though there would still have been choice with Jule. I was going to rape her."

Clara swallowed. "Daniel caught up to you in time?" she asked.

210

"Only because we were heading back toward home," he said. "I could not go through with it, you see. A villain without backbone."

"A would-be villain with a heart and a conscience," she said.

He laughed again.

"If you had no conscience you would not be suffering, Freddie," she said.

"So then I dashed off to Bath, suitably chastened," he said, "sought out the rich unmarried women, narrowed the choice down to you, and laid determined siege to your heart and hand with my charm again, Clara. A man of heart and conscience indeed."

"You did not deceive me, as I have told you before," she said. "I married you because I wanted to, Freddie. I did not marry for love any more than you did. I did not love you when I married you."

"It is as well," he said. "You would have discovered your mistake soon enough."

"Love grew later," she said. "During the week we had together here, I think, and every day since. You are far more lovable than you know."

"I have been told that I am a handsome man," he said. "My glass tells me that it is not conceited to believe what I have been told. You have been seduced by looks, Clara. You love a handsome nothing."

"You were unfailingly good to me during that week," she said. "It was without any doubt the most wonderful week of my life. If there were never anything more to match it, my life would have been worth living. I would consider that I had known happiness. I know you were pretending to a love that you did not feel, Freddie, but you lived that pretended love. You spent your time with me. You gave me the delirious pleasure of those horseback rides and that wonderful afternoon at the summerhouse. You talked and talked to me and smiled at me. You made me feel almost beautiful. And you made love to me. I cannot describe how wonderful that has been –

211

to know physical love after all the years that have gone before."

"Clara," he said, "don't make a saint of me. I abandoned you. I have lived a life of horrible debauchery in town while you have been here."

"But you wrote to me," she said, "because you wanted to ensure that I stayed healthy. And you sought out Dr. Graham and came for me to take me to him. You wanted to give me a chance to walk again. Without you, Freddie, I would never have known that it was possible. I'll not have you convince yourself that you have been a force of destruction in my life when quite the opposite is true. You have been all that is wonderful and life-giving to me. Best of all, you have caused me to know what love is. Not just physical love, but all of it. And perhaps best of the best, you have put life in me. You have made it possible for me to be fully and in every way a woman."

He stood silently, still propped against the doorframe, his eyes opaque. She had not got through to him.

"I know I am but a sorry creature," she said, "but you have brought me happiness, Freddie. Don't think of yourself as a total failure."

"A sorry creature!" he said softly. "You are the one touch of beauty in my life, Clara. You have grown beautiful in my eyes. If it were not for you, I think I might have taken my life by now."

Her own eyes blurred with tears. "Oh, Freddie," she said. "I love you. I need you."

"I can't seem to change," he said. "Willpower will not seem to do it, Clara. I seek out card games with a sort of sick dread. And I seek out other women when the only one I want is my wife. How can I offer myself to you? How can I commit myself to you?"

"Do you want to, Freddie?" she asked.

"Yes," he said.

"Why?" She blinked to try to clear her sight.

"Because I love you," he said.

212

"Let me tell you something, then," she said. "Something that is not really important except that I think you must need to hear it. If you have ever wronged me in any way, Freddie – as I suppose you did by trying to deceive me at the start, and as you have by committing adultery against me over and over again. Yes, you have wronged me. But I forgive you. And I will keep on forgiving you as many times as you wrong me. For I love you and I know you will always be sorry if you stray. Don't punish yourself any longer. By punishing yourself you will be punishing me."

"Can it be done, then," he asked, "by just trying and trying and trying? Failing and trying again? And so on?"

"I don't think there is any easier way, Freddie," she said. "Just a day by day effort. I want to show you that it can bring results. Promise me not to move?"

He did not answer, but she did not press the point. Her heart began to thump painfully and she wanted suddenly to change her mind. If she failed now, all might be lost. She would merely have proved that long hard effort brought only failure and humiliation.

She set her hands on the arms of the chair and gripped them tightly. She positioned her feet firmly and slightly apart on the floor and moved herself closer to the edge of the chair. She watched the floor a few feet in front of her and concentrated fully. She tried to forget that there was anyone else in the room. She tried to forget that success now was so important. She put from her mind Robin's warnings. She pushed herself slowly upward, all her weight on her arms. And then, when her arms were fully extended, she had to let the muscles of her legs and ankles do the work.

And finally she was standing. Upright and still. She was not even swaying. She turned her head slowly so that she would not lose her balance, and smiled brilliantly at him.

"I cannot walk yet," she said. "I am not even supposed

to stand yet. Robin will be very cross with me. And I have no idea how I am to sit down again. Come to me now, please, Freddie. I need you."

He moved for the first time since she had woken up. He was across the room even before she had finished speaking and caught her up against him in such a bruising hug that she was no longer supporting herself.

"Oh, my love," he was saying against her hair. "My love, my love, my love."

"And it is all your fault," she said, laughing. "It is all your fault that I am on my feet, Freddie. And that I am increasing. And loved. And happy. All your fault. Say it again. Please say it again."

"That I love you?" he said.

"Yes, please." She tipped back her head to gaze up into his dark eyes.

"I love you," he said. "Does it make you happy to hear it, Clara? Is it so easy to make someone happy?"

"Tell me you are happy about the baby." She had got her arms up about his neck and was hanging on for dear life. "I want so badly to be able to bear you a son. Or a daughter. A healthy child, Freddie. Tell me you are happy."

"I turn weak at the knees at the very thought," he said. "Is it so easy to make a child, then?"

"And so very pleasurable." She laughed again. She was beginning to feel almost delirious with laughter. "Don't go weak at the knees, Freddie. They are the only reliable pair we have between us."

"You are taller than I expected," he said, scooping her up in strong arms and sitting on the sofa with her on his lap. "Clara, my love, I want so much to be able to pledge my life and devotion to you and our child. Our children. But how can I be sure that I will not slip again and again into my old ways?"

"You can't be sure, Freddie," she said. "And I cannot vow to be always loving and kind to you. I wonder if happiness would be worth having if it did not have to

214

be constantly worked on. When there is a quarrel or something worse between us, there will always be the joy of making up and the soothing balm of forgiveness. But I won't ever allow you to feel worthless. You are worth everything in the whole world to me."

She felt him give in finally to contentment as he settled her head against his shoulder and sighed.

"Besides," she said, "I want to dance for Christmas and it will have to be with you, Freddie, because Robin claims to know only the Highland fling. I don't think I will be quite ready for that this Christmas at least."

They chuckled together and then she raised her face to him. They kissed each other with deep hunger and with warm affection.

"And I want to go out riding with you," she said. "With you and beside you when I gain more courage. And I want to lie in the grass beside the summerhouse with you when spring comes, among the crocuses and snowdrops. I will be getting large by that time. Oh, Freddie, I have done so much dreaming alone during the last few months."

"Dream aloud to me now, then, my love," he said, "and I'll make your dreams mine."

"I want to spend all night every night in bed beside you," she said.

"Mmm," he said.

"I want you here in the house with me when our baby is born," she said. "I want to put him into your arms almost immediately afterward. I want to watch your eyes when you see him for the first time."

"Or her," he said.

"Or her. I want to go to London with you and meet your family. I want to go to Camilla's wedding. I want to go to Primrose Park and see all the places where you played as a child. I want our own children to play there sometimes. With Daniel and Julia's children. And Camilla and Malcolm's."

"Clara," he said, "my neck is wet. You are not crying, are you?"

"Yes, I am, Freddie," she said. "I have tried to suppress my dreams all this time. Now they are running riot."

"Silly goose!" he said softly.

But when she raised her head to look up at him, it was to find that his own eyes were wet too. "A pair of silly geese," she said. "Kiss me again, please, Freddie. But first say it once more."

"I love you, silly goose," he said and kissed her again.

Harriet waited until she knew Clara was alone the next morning. Clara had just finished her vigorous exercise program with Robin – and with her husband in attendance.

Harriet did not know what had happened, but she did know that Clara and Mr. Sullivan were very happy over something. At breakfast Clara had looked like a woman who had just emerged from a long night of love. Harriet did not know a great deal about nights of love, but she knew that she had felt the stabbing of a deep envy for her employer. Even though she was married to a wastrel. But perhaps even that was no longer so. People changed, and Mr. Sullivan was looking quite as happy as Clara. It was not a feigned happiness, either.

Yes, perhaps things had changed. And if they had, then Harriet was glad. Very glad. She loved her friend, and she knew that Clara had loved Mr. Sullivan almost from the start. She knew about Clara's pregnancy too.

But it was of herself she was thinking this morning. Of herself in contrast to Clara. She was feeling a little self-pitying if the truth were known.

"Clara." She sat down in the sitting room when her employer smiled at her with luminous eyes. "You are going to London tomorrow?"

"*We* are going," Clara said. "I daresay you will have an invitation to the wedding too, Harriet."

"I want to go home," Harriet said in a rush. "Home to Bath, Clara. The time has come. You do not need me as much any longer now that you have Mr. Sullivan and now that you are going to London. Soon you will be needing a nurse, not a companion. I want to go home to spend Christmas with my mother and to look about me for a new position."

She saw some understanding in her friend's eyes. And a protest dying into acceptance. "Harriet," Clara said, "you are my friend and very dear to me. I don't want to lose you. But it would be selfish to try to keep you, would it not? You must do what you wish, what is best for you. You will write to me? Every week? And visit frequently? You must come to see the baby when he is born."

"Yes," Harriet said. "I will come. I am going to leave tomorrow, Clara."

And then they were both weeping and mopping at their eyes and laughing.

"Harriet," Clara said, "I won't talk about what I know is painful to you. But one day you are going to be happier than you dream it is possible to be. I know. I promise, dear. I wish I could wave a magic wand and make all well for you without the delay of time."

"I am happy to be going home," Harriet said, "and only sad to be leaving you."

That sadness displayed itself the following morning in a storm of tears when she was finally alone in the private carriage that Clara and Mr. Sullivan had insisted she allow them to provide to convey her to Bath while they were on their way to London. Tears for the end of a chapter in her life; tears for the loss of a friend; tears for the dreary life she had to look forward to; tears at the knowledge that she could be going to London too and the chance of seeing *him* occasionally.

She dried her eyes after ten minutes and set herself resolutely to watching the scenery. Harriet was ever a sensible and a practical woman.

She could not know that Frederick would find a note from Sir Archibald Vinney awaiting him on his arrival in town, announcing the serious illness of his grandfather. It was likely, he wrote, that he would be gone from London for quite a while, maybe even a year or more if the old duke decided really to die this time.